NIGEL McCRERY
THE THIRTEENTH COFFIN

Quercus

First published in Great Britain in 2015 by

Quercus Publishing Ltd
Carmelite House
50 Victoria Embankment
London EC4Y 0DZ

An Hachette UK company

A CIP catalogue record for this book is available
from the British Library

PB ISBN 978 1 78429 482 3
EBOOK ISBN 978 1 78429 481 6

10 9 8 7 6 5 4 3 2 1

Typeset by Jouve (UK), Milton Keynes

Printed and bound in Great Britain by Clays Ltd, St Ives plc

THE
THIRTEENTH
COFFIN

For my daughter Elizabeth and granddaughter
Samantha for all their love and care

*

Nigel McCrery is the creator and writer of some of the
most successful television series of the last ten years –
his credits include *Silent Witness, Born & Bred, New Tricks,
All the King's Men* and *Backup*.

Also by Nigel McCrery

Scream
Tooth and Claw
Core of Evil
Still Waters

AUTHOR'S NOTE

In 1836, five boys were hunting rabbits on the north-eastern slopes of Arthur's Seat, which is the main peak in the group of hills in the centre of the Scottish city of Edinburgh.

In a small cave in the rocky side of the hill, the boys stumbled across something incredible and macabre: seventeen miniature coffins. Each coffin was carved from pine, and each was decorated with ironwork. The coffins were stacked in two neat rows of eight, with one lonely coffin beginning a new row on top.

Bizarrely, each coffin contained a small wooden doll. Each doll was dressed with painted black boots and individually crafted clothing. The dolls were about four inches long.

Even more bizarrely, the coffins appeared to have been buried over a long period of time, with the top ones fresher and the lower ones more decayed.

In the nearly two hundred years since these toy

coffins were discovered, no clue has been unearthed to explain what they were made for, who made them and who hid them. I'm sure other writers have, or will, use this bizarre historical story as the basis for their own novels. This is my attempt to put some flesh on the bones, if you will forgive the phrase.

Nigel McCrery, May 2015

PART ONE

It was strange the things you notice when death is close. Everything becomes clearer; somehow more real. Children screaming with delight as they play. People chattering about nothing in particular, just whiling away a few hours with friends. The wind blowing through the trees, rustling the leaves. Those things that you take for granted when life is passing you by. She even noticed the scent of the roses that were growing close beneath her bedroom window, and the aroma of next door's freshly cut grass. They all drifted, the sounds and the smells, in through the open window, and filled her senses.

That damn window. If she hadn't left it wide open, so she could keep cool on what felt like the warmest afternoon of the year, she might not be in this situation now. She needed to sleep during the day; she was on night shift and if she didn't get some rest she would never get through her shift, but if she had left it closed and locked as she normally did she wouldn't be having the life squeezed out of her now by a pair of very powerful hands.

Why, her mind screamed, hadn't she picked up that room fan last Saturday? It was in the sale – why had she been so mean with herself? Everything would have been okay if she had just indulged herself by splashing out a little cash. That way she wouldn't have needed to leave the window open.

Strange, she pondered as the hands shifted their grip on her throat, how even the most trivial decisions, made days, weeks or even months before, could affect your future in such a dramatic way.

Not that it looked like she had much of a future left. While the world went on normally outside her room, inside it a man was ending her brief life. She had tried to fight back at the start, but it had happened so quickly and he was too strong; then as he gripped her the injection went in. Seconds later she could feel her senses swimming and any remaining strength washed away.

Had the drug caused her thoughts to drift so aimlessly? Or was it just because her mind remained the only functioning organ, and there was little else to do with no other nerves or muscles responding?

Muscles responding. *It was then that she felt a faint tingling in her right hand. She moved a couple of fingers and felt her hand respond too. Obviously the drug hadn't completely taken control, which she should have known from her medical knowledge. It took longer to reach the body's extremities. But she wouldn't have long, and would she be able to move her arm enough to swing it, even if she was able to reach the iron-based lamp to one side? She tentatively reached for it, careful not to glance in its direction and alert him. But his eyes seemed fixed on hers as the pressure grew against her throat. She stretched her hand out; only another inch and she'd have the lamp in her grasp.*

The storm came out of nowhere.

DCI Mark Lapslie looked up at the heavily greying sky as the first strong bite of wind caught the sails and then as quickly changed direction. The mainsail whipped sharply back and forth in protest.

'I don't like the look of this. Could get nasty.'

His companion Charlotte eyed the sails and the sky beyond. 'Are you sure? Might be just a squall.'

'Might be.' Lapslie studied the sky more intently, trying to gauge the direction of the ominously dark cloud layer. It appeared to stretch at least five or six miles, filling the visible skyline over the Solent behind them; and while its epicentre might miss them by half a mile, the wind whipping up at its edges seemed equally fierce.

It seemed odd. Just two hours ago they'd been moored

peacefully in Osborne Bay, a few hundred yards offshore from Queen Victoria's old private beach, enjoying strawberries and cream washed down with chilled champagne. They'd broken their pre-lunch 'no-drinking' rule, but then that was the sort of rule you broke on holiday, even if it was just a long weekend break. With his own haphazard schedule in the police force and Charlotte's as a doctor, they didn't get to see each other as much as they liked, and a long weekend away together was a rare treat indeed.

The water had lapped gently at the side of the boat, a 24-foot Mazury that Lapslie had owned the past two years, and the scene was as close to the Mediterranean as UK shores offered. Charlotte loved it, quickly embracing the mood and setting, so perhaps now she was having an equal problem adjusting to the sudden change in conditions and ambience. Whereas, with almost three years' sailing under his belt, he'd become more attuned to sudden changes in weather conditions.

Lightning forked out of the approaching dark clouds, followed seconds later by a rumble of thunder, and the boat lurched sharply leeward as the mainsail was hit by a heavier gust.

'We're going to have to pull the sails in.' He had to

almost shout to be heard above the billowing wind. 'I'll need a hand. If you hold the main boom over to port aft, I'll—' He broke off as he realized the only sailing term she'd likely grasped was 'boom', from having to dodge it as it swung across. 'Uh, back towards your left side – I'll meanwhile winch the sail in.'

Halfway down there was an anxious moment as a fresh gust caught the sail full on, almost wrenching the boom rope from Charlotte's grasp.

'Hang on!' Lapslie shouted above the heavy wind. He reckoned it had already risen to 60 miles per hour, with gusts of 80 to 90. 'It's almost down now.'

As he winched in the last of the mainsail and furled and tied it, a steady rain started to fall, becoming a deluge within seconds.

'Okay, now the jib sail. Don't worry – it'll be easier. You pull hard right this time while I winch and furl.'

It took only a couple of minutes, but in that time the wind had whipped the sea up into a vicious chop, tipping them back and forth.

Lapslie wished George was with them. Not that Charlotte wasn't coping well, given her limited sailing knowledge, but mainly because she now looked anxious. This wasn't an interlude in their romantic weekend he'd planned. George, a retired Royal Navy man, was Lapslie's part-time skipper who'd sailed the Mazury from its mooring in Clacton harbour so as to maximize their time sailing round the Isle of Wight and along the Dorset coast. George not only had long experience of sailing in storm conditions, he'd have been able to offer the right assurance to ease Charlotte's worry lines.

Lapslie started the engine and turned the tiller so that they were heading back the way they'd come. But it meant sailing into the heart of the storm; it would get worse before it got better. The chop of the waves seemed to be striking the boat's hull midway each time, so there was a sharp pitch and toss to cope with along with a heavy roll. They were getting soaked from waves washing over the bow and side as much as from the heavy rain.

'I think maybe you should go below,' he called out to Charlotte. 'Get inside.'

'What? And leave you all alone with the main excitement out here?' She attempted a sly smile which wasn't wholly convincing, and then two sharp flashes of lightning close together, only a mile away now from the following thunder, highlighted the underlying fear in her face.

'I'll be fine. I've seen worse.' Although he hadn't, and he wasn't sure he'd been any more convincing.

If they could just get past the point at Ryde, it should get calmer after that. But that five miles might as well be a hundred in this weather. He could hardly see the coastline any more through the heavy rain and flying sea spray.

She managed to swing the lamp, but not fast and hard enough. And as her attacker saw her intention in his side vision, he leant away from the lamp's arc. It brushed with hardly any effect against one shoulder, and then the pressure on her throat increased threefold.

She tried to swing again, but suddenly all her strength had gone, her emotions too seeming to drain away like dirty water from a bath.

She idly wondered why she had been the one chosen, why it hadn't been someone else, someone in a different block of flats, on a different floor. It seemed so unfair: she had never harmed anyone in her life. In fact she was a nurse, and that involved helping people. As far as she was aware, she didn't have an enemy in the world.

The other thing that flashed through her mind was that she thought she recognized her murderer. In fact, she was sure that she knew him, and of all the people in her life he was the last one she would ever have considered a threat or a danger. But here he was: her nemesis. She had always been such a bad judge of character.

These were her final thoughts. A few moments later, everything that she could see, smell, hear and feel just folded up on itself and vanished into the darkness.

Lapslie continued battling against the storm in his dream, and so he wasn't sure if they'd actually made it or the storm had won and he was going through his version of a drowning man's reflections.

All due to his recent obsession with sailing. It had started simply enough, when he'd gone for a day out on the North Sea with a friend, and the odd thing was that he hadn't been sure about the idea in the first place. The thought of bobbing around on grey water under grey clouds for hours on end really didn't appeal to him. Finally and reluctantly he was persuaded, and he had enjoyed it so much that he'd enrolled at a sailing school in Clacton-on-Sea and become a qualified sailor.

Once the training was out of the way he then brought his 24-foot Mazury. Made of fibreglass, beautiful lines, teak decks, four berths, and it hadn't cost him an arm and a leg. It even had a 6 hp outboard motor, not that he used it much – he was far too concerned about the effect its distinctive sound would have on his synaesthesia, which transformed and merged noise with smell and taste. Besides he hardly needed it, the boat had sailed like a dream. When he was out on the water all his troubles seemed to drift away. They all seemed land-bound, unable to follow him across the water. As he looked back at the disappearing horizon he knew he couldn't be troubled any more.

It was strange: none of the numerous and particular sounds that surrounded him when he was at sea seemed to have any effect on his synaesthesia. The splash of the water against the hull, the wind in the sails, the flags and pendants fluttering out until the halyards rattled. Even the screeching of the inquisitive and ever-hungry seagulls that occasionally followed the boat didn't seem to translate into tastes in his mouth the way that traffic noise, conversation and all the other sounds on land did. There was nothing, not a single discernible effect. In the water he was free, free to think, free to calculate, free to be himself for the first time in many years.

Maybe it was something to do with the drug he was taking to counter the effects – thorazitol. At first the pills had almost completely suppressed the synaesthesia, but he had began to experience side-effects – hallucinations and strange random thoughts – and so, on his consultant's advice, he had cut back on the dosage until the side-effects stopped. That still left him with a stub of synaesthesia, but nothing like the scale that he had been experiencing over the past few years.

Lapslie had become used to his own company through necessity. At first he hated it, but as months drifted into years, he had grown to love it, and now even craved it. Being alone, surrounded by water, with a calm and untroubled mind, was the pinnacle of everything he'd searched for. A sort of natural healing.

Alone. Reflecting on how sailing had served at first to heal his own personal ills, he found himself self-castigating for now bringing Charlotte along, putting her through this nightmare ordeal. What had he been thinking of? Or had his desire for them to have a weekend away together prevailed over his thirst for quiet personal space when sailing, one selfishness winning out on the other?

The vibration from his mobile phone broke into Lapslie's sleep, startling him, sending a wash of bitter coffee across his taste buds. He was slow to rouse, pulling the covers over his head for a moment. The phone kept vibrating insistently until finally he reached out for it.

'Lapslie.' As he answered it, his voice husky and still sleepy, he glanced across at the clock: 5.40 p.m. Two hours' nap since Charlotte had gone ashore. The last of the storm had blown through hours ago and was now no more than a gentle lapping against the hull in the Cowes harbour mooring. Charlotte had taken a taxi to the Villa Rothsay Hotel while Lapslie had elected to stay aboard and wait for George.

Thankfully George had stayed in Portsmouth over-night to catch up with some old mates and would inspect any damage before sailing the boat back to Clacton. And having made all the arrangements, the exertion of battling the storm and the pre-lunch wine had caught up with him and he'd fallen into a deep sleep. He glanced through the porthole towards the dockside. George should be here soon.

Lapslie recognized the voice at the other end instantly. Although the taste of her voice had shifted over the years, it always had a sort of citrusy tang to it. Of all the voices he had tasted over the years her voice was the only one that had that taste. It was Emma Bradbury.

'Sorry to disturb you, sir . . .'

Lapslie cut her short. 'But not sorry enough to avoid doing so? You know I'm not on call and this is a weekend away for me.'

Bradbury acknowledged with a sigh. 'No, sir, I realize that, but Chief Superintendent Rouse sends his compliments and says that he would like you involved in this.'

Lapslie sat up sharper. 'What exactly is "this"?'

'A possible murder, sir.'

Lapslie wasn't impressed. 'Possible? I tell you what, when it's definite then call me back. And where the hell is Chalky White? – he's the one on call.'

'Already committed with a stabbing, I'm afraid . . .'

'Is that a "possible" too?'

'No sir.' The citrus of her voice was tinged with strawberry – a sign of irritation. 'The victim is dead, it *is* a murder, and an arrest has already been made.'

'Well that makes things easy for him. What's that, his first murder this year?'

Bradbury didn't reply, not wanting to get involved in office politics or rivalries. Lapslie couldn't blame her. 'Okay,' he said, trying to be conciliatory, 'where is it?'

'A few miles from Abberton Reservoir.'

'Where's that when it's at home?'

'The nearest village is . . . give me a second . . .' She

paused for a moment, consulting someone out of range of the microphone. 'The rather improbably named Layer de la Haye. I'll text the postcode through.'

'Okay. But I'm on the Isle of Wight right now, so it'll take me a few hours. You'll have to hang on meanwhile.'

'Understood. I'll grab some tea and leave a constable to secure the scene.'

Lapslie hung up. Well, that was the end of his weekend plans – though any more sailing had been scotched in any case. It was at times like this that he seriously thought about resigning or going off on extended sick leave. Christ, if *he* wasn't entitled to sick leave, then surely no one was. The trouble was he could really do with leaving due to some injury he had received while on duty, rather than thanks to a personal condition. He would get more money that way. With an early pension and a large lump sum he could upgrade his boat and just fuck off into the sunset.

Lapslie pulled himself back to reality. It was a stupid idea, if for no other reason than the fact that he needed a bit more sailing experience under his belt – as the storm had made patently clear. No, it would be at least another year before he was in a position to realize his dream. He would have to tread water until then.

Half-smiling at his own inner joke, he looked up as a rapping came against the porthole and George's face beamed from the other side.

It took just under three hours to make the journey, and Lapslie's senses were sharpened rather than jaded from having driven flat out; he knew it would catch up with him later that night and he'd no doubt crash out.

A familiar sight met him at the crime scene. Arcs of white and flashing blue lights illuminated the area, giving it a surreal look. More like a street in Las Vegas than a British murder scene. White-suited SOCOs moved around with purposeful energy, while detectives in ill-fitting suits seemed to be wandering at random, looking for their next mug of coffee while trying to appear interested and useful. Lapslie drove slowly up to the checkpoint. He flashed his ID at the young pale-faced uniform on the gate. The lad was only there keeping the log because no one had any idea what else to do with him.

Most of the constabulary knew who Lapslie was by his reputation alone, but this young probationer clearly didn't. 'Can I have your name for the record, sir?'

Lapslie stared at him. 'Chief Inspector Lapslie,' he said, after a marked pause.

Lapslie's name at least seemed to spark some recognition. 'Oh right, sir, yes, please go through.'

The lad stood back and saluted. It was the first time Lapslie had been saluted for a long time, and he found he quite liked it. He nodded and drove through the taped cordon. Rank he considered allowed you a few privileges, like not having to stop and answer questions from some snotty-nosed probationer standing at a checkpoint in the middle of nowhere. Still, Lapslie supposed, he was only trying to do his job.

He parked his car by the sign marked 'Senior Investigating Officer' – another perk he enjoyed and appreciated. Wherever he went these days there was always a special parking place for him. On this occasion he was impressed at the speed with which the sign had been erected. He probably had Bradbury to thank for that.

As he stepped from the car and looked around he had a sudden feeling that people were moving away from him, not wanting to get too close. It was as if he was infected with some nasty and very contagious disease. In a way he supposed that he was, only it wasn't contagious. There was a time when only he and Rouse had known about the synaesthesia, but now it was common knowledge. Still it was good to see his detectives moving with some purpose, even if that purpose was only to get away from him.

A figure emerged from a dark corner of the field. Lapslie had trouble identifying it at first due to the glare of one of the powerful arc lamps he had stupidly stood in front of.

'Bradbury?'

'Sir.'

'How are you?'

'Tired. It was my day off too. They called me in about an hour before I called you.'

Lapslie looked at her for a moment. 'Clearly Rouse thinks you are more important than I am. Should I watch my back?'

Bradbury stared at him for a moment, unsure if he was joking or not. 'They always like to get me here before you, sir, so I can get your parking space ready.'

Lapslie cut her short. 'And tell everyone to move away from me when I get out of my car?'

Bradbury hesitated. 'Fewer people make less noise. I know how you react to noise.'

Lapslie smiled at her. 'Yes, I do. Doesn't mean I have to like it though. Makes me feel like a leper. '

Bradbury remained silent. There was nothing she could say, really. Lapslie continued: 'So what have we got?'

'Dead male. Been dead a while from the smell of him. Looks like a tramp and it's probably natural causes.'

There was that word again: *probably*. He hated it. Either it was murder or it wasn't, and if it wasn't then he shouldn't be here. The pale-faced kid on the gate should be dealing with it.

'The police surgeon's examining the remains now,' Bradbury said.

'Is he? Well, perhaps a *possible* will turn into a *definite*. Let's see what he has to say.'

Bradbury interrupted. 'There are some other things you need to know. I—'

Lapslie cut her short. 'Let's go and have a look at the body first. You can tell me the rest after that. Now, where to?'

Bradbury pointed to a large bunker at the edge of the field. 'It's over there, sir.'

Lapslie looked over to where a large oval shape, covered in grass, was sticking out of the ground. Some kind of natural feature, or an artificial mound? 'Will I need to suit up?'

Bradbury shook her head. 'I've had a word with the

Scene of Crime manager, and he doesn't seem to think it's necessary to wear a suit – just cover shoes for now.'

Lapslie nodded. 'Well, it's his decision. Lead on.' He followed his sergeant along a well-used dirt path to the front of the mound where a large iron door was set into a flat face of earth. So, it *was* a bunker – a large one. As he entered he turned to Bradbury. 'So, what is this place?'

Bradbury looked up at him. 'It's an old fall-out shelter from the Cold War. Built in the fifties for local politicians and dignitaries to keep them safe and running the country if the Russians had ever dropped the bomb.'

'Local politicians and dignitaries? Brilliant – they cause the bloody war, then they make sure they have a safe place to hide when it starts. How democratic.'

Looking up at it now that he was close, Lapslie was impressed by the size of the bunker and the huge iron doors that secured it. 'How did you get in?'

Bradbury answered quickly. 'Locksmith, sir. Apparently took him over an hour – they were considering blowing it off at one point.'

Lapslie looked down at the giant lock still hanging from one of the metal loops. 'Which I suppose begs the question: if we had trouble getting in, how the hell did the tramp do it?'

Bradbury nodded. 'Yes, sir, that *was* one of the other questions we . . .'

Lapslie cut her short again. 'Who found the body?'

'A man walking his dog. Well, he smelled the body really: the dog was scratching at the door, and when its owner came to pull him away he could smell the corpse.'

Lapslie looked across at her. 'Through these doors? Weren't they designed to stop radiation? How the hell did a smell leak out, even one as gross as a decomposing body?'

'The bunker hasn't been maintained, sir. The seals have either perished or just dropped off.'

'Council money well spent.' He paused, thinking. 'How did he know it was a corpse he could smell?'

'He was an old soldier. He'd smelled a few before.'

Lapslie nodded. Forget about faster cars or more capable computers: the thing the police needed the most was a squad of people walking their dogs. The amount of crime they turned up was extraordinary.

Before they went any further they were stopped by the white-suited presence of Jim Thomson, the Scene of

Crime manager and senior SOCO. He gazed across at Lapslie.

'If you wouldn't mind slipping a pair of these on, Chief Inspector.'

Petrol. Lapslie licked his lips to be sure. Yes, Thomson's voice definitely tasted of petrol. Lapslie turned to face him, trying to wipe the taste from his lips with the back of his hand. Taking a pair of the transparent plastic overshoes from Thomson and slipping them over his Timberlands, Lapslie looked at the man one more time and wondered why he tasted of petrol, of all things. Did his mind just randomly assign tastes to sounds, or was there some deeper underlying logic?

He pulled himself back to reality. 'Thank you. Are you sure you don't want us suited up?'

Thomson shook his head. 'Quite sure. Well not at this stage, anyway. The overshoes will be enough.'

Lapslie nodded his understanding before he turned to follow Bradbury into the bunker.

The interior was more basic than Lapslie had imagined. Nothing high-tech – just what appeared to be concrete wall, a concrete floor and piles of old tat, most of it broken. The smell of the decomposing body was strong, however, and seemed to fill the entire room with a thick, unseen fog, refusing to drift away even though the large metal security doors had been left open. Lapslie had never really got used to that smell, even though he lived in a world of tastes and smells. The instant desire to be sick faded quickly, and he wondered idly why no sound he had ever heard had provoked the taste of rotting human flesh.

He looked around. 'A bit sparse, isn't it?'

Bradbury nodded. 'This is just the top level. It goes down several more floors. There are bedrooms, kitchens, command and control centres, even broadcasting facilities. Five hundred people could stay down here for over five years, apparently.'

'As long as they don't mind the taste of corned beef. Didn't know we had that many important people in the area.'

'With their families.'

Lapslie smiled. 'Of course. Now it makes sense.'

Lapslie noticed that arc lamps had been positioned at intervals with cables running through. As they reached the far end of the room Lapslie saw a familiar figure packing up his medical bag and standing away from what seemed to be a pile of old rags lying on the floor, but which Lapslie knew to be a body. It was odd, he considered, the strange shapes, positions and appearances people took on after death. So many looked like mannequins: white and stiff, all the life taken out of them. Others died with their mouths wide open in one last desperate scream at the cruel trick that fate had played on them. So few went gentle into that good night, he pondered. Mostly they raged against the dying of the light.

Jeff Whitefoot was the police surgeon for Essex, and had been for years. He tended to share duties with the pathologist, Jane Catherall, and Lapslie usually bumped into one or the other at scenes such as this. He had always liked Whitefoot because he was his own man, and had been even in the bad old days, when the relationship between police surgeons and forensic teams was a little too cosy and often resulted in evidence being altered to fit the circumstances. So many innocent people had been sent down, many for life, because the various people investigating the crimes knew each other, drank together or could be easily bullied or manipulated into saying what was necessary. Whitefoot had always been above all that. Kept himself to himself. Never attended social events, and it would be a brave investigating officer that tried to intimidate him.

As he approached, Lapslie stuck his hand out. Peeling off his white latex protective gloves, Whitefoot took it and shook it enthusiastically.

'Jeff. Good to see you again. It's been a while.'

'Chief Inspector. It's been a while and a half.' He gazed up into Lapslie's eyes. 'You okay? I heard you'd been ill.'

His voice tasted of dark chocolate with a touch of something else which Lapslie struggled to identify. Lavender, maybe? Whitefoot was always formal, never used first or familiar names. He kept his private and professional lives separate and would never compromise.

'Under control,' Lapslie said shortly. The last thing he wanted was a forensic cross-examination of his symptoms by a medical man. Well, not this medical man, anyway. 'What about you?' he added quickly. 'I heard you were on short time?'

Whitefoot shrugged. 'I work two and a half days a week. I haven't got the stamina to run with the young bulls any more, but I like to keep my hand in. Keep involved, if you know what I mean. And there were . . . family issues.'

Lapslie nodded. 'So what do we have? Was he murdered?'

Whitefoot shook his head. 'I doubt it. Looks like

25

natural causes – well, as natural as the death of a man who lived rough, clearly drank too much and had done for a number of years can be. Won't really know until after the post-mortem, but there are no signs of violence, no bullet holes, knives in the back, depressed fractures of the skull, that sort of thing.'

Lapslie gave Bradbury a sideways glance. She knew what he was thinking and looked down at her feet.

'Okay, well thanks for turning out.'

Whitefoot nodded. 'I thought Inspector White was on call-out?'

'He is, got a stabbing to deal with.'

'Really? That I suppose would also explain why I'm here. Doctor Catherall is presumably at the stabbing.'

'We all have our cross to bear, Jeff. Let me have your report as soon as you can.'

Whitefoot looked slightly indignant. 'It will be on your desk first thing, as it always is and always will be.'

Lapslie nodded his appreciation before walking past him to where the body was lying. He looked down at the pile of rags that had once been a human being. He often wondered how and why people ended up like this: what it was within their personalities that had allowed this to happen. But then, perhaps they were just unfortunate.

He remembered his first sergeant, Fred Gimber. Gimber had been his sergeant when Lapslie was still a probationer. He had been a sergeant in the Royal Marine Commandos during the Second World War. Hard as nails, a man you didn't cross lightly. Local villains were terrified of him. Yet there was this one old tramp that he looked after as if they were related. Lapslie had been with him one Christmas Day when Gimber had searched and found the tramp just so he could give him a bottle of whisky and a hundred cigarettes before driving him to a shelter in the area car to make sure he had a decent Christmas dinner. Later Lapslie had discovered that the old tramp had served with Gimber during the war and had won the Military Medal for bravery. He had stayed in the Army after the war, but had been kicked out a few years later due to a stomach ulcer. Without the formal structure of the Army, he had quickly fallen apart. He died a few years later and Gimber had paid for his funeral. Such was the man. Small gestures. If everyone took responsibility for what was within the reach of their arm then the world would be a better place.

Lapslie guessed that if you scratched the body of the man lying before him there might well have been a similar story. Around the corpse was an array of food wrappers, old papers, empty and broken bottles, and a worn-out haversack with ripped seams. He looked across at Jim Thomson, who had followed them to the scene. 'So what do we know about this poor old sod?' Thomson shook his head. 'Nothing much. Just these.'

He handed Lapslie several old black-and-white photos of a man with a pretty wife and two small children. It was impossible to say if the man decomposing at his feet was the same one in the photo. He turned to Bradbury, handing her the photos. 'Try and find out who he was. Natural death or not, I would like to know.'

Bradbury dropped the photographs into an exhibit bag that Thomson handed to her.

'I'm still wondering how the hell he got in,' Lapslie said.

'We are working on that, sir.'

'Don't suppose for some bizarre reason he could have had a key? Maybe he used to be a local councillor.'

Bradbury shrugged. 'No idea, sir.'

'Well, when we find out who he is we might have a better chance of finding out how he got in and what he was doing here, besides keeping warm and drinking.'

Bradbury nodded. She glanced away, awkwardly. 'There's something else I'd like you to see, sir.'

'Something connected to this body?'

Bradbury shook her head. 'No, I don't believe so, sir – but odd to say the least.' She moved away and Lapslie followed when she walked into a small antechamber just off the main room. She turned to Lapslie. 'This room had been locked, sir—'

'Nothing odd in that, Emma.'

'No, sir, but it was locked with a new-style Chubb lock. Took our locksmith longer to open this door than it did the main door. Someone's been using this room on a regular basis.'

Lapslie nodded. 'Okay. Lead on.'

As he entered the concrete room, Lapslie glanced around. It looked like it might have been a storeroom. Empty metal racking lined the walls. At the far end, lined up on one of the shelves, was what Bradbury wanted to show him. Lapslie moved close, and stared in bewilderment.

Stretching along the entire length of the shelf, standing upright, were twelve small wooden coffins. They were perfectly shaped, and about twelve inches tall. Nine were closed, and three open. The open coffins had what looked like dolls standing up inside them.

Lapslie moved forward for a closer look. The three

dolls he could see were dressed bizarrely. The first wore a beautiful lace wedding dress. The second was dressed as a soldier; on his shoulder was a small carefully stitched crown indicating the rank of major. The third and final doll was dressed as an old-fashioned teacher, with a black gown, and a mortar board perched on his head. The dolls seemed to have been made of wax, or something similar, judging by the gloss of their skin. Whatever the material was, they had been well made.

'"There will be time to murder and create",' he murmured softly.

Lapslie slipped on latex gloves, picked up the doll dressed as a bride and stared at it for a moment, running his thumb across the lace and the material that made up the dress. The clothing was well tailored, and the material of a fine quality. He put down the bride doll and went on to peer at the soldier and the teacher. When he leaned over and opened one of the closed coffins it revealed another doll; this one dressed as a mechanic of some sort. It was wearing stained blue overalls and carrying what looked like a small model spanner. The difference between this doll and the ones in the open coffins was that this doll had been crushed and twisted into disfigurement.

As Lapslie watched, Bradbury opened each of the coffins. Within each of them was another doll, each dressed in different clothing. There was a fireman, a nurse and six others. The neck of the fireman had been crushed, falling limply onto its shoulders. Every other doll had been badly damaged in some way. All differently, but all damaged.

Numerous questions raced around his mind. Why were some dolls inside their coffins and not others? Why were the ones inside the coffins damaged and those outside them perfectly fine? What did the costumes signify? Why had they been left here, and did the dead tramp have something to do with it? Were they just dolls someone had made for a horror film, or was there something much more sinister about them? And what was the significance of the number twelve? Twelve apostles; twelve angry men; twelve days of Christmas?

The smell of lavender reached him, and he wondered just which of the dolls might be triggering that smell in his mind: the fireman, the bride, the nurse? Or maybe it was simply coming from the cloth they were made with, somebody impregnating it with lavender to keep moths away.

He turned to Bradbury. 'I don't suppose we know anything about the dolls, do we?'

Bradbury shook her head. 'No, sir, nothing. I was about to get the SOCOs to bag and tag them.'

'No, don't do that. Well not for now, anyway. Do the media know about this yet?'

Bradbury shook her head again. 'No, sir, not yet. Seems little point in telling them now. I don't suppose there's much of a story in "alcoholic tramp found dead".'

Lapslie looked at her for a moment. 'Everyone has their story, Emma – even alcoholic tramps.' Before she could reply he changed the subject. 'Let's wrap up the body ready for removal and run this operation down.'

'Before we are sure of the cause of death?'

Lapslie nodded. 'Yes. I'm pretty sure Whitefoot is right, but just in case, no one goes in or out until we have the final results. I want the placed resealed and any sign that we have been here gone. If we do have a suspicious death then there's no harm done because the evidence will still be intact. If, as I suspect, we don't, then I want the place watched to see if our doll-maker returns. There are a few questions I would like to ask him.'

Bradbury seemed unsure, but nodded her acceptance.

'I want the surveillance on for a week, twenty-four hours a day. If anyone is picked up, I want to know at once. There's something odd about this and I want to know what it is.'

'Chief Superintendent Rouse isn't going to like this, sir. He'll want to know why we're spending money on surveillance when there's no obvious crime.'

'Do it anyway. By the time he finds out it will all be over – unless someone tells him.'

He turned to Bradbury. She held defensive hands up. 'Not me. I won't breathe a word.'

Lapslie stared at her for a long moment. 'It might be nothing,' he said finally, 'but equally some important investigations have started out with something small like this.'

Before she could respond, Lapslie moved off, heading out and towards his car. As he left, he heard Emma talking with Jim Thomson, the senior SOCO.

'Did you hear all that?'

'I did.'

'Then we'd better get on with it, hadn't we?'

'We had. I know the name of a good doll-maker, if it would help. Big hobby with my wife. She has dozens of them.'

Either Bradbury didn't reply, or her words were lost as Lapslie walked outside.

They say it takes at least a year to arrange a wedding. As far as Leslie Cooke was concerned, it had taken at least three of them. Well, that was how long they'd been engaged; straight after the split from her previous boyfriend, in fact. They had talked about getting married six months after the engagement, but there always seemed to be a reason they couldn't. A reason to put it back, to delay. In the end, Leslie began to wonder whether she should scrub not only the wedding but also Nathan, her boyfriend, too. Third time lucky, perhaps. But after dropping some broad hints, and telling him she wanted a trial separation, Nathan had come up with a date, and here they were.

She looked at the dress in the mirror for the hundredth time. It was truly stunning – just what she had always wanted – but then it should be for what it cost. Even with the damage, which her aunt had very cleverly managed to hide, it still looked wonderful.

A voice from behind cut into her thoughts.

'My God, lass, you look as good as your mother did on her wedding day, and that's saying something.'

Leslie Cooke turned to face her father. 'Do I really?'

Her father nodded, a broad grin across his face. 'You

certainly do. I just wish she was here to see you now. She would have been that proud.'

Leslie moved across to her father and, picking up a hanky from her dressing table, wiped away the tears from his eyes. 'She is here, Pa. Don't worry, she is.'

A grinning face suddenly appeared at the doorway. 'Are you coming? Cars are here. By heck, you look good, sis. He's a lucky man.'

Leslie smiled across at her brother. 'So I keep telling him.'

She looked at her father one more time, straightening his bow tie before taking his arm and making her way down to the waiting cars.

Lapslie's sleep was fitful that night, his dream a medley of the day's events. He was back in the fall-out shelter, this time alone, walking slowly into its dark depths and seeing once more the dolls lined up against the wall. Some, the more grotesque and damaged dolls already in their coffins, slowly opened their lids and stepped into the dim light. As Lapslie watched they began to dance, alone and with each other. After a while the dance changed its stately and organized rhythm into something darker and more chaotic, and eventually the grotesque dolls abandoned the pretence of the minuet entirely and began attacking the dolls not yet in their coffins. They began to stab and beat them, tearing at their waxed faces with their fingers. Finally the last three unscathed dolls were pushed into their small coffins and the lids slammed shut.

It was then that Lapslie noticed a thirteenth coffin, one that he hadn't seen before. And there seemed to be an intense light on it, almost like a spotlight picking it out from the others; then, as the light flickered and faded and instantly returned in a blinding flash accompanied by a rumble of thunder, he realized the storm had returned. He'd survived sailing through it, but now it had come back to show him something. Something important.

The dolls gathered around the coffin, pulling at the lid until it finally opened. They dragged the doll out and held it up for Lapslie to see. But at that moment the lightning abated, and in the gloom that followed he couldn't make it out – although he sensed it was vitally important he viewed it. He edged closer, praying for another lightning flash so that he could see it clearly.

But as the next lightning flash came it was accompanied by a heavy boom of thunder which awoke him. He sat up sharply, but there was no thunder from outside, just the heavy thud of the bin men loading the week's recycling. He glanced at his bedside clock: 6.52 a.m. He blinked heavily; only twenty minutes from when his alarm was set, so he might as well get up.

Two hours after leaving the bomb shelter he'd received a call at home from George, at that point only half an hour's sailing from Clacton harbour. Too late and too dark to start work on any storm damage to the boat, they'd agreed to meet back at the harbour late the next morning. Give George a few hours' more good daylight to assess any repairs needed.

He ran one hand brusquely through his hair as he padded to the bathroom. He had once been told that dreams were nature's way of clearing all the crap out of your brain – like Peter Pan's nanny brushing his mind clear every night, ready for a new day. He also remembered how Sherlock Holmes had dreamed about the drawings of the Dancing Men as he tried to decode what they meant. Dreams could sometimes be a way of making sense of things that seemed senseless.

He wondered why he'd been unable to see that final coffin figure, why that might be significant. Or maybe it was just the number thirteen that was significant – that harbinger of doom, unlucky number ever since

Judas and the Last Supper – and having filled that final number, he was unable to match it with a face or costume.

With no ready answer, Lapslie contemplated himself in the mirror and started cleaning his teeth.

The wedding had been a great success. Nathan had arrived on time, despite his friends and what looked like a stag night they would never forget but would like to. As Leslie walked down the aisle towards him, and he turned to face her, she had never been so happy. After that it was easy. Just a hard stare at her brother during the 'If anyone can show good cause' bit.

She had never seen her dad so happy. He'd had a hard time of it since the death of her mother, two years before, and it was good to see him smiling and happy again. The walk back down the aisle was wonderful. All her family and friends were there, wishing her well, giving her decorated horseshoes and painted wooden spoons.

'This way! Look this way!'

It was the photographer, trying to get everyone to be serious, if only for a few moments. As Leslie turned to face him, her face glowing with all the happiness that was blossoming inside her, she felt a sudden impact on her chest. It didn't seem anything much at first: she thought perhaps one of the pageboys had run into her, but she hadn't seen anyone. Then she realized it must have been harder than she thought when she found herself thrown backwards and falling. Nathan's hand was ripped from hers. Someone screamed as she fell, face upwards, onto the cold church floor. The impact knocked the breath from her body, and she felt silly and embarrassed. She hoped no one had captured the moment on tape so it would appear on one of those 'pratfall' programmes that were so popular on television at the moment.

The impact must have been harder than she expected, because she was struggling to breathe. She hoped that the little pageboy, or whoever it was that had bumped into her, was feeling all right.

The next thing she knew her father was by her side, holding her up and talking to her. His face was red, bright red, and whatever it was seemed to be dripping off his chin. She wanted to wipe it off, but couldn't move.

Her father began to speak: 'You all right, lassie? What's happened? Oh my God, what's happened?'

Leslie Petersen never heard his next words. Her eyes were wide open and staring but she could see nothing. Her father, unable to protect her any more, pulled her closer to him.

'Oh God, no, no, no, no. Not Leslie, no!'

Lapslie was still officially off duty, seeing that he had curtailed his weekend away with the bunker investigation. Still, he put in a call to Emma Bradbury for any case updates while availing himself of a full English breakfast at his favourite café. Nothing pressing to report, so he browsed the day's newspaper, finished his tea and headed to the harbour. When Lapslie parked his Saab at the dockside, George was already there. George nodded in greeting, and as they headed along the jetty towards the boat, Lapslie asked, 'So what's the damage?'

'Looks like you were lucky. Like I said last night, the only thing is some loose play in the rudder.'

'Will it take much to fix?'

'I think a bit of tightening will see to it. You won't need a new coupling.'

'What about the inch of water in the galley?'

'It didn't increase on the sail back from Cowes and from what I can see the hull looks fine. No leaks. Looks like it came in from water swilling over the deck during the storm. Probably that aft hatch seal I felt had seen better days.'

'Yes, you're probably right. I should have had it replaced earlier.' George had mentioned the wear on the seal almost a year ago, but with no rough-weather sailing to test it out it hadn't seemed so urgent. Until now.

George looked back towards the boat, as if gauging whether there was anything he'd missed. His face was worn and lined and he had only a few remaining wisps of grey hair, but his pale blue eyes seemed as sharp as ever; as if constantly scanning the horizons had kept his vision honed. 'Should only take a couple of hours to pump the water and tighten the rudder. But if you want the hatch seal replaced, best I get that first so it's all done at the same time.'

Lapslie nodded after a second. 'Yes. Go ahead with the seal too. I don't aim to be facing more heavy storms any time soon, but it's not worth taking the risk.'

Lapslie joined George in looking thoughtfully towards the boat, as if he too was considering anything that might have been overlooked. Where a name should have been painted there was just a white blank, replacing the previous owner's rather unimaginative name of *Seagull*. He supposed he could name her *The Busted Flush*, after the boat owned by 'salvage consultant' Travis McGee in the books by John D. MacDonald.

The arrangement with George worked particularly well. Retiring from the Royal Navy, George couldn't afford his own boat and Lapslie couldn't afford a captain – either full- or part-time. So the arrangement was that in return for a few days' sailing here and there, George would maintain the boat and sail it to more favourable sailing grounds for when Lapslie wanted to use it, so that he wouldn't lose precious hours getting there; his preferred grounds of the Isle of Wight or Norfolk were almost a full day's sailing away from Clacton harbour, but George had old Navy mates he could look up in both, so the arrangement worked well for both of them. All Lapslie had to shell out for was any parts needed.

'Might have helped if I'd stayed with you,' George commented. 'Less panic.'

Lapslie smiled wryly. 'I'd have been all right on my own. My main concern was Charlotte being with me.'

George looked as if he was struck with another thought, but finally decided against voicing it.

They spent ten minutes more going round the boat while George went through his notebook checklist of damage, before concluding, 'I think that's it.'

'Looks like it.' Lapslie joined George in a final visual once-over of the boat from the dockside, then George took a fresh breath.

'Well, it's not going to get fixed with us just staring at it. So I'll nip down to Griffin's chandlery and—'

Lapslie held a hand up as his mobile phone buzzed in his pocket. When he saw it was Emma Bradbury calling, he moved two paces away to answer it.

'Sir, I thought you'd want to know straight away. Something has just come up – a murder at a wedding. The bride, no less.'

'My goodness.' Lapslie felt his chest tighten, his breath suddenly short. A bride had been among the dolls he'd seen in the bunker, but that could be just a coincidence. Impossible to make either assumptions or conclusions. Too early. 'Where's this happened?'

'St May's Church, Finchingfield.'

'And you're on the scene now?'

'I'm on my way. Should be there in about fifteen minutes.'

Lapslie could hear the siren in the background her end. He did a quick time and distance calculation. 'I shouldn't be too long getting there. An hour at most from now.' He rang off and peeled a twenty-pound note from his wallet. 'Sorry, George, got to run. Duty calls! Hopefully that should cover the hatch seal.'

Foot hard down, he made the drive to St May's Church in just fifty minutes. The place was teeming with the usual suspects. SOCOs, detectives, uniforms.

The press were also there in force, both TV and papers. The mobile incident room had already been established and there was yellow incident tape everywhere. For once everyone, including the detectives, really did seem to have a purpose. There was a palpable air of urgency and professionalism. This had to be a bad one.

As Lapslie went to drive through the checkpoint he was stopped for a second time, this time not by a pale-faced probationer but by an experienced uniformed sergeant. The man's voice tasted of something simultaneously creamy and greasy, like avocados. Lapslie had never liked avocados. His identification was noted and verified, as well as the time he arrived at the scene, along with the registration number of his car. Before he could drive towards the church car park the passenger door was opened and Bradbury got in.

'I've got you a spot over by the church wall, sir, but you'd better be quick before it gets taken.'

Lapslie looked at her. 'What happened to my sign?'

Bradbury shrugged. 'Disappeared, sorry. Some scrote took it away with them. It's probably hanging on their living-room wall right now.'

Lapslie frowned. Yet another perk gone. There would

be no point to it all soon – everyone would be equal in a flat management structure. Apart, of course, from Chief Superintendent Rouse.

He followed Emma's directions to the parking spot. Fortunately the gap was still free. Lapslie pulled into it. He turned to his sergeant. 'So what have we got? It's obviously bloody serious.'

Bradbury paused for a moment, determined not to get a thing wrong. 'The girl . . .' she looked at her notebook '. . . is Leslie Cooke, aged twenty-two years, who got married here today and was shot and killed shortly after the service concluded.'

Lapslie was impatient. 'By who? Husband, former husband, boyfriend?'

'No none of those, or we don't think so. She was shot by a sniper . . .'

'A *sniper*? What is this, Iraq?'

Bradbury shrugged. 'The Army have provided a Special Forces contact. He's trying to establish where the shot came from. We know it came from some considerable distance, and the person pulling the trigger must have been well trained.'

Lapslie was now all attention. 'How many shots?'

'Just one: through the heart. She died very quickly.'

Lapslie sighed. 'Sounds like someone knew what they were doing. Is the body still here?'

Bradbury nodded. 'Yes.'

'Witnesses all still here?'

Bradbury nodded again. 'They're all giving statements, sir. Her father is in pieces. Tried to get him to hospital, but he won't leave the scene.'

Lapslie let out a deep sigh. The trouble with murders like this, he thought, is that they become relatable. You wonder how you would feel if it was your child lying dead in their own blood. Lapslie had two sons, and the thought of anything happening to them kept him awake at night, especially as they lived with his ex-wife rather than with him. He knew, however, that he mustn't let emotion interfere. The most he could do for the relatives now was to catch the bastard that did it.

Stepping out of the car, Lapslie followed Bradbury first to a large white tent established by the SOCOs, where he was supplied with a white disposable oversuit, a pair of overshoes and a green facemask. From there they went to the crime scene itself, just outside the doors to the church. The body of Leslie Cooke was still lying there. It was just how Lapslie had imagined. There was a lot of blood. It spread in pools congealed around the body, small streams spilling and meandering along the cracks in the stonework and down the steps like a glutinous red waterfall. Her wedding dress was a bizarre jigsaw of maroon and white.

'Who would have thought her to have had so much blood in her?' he murmured.

Lapslie stood on the plastic panels which had been laid around the body in order to stop any contact with the floor, and potential evidence. He looked down at the discolouring face of a once beautiful young girl. Her eyes were still wide open and staring blankly ahead into a future that must have seemed so promising a few hours before, but now was just darkness. He knelt down and gently closed them. As he did so, he was interrupted by a young female SOCO. 'I wouldn't do that if I were you. Continuity of evidence.'

He looked up at her. Her voice tasted of bitter almonds, which made sense to Lapslie. 'When science gets in the way of common decency, that's the day I walk away from this job. Closing her eyes will make no difference to anything, except maybe to give her a little of the respect she deserves.' He stood up slowly, not taking his eyes off an increasingly uncomfortable-looking SOCO.

'And the next time you address me, it's "sir". Do you understand?'

She nodded, turned and walked away. Lapslie was glad to see the back of her. He returned his attention to Bradbury.

'Where do we think the shot came from?

Bradbury pointed to a small medieval tower some way in the distance.

Lapslie strained his eyes. 'Bloody hell, are you sure? That's one hell of a shot.'

'Special Forces, SOCOs and the ballistics boys are trying to determine that right now, sir. We're pretty sure the shot came from there, though.'

He looked around. There was no sign of any officers with guns. 'What about the Firearms Unit? We've got an armed criminal somewhere in the vicinity. That's not something that makes me comfortable.'

'SCO19 has been called in,' Emma confirmed, 'but you know how long it takes them to get to anything that doesn't involve a man standing in the High Street with a gun actually in his hand. The assumption is that chummy with the sniper rifle had it away on his toes straight after the shot.' She gestured around. 'No other fatalities or injuries occurred before the emergency services turned up. If the sniper had hung around look-ing for new victims then the paramedics and the wedding guests would have been decimated.'

Lapslie looked towards the tower again. To make a shot like that you really had to know what you were doing, but why would someone with that kind of know-ledge and ability murder a young bride on her wedding day? Maybe that was the question that would help them catch the killer.

A voice broke into his thoughts. 'Can we remove the body now?'

Lapslie licked his lips; the same smell as the day before – petrol. He knew who was posing the question before he turned to face him: Jim Thomson, Scene of Crime manager and senior SOCO.

'Has the police surgeon been?'

'Yes, sir. He pronounced death a little while ago. We were just waiting for you.'

Lapslie nodded. 'In that case, fine, let's get her to the mortuary and see what Doctor Catherall can tell us.' He looked back at Bradbury. 'So where are the witnesses?'

'In the church hall, giving statements. We've taken it over as an incident room.'

'I take it we managed to hold everyone here?'

Bradbury nodded. 'As far as we know. Even had to cancel the next wedding. That didn't go down well.'

'Funny, isn't it, how one person's tragic death affects so many people. Let's go and talk to the witnesses.'

Lapslie followed Bradbury back down the church steps, across the church yard and into the hall. It was a large, well-lit and well-ventilated room with a balcony at one end and a stage at the other. Pantomimes and carols at Christmas; Agatha Christie and giant marrow competitions in the summer. English village life.

Scores of tables had already been set up around the room. At each one sat a distraught witness and a police officer who was busy scribbling down their description of events. It would mostly be a waste of time, but it had to be done for completeness's sake, and occasionally there was something there, some scrap of usable evidence. The support group were setting up a computer section and getting ready to collate the incoming information. Boards were being erected and a small briefing room established. Just after any murder it was always like this; then, as time went on and no one was caught, things became more routine until they were scaled down and the murder ended up as a cold case. In most cases, if the murder wasn't solved within the first seventy-two hours the chances of ever solving it were halved. Lapslie was determined that this one wouldn't end up in a brown box stored in some forgotten cupboard. The one thing the family would need was justice and he was going to do his best to give it to them.

'Where are the groom and her father?'

Bradbury pointed to a man with his head in his hands. As he looked up, he caught Lapslie's eye for just a moment and moaned like an animal, and in that moment, and despite his medication, Lapslie felt all the grief and hurt he was suffering as a wash of something across his tongue. It was a taste he had never experienced before, and had no way of describing. It was the most intense, most complex, most subtle flavour he had ever tasted: sorrow and agony expressed as a single incredible essence. For a moment he had to grab Bradbury's arm to stop himself falling. The intensity lasted only a moment and he pulled himself together quickly.

Before Emma Bradbury had a chance to ask Lapslie what was wrong, Detective Inspector Alan Shaw walked across the hall to join the two of them. Lapslie looked across at him, surprised to see him there.

'Thought you were on night crime, Alan?'

'I'm standing in for you here. You're wanted back at the bunker. There's been some kind of incident.'

Shaw had a bitter, musty taste to him, like sweat. His voice made Lapslie wince.

'What kind of incident?'

'The doll – the one in the bride's dress. Someone's played out its murder.'

PART TWO

8 August 2008

The fire, as far as it went, wasn't a bad one. He'd seen far worse during the ten years he had been a serving fireman. For some reason, though, the heat from this one seemed to belie its ferocity. Richard Dale had never known a fire quite so hot, while at the same time being so small. There must be something within the building causing the heat, and they had no idea what it was. Maybe some sort of accelerant.

If it hadn't been for his friend Niamat, who had been a fireman since he left school, Dale would still be stuck in a never-ending round of worthless going-nowhere jobs, or sitting at home wondering where the next job was coming from. Niamat had had words with a few people within the Fire Service, and before Richard Dale had realized what was happening, he was in. Not only did becoming a fireman give him a regular job with career prospects and a pension at the end – the working man's Valhalla – it also delighted his girlfriend Cat no end. She had been fed up with his easy-going, 'Something will turn up', attitude to work. Truth be told, she felt a little ashamed of him, and he couldn't blame her. Now she had something to hold her head up about. Even the kids seemed pleased, and loved to brag that their dad was a fireman.

There had been no explosion, and the fire seemed to be generally under control, when Richard Dale felt a sudden sharp pain on the left of his forehead. He tried to sort out in his mind what the hell had just hit him. He raised a hand to the side of his head and realized that blood was streaming down his cheek. The moment he touched the blood, a feeling of nausea overwhelmed him. The combination of pain, shock and nausea finally made him lose his balance. He fell back off the ladder.

He should have been wearing a safety harness but it had been all tangled up, and on this one occasion, and despite all the rules, he had disregarded it. The bottom line was the fire needed to be put out, and put out quickly, so he'd cracked on without securing the harness. He'd done it a dozen times before without a problem. They all had.

Richard Dale was still alive when he hit the floor in the middle of the burning building. Both his legs, his right arm and several of his ribs were broken, along with his pelvis. He couldn't move, but he was still conscious and aware of everything that was happening around him. He tried to call for help, but the *smoke was too strong. It got inside his throat, his lungs, choking him.*

Outside his colleagues, seeing what had happened, did all they could to get to him, but it was hopeless. The heat was too much and parts of the building had already begun to crumble. Inside, the flames enveloped Richard Dale. His coughing screams were the last thing his colleagues heard, before the stricken building collapsed over him.

Lapslie had never liked Alan Shaw. He was a chancer, spent most of his career looking for the right arse to kiss. He had even asked Chief Superintendent Rouse to be his son's godfather, and, what was worse, Rouse had accepted. Lapslie had known Rouse ever since they were both raw woodentops at Brixton nick, and it hadn't even *occurred* to him to ask Rouse to be the godfather of his sons, Jamie and Robbie. After that, of course, Shaw was untouchable. Lapslie was positive that over the next few years his promotion would be rapid until finally he would turn up as the new head of CID. With luck, Lapslie would have retired by then. The idea of calling Shaw 'sir' was more than he could stand, now or in the future.

It took Lapslie and Bradbury just over forty minutes to get back to the decommissioned nuclear bunker. Jim

Thomson had wanted to come, but Lapslie wasn't sure he could stand the continual taste of petrol. Besides, why would he need a senior SOCO at the scene of a murdered doll?

When they arrived, two DCs were waiting for them: Parkin and Pearce. Lapslie looked around: the police presence was low – the squad car was out of sight and the two coppers had been observing from a distance. It was what he had wanted – the bunker left invitingly alone – but now he wasn't sure that it had been the best idea. Something had happened, and it had gone unobserved.

They all walked across to the large metal doors together. As they began to move inside the shelter, Lapslie stopped Pearce. 'No, you wait here. Don't want any unwelcome visitors barging in.'

Pearce nodded. 'Yes, sir.'

On entering the shelter the first thing Lapslie noticed was that the smell of the tramp's decaying body had disappeared and been replaced with an odd musty smell that he normally associated with damp cellars.

Lapslie turned his attention to DC Parkin. 'So what have we got?'

Parkin looked uncomfortable. 'Think you had better have a look, sir.'

Parkin switched on a small hand torch, and both Lapslie and Bradbury followed him through the dank darkness of the interior. This time there were no arc lamps to guide them: just the natural light spilling in from the door and Parkin's torch.

On reaching the storage room Parkin pulled open the door and shone his light inside. At the far end of the wall, still perched on the metal shelves, were the coffins, only this time there were only ten of them. Two of the dolls and two of the coffins had disappeared.

Pulling the torch from Parkin's grasp, Lapslie made his way slowly towards the small line of wooden coffins. Using only the tip of his index finger he opened the small coffin lid on the last of them. Standing upright inside it was the bridal doll he had seen earlier. The doll had a large hole on the left side of her chest from which a red substance had been oozing, and the once brilliantly white dress had turned a mottled red.

Lapslie leaned forward, sniffing at the dress. He had wondered at once whether the red liquid was a dye of some sort, or ink, or even tomato sauce or raspberry jam, but it was none of those. His nose was quickly filled by the hot copper smell of blood, and Lapslie had a bad feeling that when the blood was analysed it was going to have come from the body of the girl at the church – Leslie Petersen. He felt a shiver run through him. This case grew more bizarre by the day.

At least only two of the dolls and their coffins had disappeared. Was the killer sending some kind of message? Challenge the police; get them involved in some bizarre deadly game? Still, the good news was that Jim Thomson and his team had already photographed the two missing dolls, so at least he would have some idea of what they looked like, and hopefully their significance to the murder inquiry.

He felt an almost overwhelming urge to remove all the dolls from their coffins and examine them himself, but he knew at this stage that it would be a big mistake. As he took a step away, the scent of lavender reached him again. He scanned the row of coffins containing dolls, wondering again which one of them was triggering that smell in his mind.

He turned to Bradbury. 'Get Thomson and his team back up here. I want this place treated like a murder scene. No half-measures this time – I want everyone suited and booted. I also want all these dolls and the coffins they're in bagged and tagged.'

'Yes, sir. Because of the tramp?'

Lapslie shook his head. 'No, because of the dolls. I also want the blood on the wedding dress matched with that of the murdered girl. Get a DNA comparison: I need to be sure about this.'

Bradbury was obviously taken aback by his last request. 'Sir, you think the blood on the doll's wedding dress is the murdered girl's? How the hell would that be possible?'

This time it was Lapslie's turn to shrug. 'I've no idea, but then there are a lot of things about this case I have no idea about, and I'd like that put right.'

The atmosphere inside the bunker was cloying, so while they awaited the SOCO team Lapslie decided to grab some fresh air and phone Charlotte.

'Hi, I thought I'd give you a call to find out how you were after yesterday's ordeal.'

'I'm fine. Stirred but not shaken.'

Lapslie smiled and glanced back towards the bunker. He'd made his way to the far side of the car park forty yards from its entrance; far enough away not to be overheard.

'I'm sorry. If I'd known the weather might turn like that, I'd never have gone far from the harbour.'

'That's okay, you weren't to know. You're not Michael Fish.'

'Now if he'd said that a light wind was expected, I'd have definitely not even ventured from the harbour.'

Charlotte joined him in a light chuckle, which reassured him far more than her seemingly stock response that she was 'Fine'.

'Was there much damage to the boat?' she asked.

'Not much. George is seeing to it now. Should be all sorted within a few days.'

'Shipshape again.'

'Yes.' With a brief lull in the conversation then, the background echo of voices on a hospital corridor drifted in from Charlotte's end. Lapslie was reminded that she must be busy too, but she'd still made time to take his call. 'I'll make it up to you with another couple of days away next time I'm able.'

'Look forward to it.'

Signing off, Lapslie reflected that he probably would never have bothered to put in a call to Sonia, his ex-wife, the day after an interrupted day out or romantic evening, which sparked a second thought: was he now trying too hard, making up for all the mistakes of his past failed marriage?

The fact that Sonia and Charlotte were very different people was no doubt a part of that. Sonia would probably have been less accepting of his apology, or might have asked, 'If it hadn't been for the rough weather interrupting our weekend, would you still have gone off when Emma called you?' – already knowing the answer from his actions with countless previous interruptions. Whereas Charlotte would never ask that; her own work would often drag her away for emergencies at short notice, so in turn that was a question he'd never ask her. Common ground. Unspoken understanding.

But he'd never troubled to put in those day-after calls to Sonia to find out. Perhaps because he already knew. Copper's gut instincts. And not just because of all the other coppers' marriages he'd seen go down the pan the same way due to the irregular hours and string of interrupted dinner dates and family outings – but because of how his condition had compounded that. The sound of laughter or children playing – which would be a joy to many a father's ear – would leave him with a bitter taste and his head reeling. So even quality family time with his kids, Robbie and Jamie, would become an ordeal, making him crave solitude.

And upon his return from that solitude, or the

inspection of a corpse which had interrupted a romantic dinner, Sonia's voice would be sharper, more incriminating, giving an ammonia undertone to its normal blueberry taste which would make him cringe. The expression, 'What's wrong? Did what I've just said leave a bad taste in your mouth?' would be literally true in his case.

So all of that – the knowledge of what her reaction would be, the sickening ammonia–blueberry aftertaste – would lead him to seek more solitude, more refuge. Until there was no refuge left for him to take, and the only one left for Sonia was the arms and solace of another man; the final camel's-back straw in their marriage.

The sound of footsteps interrupted his thoughts, and he looked up to see Emma Bradbury approaching.

'Sir. Jim Thomson just called. He's just turned off the A12. Says he'll be here in ten or twelve minutes.'

Lapslie nodded with a strained smile and followed her back towards the bunker entrance.

Jim Thomson and his team arrived remarkably quickly considering the seriousness of the job they had just been working on. Sniper killings were not common, but Lapslie supposed that with a constrained crime scene and an obvious point of vantage for the sniper, there wasn't actually that much to check.

Lapslie left it to Bradbury to brief the SOCO team, but watched from a distance. Judging by his expression, when Thomson discovered why his team had been called away from one of the most serious and bizarre murders they had ever dealt with, he was bemused. He took it in his stride, however, and within half an hour the area was taped off and everyone was made to wear disposable white overalls and shoes. The arc lamps were moved back into the shelter and the whole process started again.

While the crime scene was being established and the boundaries set, Lapslie walked outside to where DCs Parkin and Pearce were standing. Lapslie wasn't in the best of moods; he never was when he had a problem and was struggling to solve it. It irritated him. 'So, you two saw nothing?'

Both detectives shook their heads.

'No, sir,' Pearce replied, 'well, not until Dave went for a slash. It was Dave that noticed something was wrong.'

Lapslie turned to face DC Dave Parkin. 'Was that the first time you got out of the car since I last saw you?'

Parkin shuffled his feet like a naughty schoolboy

caught with his hand in the sweet jar. 'Yes, sir, but we had a good view of the front of the building and we knew it was impossible for anyone to get into it from any other place.'

Lapslie continued to stare at him. 'Really? Yet not only do we have a dead tramp who obviously got in without using the front door, we also now have one doll seriously damaged and two others gone, both of them major exhibits and linked to a murder that has occurred elsewhere?'

Met with silence and an awkward look exchanged between the two detectives, Lapslie reflected that perhaps he should have turned it into a major crime scene with more cover; with only two men on such a long shift, during forced breaks effectively only one man would be on duty, so there were limitations. But extra manpower would require approval from Rouse, which could prove problematical given what they had so far. He took a fresh breath. 'So what made you suspicious?'

DC Parkin answered. 'Thought I heard someone moving about inside the bunker.'

'You *thought*?'

'Like Carl – DC Pearce – said, I was having a slash down by the security doors when I heard the sound of a door being slammed shut from inside the bunker. I thought it *had* to be the door to the cupboard where the dolls are kept; it's the only other door in there. Well, on the first floor anyway.'

'And you did *what*?'

'I banged on the door and told them to come out. Said the place was surrounded.'

Lapslie shook his head. 'Surrounded, by you two?'

Both detectives nodded simultaneously. 'Thought we would try and bluff whoever it was.'

'Bluff them into thinking you were detectives. So what happened then?'

Parkin continued: 'I ran back to the car to get the key to the door—'

Lapslie cut in. 'Why didn't you call Pearce over? It might have been quicker.'

'I tried, sir, but—'

This time Pearce cut in. 'I had the radio on, sir. Didn't hear him.'

As Lapslie shook his head, Parkin grimaced awkwardly. 'The arrangement, sir, was that one of us rested while the other kept a watch.'

Lapslie sighed deeply. 'Go on.'

'When we got the key we went into the bunker and

searched the top floor and the storage cupboard; that's when we noticed the bride doll was missing. Thought it had been stolen at first, but then when I looked inside the coffin she'd been standing in front of I saw the state of the dress . . .'

'And you did . . . ?'

Parkin shook his head. 'Nothing, sir. Carl stayed inside the bunker while I got on the radio and asked for help.'

Lapslie turned to Pearce. 'Anything else happen after Parkin had gone?

This time Pearce shook his head. 'No, sir. Well – there was a sound from the floor below . . .'

'What kind of sound?'

'Like something heavy being moved . . . perhaps metal or heavy wood.'

'So you went downstairs and checked?'

Pearce looked down at his feet for a moment. 'No, sir.'

'Why not?'

'It was dark and my radio and my mobile didn't work inside the bunker, so I couldn't call for back-up. I didn't think it was advisable.'

'You didn't think it would be advisable?' Lapslie repeated heavily.

Pearce shook his head. 'No, sir, sorry.'

Without another word Lapslie turned away from them and walked back inside the shelter. When he had moved no more than a few steps into the shelter Jim Thomson's voice called after him. 'Sir! You need to be suited and booted.'

Lapslie stopped dead in his tracks. He couldn't argue with the man – after all, Lapslie had given the order in the first place. By the time he had pulled his overalls on and slipped the plastic covers around his shoes, Bradbury, similarly attired, had joined him.

Lapslie stared across at Thomson. 'I want all the dolls bagged up, and the coffins bagged up separately. I want the entire place photographed and gone through with a fine-tooth comb.'

'Already in hand, sir. Are we looking for anything in particular?'

Lapslie shrugged. 'I'm not sure yet. But I want the scene treated as if you were dealing with a major murder inquiry, which if I'm right you may well be.' Before Thomson had the chance to ask any more questions, Lapslie turned his attention to Bradbury. 'We need to go down a few floors. Got a flashlight?'

Jim Thomson handed Bradbury a large Dragon Light, which was attached to a multicoloured strap. Slipping the strap over her shoulder, Bradbury looked across at her boss. 'Ready when you are, sir.'

Lapslie thought the lamp looked more like a search-light than a flashlight. Still, if it did the job, he was happy.

Thomson looked across at him. 'Want any of my boys to come down with you?'

Lapslie shook his head. 'No, there's already been enough size twelve boots down there. I'll be okay with just Bradbury.'

Lapslie began to descend the ladder with Bradbury standing at the top shining the lamp into the gloom and lighting his way.

The ladder had fifty-two rungs. Lapslie counted each and every one. Once at the bottom he called for Brad-bury to follow him. This time Thomson shone his light down, guiding Bradbury. When she got to the bottom she called up to Thomson, 'It's okay, I'm here, thanks.'

Thomson switched off his beam, and Bradbury began to scan the room with her Dragon Light. It was far sparser than the room above, with no furniture, or side cupboards. It looked like the place had been stripped many years before, probably after the Cold War ended, and had been left in this state ever since. Bradbury ran the light over every inch of the room but there was nothing to see.

Lapslie was disappointed. 'Okay, looks like we are going to have to go down another level.'

Bradbury nodded her understanding. Clinging tightly to the ladder's metal rungs, Lapslie started down. This time there were only thirty-one steps. His way was lit by Bradbury's lamp. As he got to the foot of the ladder he looked back up at her. 'Okay, throw the lamp down to me. I'll shine it up the steps for you.'

Bradbury hesitated. 'Are you sure? It's quite heavy.'

'I'll be fine. Played keeper for the Gentleman Players in my youth.'

'Whatever that means. It's a bad career move to kill your commanding officer, you know?'

Lying flat on the ground, she hung the lamp by its strap as far down as she could before letting go. The lamp seemed to hang there for a moment, hovering over Lapslie's head, before suddenly falling at what seemed to be a remarkable speed. In that moment Lapslie became momentarily and terrifyingly unsure of his ability to catch it. He wondered what he would do if he missed it, and it smashed to pieces on the floor, or worse, hit him. Fortunately instinct took over, and his years as a Gentleman player didn't fail him. Catching it in his arms, he pulled it into his chest with a sigh of relief. With the aid of the light Bradbury descended quickly and the two of them began to search the next level.

This level, like the ones above, was largely empty, except for a large green filing cabinet pushed tight against the wall. Lapslie played the lamp along the cabinet – nothing special about it. He moved closer and opened the door. Ten empty shelves: no dolls, no coffins.

Bradbury's voice suddenly cut through the silence.

'Sir, shine the lamp on the floor, could you?'

She must have spotted something he had missed. Once he knew where to look he could see what she had spotted. There was a mark, a scrape in the dirt in the shape of a curve, as if something had been dragged or pulled across the floor. As Lapslie crouched to examine it, Bradbury put her fingers behind the back of the cabinet and pulled. The object was heavy, but it moved. Seeing that she was struggling with the weight, Lapslie lent a hand, and eventually the two of them managed to pull the cabinet away from the wall. It turned out to be hinged at one end and came open like a door. Once they had pulled it back as far as they could, they saw it was the entrance to a tunnel. Lapslie shone the lamp into the gloom. It was about a hundred metres long, and at the far end there appeared to be a set of stone steps.

'Well, it looks like we've found out how our tramp and Gepetto the puppet-maker got in.'

Bradbury nodded. 'Yes, sir.'

The passage was oval in shape, about six feet tall and four feet wide. It was crudely made of what seemed to be house bricks. They were damp, and covered with mould. Along the length of the tunnel a row of lamps had been screwed to the wall, all linked by a looping cable.

Bradbury spotted a switch just inside the tunnel. She pushed it up and down a few times but nothing happened.

'So,' Lapslie asked, 'are you game?' He gestured to the depth of the tunnel.

Bradbury nodded. 'Yes, sir.'

Lapslie began to move into the darkness. 'Follow me then?'

Bradbury obeyed.

The tunnel was so high that Lapslie did not have to stoop, but managed to walk forward upright, scanning the beam of the light all over the tunnel, searching for anything that might do him or Bradbury harm, or might be of some interest, but there was nothing apart from beetles and other insects that scuttled out of the way of the light as if it touched them. Apart from the insects, there was just dirt and the overwhelming smell of damp and rot.

After about a hundred yards they came to a set of concrete stairs and began to ascend them slowly, Lapslie counting each step as they went. He didn't know why, but he always counted things like steps, or paces from one place to another. Maybe it was connected to his neurological condition, maybe not, but he'd done it since childhood. After he had counted eighty-seven steps they came to a halt. Above them was a large metal manhole cover. Lapslie pushed at it hard with both hands for a few moments, and it gave way. Then, slipping one hand around the edge of the cover, he pushed it sideways until blinding sunlight streamed in and there was room enough for a person to climb through.

Lapslie climbed the few steps that took him to the edge of the hole, and scrambled out. Once in the open he turned off the lamp, and took several deep breaths of the blessedly fresh air before offering his hand to Bradbury. As soon as they were out, they looked around. They were in the middle of a small copse, and just beyond it spread a large field full of lavender. So that explained the lavender smell, Lapslie considered. It hadn't been sparked by any object in the bunker, it was a real smell from outside. Although the copse was overgrown, there was an obvious path leading from the field. It was too big, too well marked to be one made by badgers or foxes. Lapslie assumed that it had been made by the comings and goings of the tramp, and perhaps also the doll-maker.

Bradbury gave a shout. 'Over there, sir! Look over there! I think it's the entrance to the bunker!'

Lapslie looked in the direction of her pointing finger. She was right. About three hundred yards on the other side of the wood he could see Thomson's SOCOs moving around the scene. So now they knew how the tramp and the doll-maker had got in and out of the bunker without being detected.

He looked across at Bradbury and chuckled. 'Have you seen yourself?'

Bradbury's face was black with dirt, and her hair and clothes covered in dusty, sooty cobwebs. She made a vain attempt to brush herself down, and then looked at Lapslie and returned the compliment. 'Have you seen *yourself*, sir?' He looked down at his own clothes and found he was in a similar state, if not slightly worse. He smiled broadly. 'What do you think – some sort of emergency exit in case the bunker was attacked?'

Bradbury wasn't so sure. 'Or maybe if things got unpleasant inside.'

Lapslie nodded. 'Maybe. We need to get Thomson and his troops over here to do a proper job on the tunnel and the woods. Our doll-maker must have got here somehow – I'm guessing by car – so a search for any tyre marks might be a good start. Also anything that might have been dumped from the car: cigarettes, cans of drink, general rubbish. Let's get Special Ops down here to do a fingertip search of the entire wood. You never know, they might turn something up. Can you get that sorted?'

Bradbury nodded.

'Also, get those two uniformed goons over here. I want them to keep an eye on the tunnel until the SOCOs turn up. Oh and get a dog. Let's put one inside the shelter, see if it can find anything else we have missed.'

Bradbury nodded with a 'Yes, sir,' and made her way towards Thomson and his team.

But Lapslie stayed where he was for a moment, looking back towards the lavender field, pondering just why this site might have been chosen.

*

Ten down; two to go.

It had taken years, but had been worth it. It was all in the planning. The police had no idea that eight of the ten of them had been murdered. It was his little secret.

He giggled to himself as he sat in his kitchen, sipping at a cup of tea: an uncontrolled noise bubbling up from deep inside. All those detectives, all those pathologists, and not one of them had ever come close to realizing what he was doing. The girl he'd shot earlier today was only the second they had ever detected; but then that one had a specific purpose set aside from the others. Eight deaths still remained listed on the books as accidents.

The first one, the Nurse, he remembered like it was yesterday. He could still see that confused 'Why me?' look on her face as he choked the life out of her. He treasured that look. It kept him warm at night just thinking about it.

She had died quicker than he imagined she would, but then he had never choked anyone to death before, so maybe it was normal. He had listened to the profiler they had brought in – Eleanor Whittley. Her theories had amazed him, they were so totally wrong, but that had the advantage that it did much to stop the police getting anywhere close to him. So a big thank you, Doctor Whittley.

He wondered how many more people had got away with

murder because of that woman's clumsy theorizing. Dozens, he conjectured.

Still, he now needed to concentrate on the last two. They would also have to be tragic accidents, of course: he couldn't chance another murder and too many links being made too quickly; that might work against the links he hoped they'd follow. He also knew they would have to be carried out quickly. This had been going on for long enough, and he was getting tired, but he couldn't rest until his task was completed.

There were two problems he had to overcome. One was the fact that the police had discovered his dolls. He hadn't wanted that to happen until after his task was complete. It was that bloody tramp's fault – and to think he'd left the tosser alone. The second problem was the involvement of Detective Chief Inspector Lapslie. Lapslie was an odd man and, from what he understood, an ill man, but he also knew that Lapslie was supposed to be the best investigator the Essex Constabulary had. Still, he'd suspected Lapslie might become involved at some stage, thus the choice of location so close to the lavender field – to hopefully work against Lapslie's synaesthesia; conflicting aromas to throw off his focus. Though if Lapslie became too much of a problem, he would have to be dealt with.

He picked up the two dolls from the kitchen table. Which next? The Teacher or the Major? Seemed like a simple decision, *but nothing had been simple so far. Killing wasn't simple. Killing so many people, and making sure that no one had any idea that most of them had been murdered, as well as obscuring and misleading where necessary, was innately difficult – but he was up to the task and so far it had all worked out well. The Teacher or the Major? He moved the two dolls up and down in his hands. He felt like God weighing the fate of two of his creations.*

His eye was caught by the local paper sitting on a corner of the table. It was open at an inside page: he'd been looking for the crossword earlier, before making his cup of tea. The headline on the most prominent article on the page read Teachers Diet for Charity! *He remembered glancing through the text: it was about a group of overweight teachers at the local comprehensive who were planning to lose weight on a sponsored diet in order to raise funds for a local charity, but the way he had left the paper folded obscured half of the words.* Teachers Die, *the headline now read.*

Teachers Die. Yes, of course. It was as if God was sending him a message, telling him that not only was his cause a justified cause, but also pointing him in a particular direction. Helping him to see which way to go.

Yes, the Teacher would be next.

Now all he had to do was to work out where, when and how.

*

Lapslie had no respect for his boss. He had formed the opinion, early in his career, that most people in any organization – and the police force was no exception – either desperately wanted to be the next grade up or desperately yearned to return to the easier life one grade down. Alan Rouse had always had his eye on higher things. The two of them had worked together as constables in Brixton, more years ago than Lapslie liked to recall, and even then Rouse had always been less interested in solving crimes and protecting civilians than in looking for opportunities to advance his status, make himself known, attach himself to the officers he thought were going to make it to higher things. Now that he was near the top of the slippery pole of police politics he seemed, on the surface, to be affable and avuncular, everyone's best friend, but Lapslie knew that he was always on guard, waiting for the officers beneath him to plot to usurp his authority, and he wasn't above wrecking an officer's career if he thought they were becoming too ambitious. He wasn't in any hurry to relinquish his position.

Rouse's attitude towards Lapslie was ambivalent, which suited Lapslie right down to the ground. On the one hand, Lapslie was no threat to him, but on the other he knew where Rouse had come from, and the things he had done to get promoted, and that made Lapslie a walking time bomb in Rouse's mind. Now he only brought Lapslie in on the most difficult of cases, the theory being that if he dropped the ball – which he was bound to do one day, because everyone did – then Rouse could get rid of him and put it down to his synaesthesia. Lapslie's view on the world was that he would rather be hated for who he was than be loved for who he wasn't. Rouse didn't quite think that way.

His office was on the top floor at the Essex Constabulary HQ. Lapslie hated going there. Too many voices, a melange of flavours, and not all of them very pleasant. It was a bit like having tinnitus of the mouth, and there wasn't a thing he could do about it.

Entering Rouse's outer office he was greeted by the great man's personal assistant, or 'secretary' in old money. She was pleasant enough, and Lapslie quite liked her. On the other hand he had once locked her in Rouse's office, following a slight disagreement, and every time she saw him now she took a step backwards and her gaze darted around as if in search of escape routes.

As he opened the door she looked up at him from behind her desk, an inquisitive smile on her face which quickly melted into apprehension. 'Chief Inspector Lapslie. How are you?'

'Very well, Helen, thank you.'

'Good. The superintendent is expecting you.'

She pressed the intercom button on her desk and announced his presence. 'DCI Lapslie here to see you, sir.'

Rouse's voice came straight back. 'Send him through, would you, Helen? Oh and could you arrange for some coffee and biscuits? I think the Chief Inspector is partial to custard creams.'

Lapslie wasn't, but he knew that Rouse was. The man couldn't stop being devious even when ordering biscuits.

'You can go right in, Chief Inspector.'

Lapslie nodded, walked past Helen and into Rouse's office.

Rouse was waiting for him. 'Mark, how are you?'

He put out his hand and Lapslie took it. He pulled out the chair on the opposite side of the desk. 'Sit you down, Mark, sit you down. So, how are things? How's the problem – any better?'

Lapslie shook his head. 'No, not really. The cognitive behavioural therapy sessions at the hospital are a waste of bloody time. My consultant's suggested a new course of medication, some experimental drug or other, but I'm not sure. I think I may just have to live with it.'

'Seeing much of the children?'

Lapslie shook his head again. 'No, not much. They're busy, I'm busy, Sonia's awkward as hell. Difficult situation.'

With Jamie and Robbie now in their teens, it was true that his sons' social schedule had become more hectic; and between his wife's busy schedule and his own demanding workload and irregular hours, time with his kids often slipped through the gaps between. He'd seen them only three times in the past year, when the original arrangement had been every month. But he couldn't help thinking that Sonia had engineered part of that, coming up with last-minute emergencies for her own work, or a skateboard or camping outing for Jamie or Robbie with friends that had suddenly come up. Perhaps getting her own back for his own past quality-time-with-family negligence.

Rouse gave an understanding nod. 'I see.'

'Ironically, she's now doing aromatherapy, so I dare say she likes to rub it in.'

A faint curl of the lips from Rouse, so Lapslie wasn't sure whether he'd got the joke or was simply offering a strained smile to shield his concern that Lapslie was still troubled by the split. Strangely enough, it had been his ex-wife's aromatherapy work which had led her to suggest that drugs would have limited effect on his synaesthesia, so it had become yet another 'I told you so' argument between them. What he hadn't told Sonia was that he took his prescribed thorazitol minimally, not just because of the regular dose's hallucinatory side-effects, but because it took all the edges off his other senses too, made them less sharp. A strange sort of subdued inner hue, as if he was mentally and emotionally just treading water. Otherwise he feared his days as a detective would have been numbered: in no time he'd have been used for no more than an internal, desk-bound, pen-pushing job – like Rouse's, in fact.

He pushed his own cramped smile in response. 'So why is it you wanted to see me, sir?'

Rouse leaned back in his seat. 'I'll be honest, Mark – it's about these dolls. Don't you think you're getting a bit carried away with them? I mean, they're *dolls*, for God's sake. I can't see how they can be significant, and yet you seem to be spending a lot of resources on them. That vagrant died of natural causes – I'm waiting for the post-mortem results but the initial analysis has confirmed it. There *is* no case.'

Lapslie looked at him for a moment, savouring the blood-connection bombshell he was about to drop. 'I think they are *very* significant, sir. In fact I would bet my pension that we have a serial killer on our hands.'

Rouse sat up straight in his orthopaedic chair. 'A serial killer? That's a bit strong, Mark. How have you come to that conclusion?'

'There was a girl murdered yesterday, shot with a high-powered rifle . . .'

'Yes, I know. Tragic. On her wedding day, I understand.' Rouse pulled on his serious face. 'But we have half the roles and professions known to man also represented with those dolls, so I don't see that we should attach specific significance to the bride doll.'

'Well, that's the point – that significance has now been taken a step further. Some time after her murder, someone entered the fall-out shelter where the tramp's body was discovered and where the dolls were found. They got in through an escape tunnel we have only just discovered, and covered one doll – importantly, the doll with the wedding dress – in blood. They also made a hole in the doll's chest right where the bullet wound was.'

'Some grotesque practical joke?'

'I doubt it. There were only a handful of people who knew where the bullet had hit, and they're either police, SOCOs or family and friends – and the family and friends have all been tied up giving statements.' He paused, and took a breath. 'I am also betting that the blood is the girl's.'

'*What*?' Rouse looked astonished, his eyes keen. 'Why would you think that? How could that possibly be the case?'

'I have no idea, sir. It's just a hunch at the moment, but the dolls have all been taken down to the labs and I've asked for a blood comparison, so we'll know soon enough. Doing a DNA match might take a bit longer.'

'And it all costs money . . .'

'Maybe, sir, but if I'm right it will be money well spent and it will prove my other theory.'

'Which is?'

'That each of those dolls signifies a victim. The bride just happens to be the latest.'

Rouse was becoming increasingly agitated. Before he could ask more questions there was a knock on the door and his PA walked in with a tea tray. She placed the tray on Rouse's desk and left. Picking up a biscuit and biting on it, Rouse looked across at Lapslie. 'Go on,' he said, crumbs spilling down his lapels.

'When I first saw the dolls, nine of them had been placed inside their coffins. Each of those nine dolls was badly damaged in some way. All differently, but all damaged. The three outside their coffins were in perfect order, with no sign of damage at all. After the girl was shot, a hole appeared in the bride doll's chest at the precise spot where the bullet entered the girl's body and killed her. The other two intact dolls and their coffins have also disappeared, although fortunately we do have photographs of them. It is my opinion, based on the evidence, that there are now ten victims, including the bride, and that there are two potential victims left out there. Unless we move fast we are going to have at least another two murders on our hands.'

Rouse leant back in his chair again. 'This is all very interesting, Mark, but it's just speculation. Morbid speculation. You don't have an ounce of actual evidence, do you?'

'We will when we get the reports on the blood samples found on the doll's wedding dress.'

Rouse nodded his head. 'True enough,' he said, 'true enough.' He steepled his hands on the desk. 'I'm sorry, but this is what I'm going to do. I don't want any more of my tightly stretched resources spent on this doll thing until you can come up with something a little more concrete. The girl's murder is eating into my budget as it is. If you and Bradbury want to poke around and see if you can put some flesh on the bones of your theory, that's fine, but you mustn't neglect the girl's murder. That has to be the top priority. The sooner we get that sorted out, the cheaper it's going to be for the force, and then I might have some money to spend on your doll theory. Are we *d'accord* on this?'

Lapslie nodded dully, feeling the familiar wash of disappointment flow through him. He'd been here before, in this chair, hearing these words, or some that were similar. 'Yes, sir. Understood.' He paused, wondering whether he had enough leverage with Rouse to push a little further. 'Is it still okay to have a DNA match done on the blood from the doll?'

Rouse thought for a moment. He finally nodded. 'Okay, but that's it. No more ordering Special Ops out and racking up the force overtime bill, okay?'

Lapslie nodded. Rouse was hedging his bets. If Lapslie was right then it would be Rouse who authorized him to investigate. If he was wrong, well, Rouse could quite honestly say that he had warned him off. The man really did take the biscuit.

As Lapslie pulled into the car park of the mortuary, he wondered if Jane Catherall would be able to add anything to what he already knew. He parked his car and made his way inside the anonymous single-storey building.

He hated visiting the mortuary, hated that lingering spell of death and chemicals, decay and cleanliness, all mixed up together. He made his way to Catherall's office. She was sitting bent over her computer typing what Lapslie assumed was a report of some sort. With anyone else, the phrase 'bent over her computer' would be a descriptive metaphor, but with Jane it was the truth. She had been one of the last children in the country to be struck down with polio before it had been eradicated. She had spent half her childhood in an iron lung, and the disease had left her with a twisted spine and a bloated abdomen. Yet despite her physical problems, she was one of the brightest and friendliest people that Lapslie knew. As well as being one of the most pedantic.

She spoke before him. 'You are being a bit premature,

aren't you, Chief Inspector? I hadn't intended starting on the post-mortem of that poor girl until tomorrow.'

'I came about the tramp, actually. The one they found in the bunker.'

She cut in. 'With the dolls?'

Lapslie nodded. 'Yes. How did you know about those?'

'It may surprise you to know that I am a great fan of jazz music. In particular, I am an aficionado of the jungle drums.'

'As played by that popular beat combo Jim Thomson and his Merry Men?'

She turned away from the computer and gazed at him with pale blue, slightly protuberant eyes. 'My lips are sealed, Chief Inspector. So you want to know how he died?'

Lapslie nodded. 'It would be helpful.'

'All quite straightforward, I'm afraid . . .'

'I'm glad that something is.'

'Old age and decrepitude. His heart gave out, although to be honest if it hadn't been his heart it would have been something else. His internal organs were in a race to see which could fail first. It was the drink, of course.'

'No indications of anything unnatural?'

Catherall shook her head. 'If you mean "Was he murdered?" then the answer is "No". No evidence for that at all. It was just his time. It was, frankly, way past his time.'

'Do you have any idea who he was?'

Catherall shook her head again. 'No, none at all. I've forwarded what details I have to the delightful Emma Bradbury: she may manage to dig something up, but I doubt it.'

Lapslie felt a sudden overwhelming sense of sadness, and it obviously showed. Jane's faced creased into a sympathetic grimace, and she continued: 'I see an increasing number of these cases, year on year. More and more people are falling through the cracks. It's very sad, but there isn't much we can do here. We are at the end of the chain. We take what details we can, in case there is a match against any missing person, but that seldom happens. If it helps, there was a postcard and a couple of old black and white photos in his pocket. The postcard was addressed to "Billy". That might be him, or alternatively he could have picked the card and the photographs up from the floor or found them in a bin. These people who end up on the streets, sleeping rough, they often start acting like magpies, picking up odd detritus and keeping it as if it's worth more than jewels.' She shrugged: an awkward movement of her twisted shoulders. 'It's only a feeling, but I think it was his. That's what we have called him anyway. Billy. A lot better than "John Smith", don't you think?'

Lapslie nodded his agreement. 'So what happens to him now?'

'We keep him for a few weeks, then the council take him away and cremate him. They put his ashes in the Garden of Remembrance and that's it.'

Lapslie looked at the two black and white photographs. One was a single shot of a young boy of about eight; the other was a family group. Mother, father and the same eight-year-old child. Lapslie wondered if 'Billy' was the young boy in the photograph, or maybe the father. He wondered what paths he had followed in order to end up dead and alone in a stinking fall-out shelter.

He looked back at Catherall. 'If you do find out anything about him, can you let me know?'

Catherall nodded. 'Of course.' She smiled at him.

'In fact, if you don't discover who he is, can you let me know that too?'

Catherall nodded again. 'No trouble at all.'

Lapslie was grateful. 'I could also do with a photograph of his face, if he isn't too badly decomposed by now.'

Catherall nodded. 'We can touch him up. I have picked up various cosmetic skills along the way. I'll get my assistant, Dan, to do it. He's getting very good at things like that. He has an artistic streak.'

'Thanks. Get a few copies over to me. I want to see if anyone recognizes him. You never know: he may have talked to a few people in the local village about what was going on inside the bunker. Could give us a lead. We could do with one before more people die.'

'You think they will?'

Lapslie nodded. 'I'm bloody sure of it.'

Catherall looked surprised and a little shocked.

'Anyway, I'll see you tomorrow for Leslie Cooke's PM?'

'You mean Leslie Petersen? She was married, you know. Not for long, but she was.'

Lapslie suddenly felt very awkward. 'Petersen. Yes, of course. Sorry. I should at least call her by her correct name: everything else has been taken away from her.'

With that he turned and left.

From the mortuary he made his way back to force HQ, a four-storey, flat-sided building in Chelmsford which looked like it had been built entirely from white Lego. Only a touch of police blue on its front insignia and entrance awning, which was equally flat and lacking in detail, offered any relief. Those wishing to be kind described it as functional and efficient, those who didn't feel so inclined used terms such as sanitized and unimaginative. Lapslie had called ahead to Bradbury to make sure there were no distracting sounds or noises near his desk when he arrived. He always went in the back way to avoid as many people as he could. Police stations were by nature noisy places: people screaming, shouting, running, dropping things, banging on metal doors. Each of those sounds had an effect on him, an effect he didn't need.

Bradbury did her job well. From the moment he entered the HQ to the time he reached his office, Lapslie didn't see another soul. He also made the short journey in total silence. He had only been in his office a few moments when Bradbury knocked gently on the door and entered.

'Everything okay, sir?'

'Yes, fine. A good job, as ever.' Lapslie looked up at her and smiled, noticing her eyes had faint red rings. 'And you? Everything okay? You look a bit tired.'

'I'm fine. Dom got a takeaway curry last night. Bit hot, and some indigestion kept me up.'

Lapslie's eyes stayed on her for a second, and she wondered what smell might have hit him if he'd detected the lie. The takeaway part was true, but the late night and fitful sleep following was due to the argument between her and Dom, her partner for the past three years, which had nothing to do with the curry. More to do with the increasing number of evenings she was spending apart from Dom, which equally she was finding increasingly hard to put down to investigative duties.

Dom McGinley had been a career villain, and understandably Lapslie had warned against the association, saying that it would never work out. But was she loath to talk about any cracks appearing in their relationship to avoid the inevitable 'I told you so' comments, or because those cracks sprang more from her own actions than from Dom's?

Lapslie's expression as quickly relaxed and he held out one hand. 'Take a pew.'

Bradbury sat down in the chair opposite Lapslie's desk. 'Any update on the tramp?'

'You mean Billy?'

She looked surprised. 'You have a name for him?'

Lapslie smiled broadly. 'Maybe. It's what we're going to call him for now. Like Doctor Catherall said, it's a lot better than "John Smith". Makes him more human.'

Bradbury was obviously confused. 'So why Billy?'

'It was a name found on a postcard in his pocket, along with a couple of old photographs. Maybe it's him, maybe not. Who knows? Anyway, there was nothing suspicious about his death. Natural causes. That said, I think with a bit of luck he might still be able to help us from beyond the grave.'

Bradbury was all attention.

'I want you to get hold of those two PCs, Parkin and Pearce. Tell them to check out all the rough sleepers known within, oh, a 15-mile radius. See if anyone knew a tramp by the name of Billy.'

'Bit of a long shot, sir, especially if that wasn't his name.'

'Doctor Catherall is having some photographs taken of his face. They should be here soon. Get Parkin and Pearce to show them around. Someone might recognize the poor sod.'

'Yes, sir. How long do you want us to do it for?'

'Seventy-two hours should cover it. After that I might release the photograph to the media, see if we can get any results that way.'

Bradbury winced. 'Bit macabre, sir.'

'A bit, but people love that sort of thing.'

Bradbury wasn't convinced. 'Really?'

'Oh yes. First time it was done was in Paris in about 1850. They found the severed head of a woman in the Seine. Had it photographed and hundreds of photographs produced. They sold out in a day and the photographs became collectors' items. People like to be shocked: it gives them something to talk about at work.'

Bradbury raised her eyebrows. 'Well if you say so, sir. Is that it?'

Lapslie nodded. 'For now. Good luck. I'll get copies of the photos to you as soon as they arrive.'

Bradbury pushed her chair back and stood. 'Thank you, sir. I'll await them with interest.'

Lapslie left force HQ the same way he'd come in. Once again he didn't see another living soul and left in total silence.

He got in his Saab 9-5 and pulled out of the car park, heading back towards Finchingfield and St Mary's Church. He wanted to see the place where the Special Operations guys suspected the shot had come from. The small tower. He still found it hard to believe that anyone could kill someone from that distance with one shot. Lapslie wasn't a bad shot himself, but he wouldn't even attempt a shot like that. Whoever killed Leslie Petersen, née Cooke, had to be some kind of an expert shot, a marksman, sniper maybe. That might provide the lead he was looking for. He doubted that there were many people in the country who could make a shot like that. Maybe if Bradbury checked the local rifle clubs she might get some names.

The tower was a well-known landmark, and all that was left of what must have been a magnificent and powerful fortress. Parts of it were over a thousand years old, according to a sign outside, and dated back to before the Normans, who had built it to keep the local peasants in order. Tom's Tower, as it was now known locally, was a major tourist attraction and thousands of people climbed the 180 steps to the top every year. However, due to restoration work, it was currently closed to the public, and no one had visited save the builders for nearly six months.

Lapslie parked his car in the small car park at the foot of the tower, ignoring the Pay and Display signs. There was nobody about: no builders, no police. The SOCOs had left, although the 'Crime Scene – Do Not

Cross' tape was still wrapped around the entrance and the ground-floor windows. Lifting up the tape, he stepped under it and began to climb the stairs to the top of the tower. It was slow going and he was obliged to stop several times to catch his breath.

As he reached the top of the tower, Lapslie heard someone walking about. He slowed his pace. It was probably some young copper who had been left there to guard the scene, but he wanted to be sure.

As his head reached the top of the stairs, he looked around as best he could, but he could see nobody. He considered shouting out, but he wasn't sure that was a particularly good idea.

As he got to the edge of the exit, he stared around the edge of the tower. This time he did see someone: a man in a long light brown coat was crouching down and looking across in the direction of the church. From the way he was standing with his arms upraised, Lapslie was convinced that he was looking through a pair of binoculars.

Lapslie moved quietly off the stairs and onto the top of the tower, determined to take the man by surprise and find out what he was doing there. He had only taken a few steps when the man spun around quickly and unexpectedly, taking Lapslie completely by surprise. He must have heard something.

It was only now that Lapslie realized that it wasn't a pair of binoculars he had in his hand, but a sniper's rifle with a large scope, and it was pointed straight at his head.

PART THREE

2 December 2008

It had taken Michael Cohen years to finally open his own garage. He had always loved cars; his parents had always said he was car-mad. If he wasn't building Airfix models or buying Matchbox toys, then he was watching Formula 1 racing on TV.

It was slow at first, but as time went on the clients came, and it wasn't long before he had three mechanics working for him and had to move to larger premises. Everything was coming up roses.

It was late on a Monday when the car came in. Michael was on his own. The garage had officially closed for the evening, but the man seemed to be in some trouble, so he agreed to help. It sounded to him as if the exhaust had blown, and until he could get under the car he wouldn't know if it needed a completely new exhaust, only part of one, or, with luck, for the customer, just a new bracket. He couldn't be bothered to open the garage and get the car over the pit so he got the driver to drive it up a couple of portable ramps. Once in position Michael crawled underneath and started to examine the length of the exhaust.

So engrossed was he in what he was doing that he didn't notice the car moving. Not at first anyway. When it jerked for the second time Michael called out to the customer, 'Car's slipping a little, can you make sure the handbrake's on?'

There was no reply. Michael glanced around the car, looking for the customer's feet, but there was no sign of him. Suddenly the car's engine started and the wheels twisted hard to the right. Sudden heat blasted Michael in the face, and he tried to scramble out of the way on his elbow.

'Look out!' he called. 'What the hell do you think you're doing?'

The mobile ramps gave way, and the car collapsed on to Michael Cohen, crushing him. He didn't die at once. He lived long enough to see the customer's feet suddenly appear in front of him as he crawled out from under the car. He lived long enough to ask for help and be ignored. He lived long enough to see the customer watching him with a sort of half-smile on his face. Dying, still unsure what had happened, his killer was the last thing he ever saw.

Lapslie looked down the barrel of the rifle, and then up at the man who was pointing it at him. The man looked back at him for a moment, then aimed the rifle back down at the floor. 'So sorry. Took me by surprise. Colonel Parr. Call me Andrew. You must be Chief Inspector Lapslie?'

Parr put his hand out and Lapslie found himself taking it. His voice tasted of a very peaty whisky, which seemed to match his character. He was in his forties, with grey-streaked hair and a firm chin.

'Have you got any identification?'

Parr looked at him and smiled. 'Yes, of course.' He reached inside his jacket pocket and handed over a small leather wallet.

Lapslie examined it carefully. It was a simple card that identified Colonel Andrew Parr as being a member of the British Army. He had never seen an ID quite like it, but it looked genuine, so he accepted it with a mental proviso that he would get it checked out later.

'Do you want to see mine?' he asked.

Parr shook his head. 'Already have, old man. Already have.'

Lapslie wasn't quite sure what he meant by that, but he let it go – for now. 'If it's not too difficult a question, what the *fuck* are you doing here? It's a crime scene! And, while I'm at it, how the hell do you know who I am?'

Wincing at the profanity, Parr put the rifle down, leaning it against a wall. 'They haven't told you, then?'

Lapslie shook his head. 'Told me what?'

'We, well, *I*, have been asked to see if a hand can be lent.'

'With what?'

'The shooting, it's my specialist field, old boy. I lecture on ballistics at the Defence Academy in Cranfield.'

'You introduced yourself as Colonel. What regiment?'

Parr hesitated for a moment. 'Royal Artillery.'

'Really. A long-range sniper then?'

Parr smiled broadly; he had obviously heard the phrase before, but was surprised that Lapslie had. 'Let's just say I serve Queen and country and live in Hereford.'

'Ah.' He dropped into a deeper, more mellifluous voice. '"An attendant lord, one that will do to swell a progress, start a scene or two, advise the prince; no doubt, an easy tool, deferential, glad to be of use, politic, cautious and meticulous".'

'I am,' Parr said, smiling slightly, 'certainly no Prince Hamlet.'

'So, what have you discovered?'

Parr turned to face in the direction of St Mary's Church,

whose spire could be easily seen. 'It was a long shot – one thousand, two hundred metres. You would have to be not only a good shot, but a very well-trained one, to make it successfully.'

'Could you do it?'

Parr glanced at him oddly. 'Yes. Of course.'

Lapslie moved over to where he was standing and also looked out towards the church. 'So you think our killer might be a military man?'

Parr looked across at him. 'Maybe, but from which country's army? But it's not just the military that are taught to shoot accurately: there are hundreds of people who do it as a sport. A lot of them are very good. What I don't want to do is steer you in the wrong direction.'

'What's your opinion?'

'I believe that you are looking either for a member or a former member of the military, and that you may have more than one killer on your hands.'

Lapslie turned towards him. 'What makes you draw that conclusion?'

'As far as we know our sniper fired one shot – the shot that killed the girl. Normally sniper teams will work in twos, one doing the AMOS—'

Lapslie stopped him. 'What the hell is the AMOS?'

'Simply put, it's judging the speed of the wind, air temperature and the angle of the shot. They can all have a significant influence on the shot if it's to be accurate. There's a big difference between, say, a down-angle shot and an up-angle shot. Once that's worked out, the other member of the team, armed as it were with that information, will do the shooting. I also think that some test shots, ranging shots, would have to have been made before the kill shot.'

'Are you sure about that?'

Parr shook his head. 'About there being two? No. It's not always so: he might have ranged it and fired it himself, although that's quite difficult because things like wind speed and temperature change quite quickly. That said, it's one hell of a shot to have got right first time on your own.'

Lapslie nodded. 'Any idea what kind of weapon he would have used?'

Parr gave a strange half-smile and picked up the rifle he had just put down. 'One like this.' He handed the rifle over to Lapslie, who examined it with the eye of an amateur – a little, he realized, like kicking the tyres when buying a car. 'Do you know much about guns?'

Lapslie shook his head. 'Not much. That's why we bring in experts like you. So what have I got here?'

Parr took to the rifle back from Lapslie. 'We have here an Accuracy International AX50 .50 BMG with a Schmidt and Bender scope. It's the big brother of the AW50, which was also a very fine rifle. Certainly, in my humble opinion, the best sniper rifle and scope around at the moment. Your man would have used something like this. He wasn't using a rook rifle, that's for sure.'

'How long would it take him to make the kill shot?'

'A few minutes, more if he was doing the AMOS himself. The place was closed for refurbishment, and there was no one around. He still took a bit of a chance, but obviously thought it was one worth taking. I was just looking around for the shell casings.'

'Do you think he would have been that stupid?'

'Probably not, but it's a single-shot, bolt-action. Common sense tells you that he would have taken the casings away with him. However, I've known situations where the case ends up somewhere stupid and they can't find it. He wouldn't have had long.' He gestured towards the edge of the tower. 'It might have gone off there and fallen to the ground. That would have spoiled his day.'

'I think you'll find Jim Thomson and his team don't miss much.'

Parr looked at Lapslie quizzically. 'Who is that?'

'The senior SOCO and his lot.'

He nodded. 'Well, as I say, you never know.' Parr continued: 'What do we know about the girl?'

Lapslie shrugged. 'Not much yet, but she seems to be just a normal, everyday girl. Why do you ask?'

'It seems odd that such an experienced shooter should go to so much trouble, take such a big risk, and use the best damned rifle on the market, to kill just some girl.'

Lapslie looked at him. 'I'm sure her family don't look at her quite like that.'

Parr looked away from him. 'No, I don't suppose they do. Badly put. I apologize, but you know what I mean.'

Lapslie nodded. 'Yes, it is odd. You have any ideas?'

Parr thought for a moment. 'Yes, I think it was a practice shot, a rehearsal.'

Lapslie felt confused. 'Explain.'

'She wasn't the real target, just someone to practise on, check if the rifle was ranged properly. I can't think of any other reason he would want to kill her.'

Lapslie wasn't convinced. 'I think before we go

jumping in that particular direction you should give me a few more days to find a more practical reason for her murder.'

Parr shook his head. 'Can't do that, old man. Sorry, too much at stake. I'll have to report this to my superiors, let them decide how to take it forward. Can't have a trained sniper running around unchecked.'

Lapslie wasn't convinced. 'I think you're wrong. In fact, I know you are.'

Parr looked up at him. 'How can you be so sure?'

'Because of the dolls.'

Now it was Parr's turn to be confused. 'Dolls? What kind of dolls? Barbie, blow-up, New York? What are you talking about?'

Lapslie knew that, to a man like Parr, what he was about to say might sound ridiculous, but there was no roundabout way of explaining it. 'Just last week we found a dozen dolls in an old fall-out shelter. Nine of them were badly damaged in some way and had been placed inside small wooden coffins. Three which were still intact were left standing by the side of their coffins but hadn't yet been placed inside. One of those dolls was dressed as a bride. After Leslie Petersen was shot and murdered, I was called back to the bunker. The bride doll, which I now know represented Leslie, had been put into its coffin. When I opened the lid I discovered a hole in the doll at the exact point the bullet had entered Leslie's body, and I also discovered that the dress was covered in blood. Her blood, I believe, although we are still waiting on forensic tests.'

Parr looked at him as if he was listening to some bizarre nursery story. 'If I may ask, how do you know it was her blood?'

Lapslie shrugged. 'Like you with the gun, I can't be sure, but age and experience tells me it is.'

'How long after the shooting did you see the doll?'

'Two hours tops.'

Parr shook his head. 'And I thought I had a bizarre job. When's the PM?'

'Tomorrow afternoon.'

'Would you mind if I came along? I'd like to see if the pathologist manages to recover the bullet. It would help confirm my view on which rifle was used.'

Lapslie nodded. 'I don't have a problem with that, as long as you keep me in the picture.'

'Certainly. I think we might need each other right now.' Parr grimaced as he was struck with another thought. 'And may I give you some advice?'

'Certainly.' Lapslie returned the grimace wanly. 'And if it's good, I might take it.'

'Get your people to search the church wall around the front entrance to the church, near to where the girl was shot. If our sniper did fire some ranging shots – and I'm bloody sure he did – then the bullets will be there or thereabouts. Might take some careful searching, but they will be there. I'd stake a good bottle of wine on it. Also, given the power and velocity of the bullet, unless it was deflected by a bone, my best guess is that it went through her. That's for the PM to determine, of course. Check the wall at the back of the church directly behind where she was shot. I think you'll be surprised what you find.'

Lapslie nodded. 'Thank you. I'll get the SOCOs on it right away.'

Parr smiled. 'Good. I'll see you tomorrow then?'

Lapslie nodded and watched as the colonel disappeared into the gloom of the tower steps, carrying his rifle. 'Just out of interest,' Lapslie called, 'you *do* have a permit for that gun, don't you?'

The only answer that came back was a fading laugh.

As Lapslie drove away from Tom's Tower he realized that he really did need to know as much as possible about

Leslie Petersen. He wasn't sure she was going to be the key to solving the problem, but her murder was certainly an important element, at least to her killer, and more facts might uncover why? He knew his next interview would have to be with her father, followed by her husband. The interviews weren't going to be pleasant, and might even be traumatic, but sometimes the close family knew things and didn't even realize it. He also needed to get hold of Jim Thomson and get him and his team to comb the church wall inch by inch to see if Colonel Parr's theory was correct. Before calling Jim, however, there was something he wanted to check with Jane Catherall.

He pulled over to a lay-by and called her on his mobile. She answered almost at once. 'Jane, it's Mark Lapslie. I need a favour.'

There was a short pause as she either pondered the request or, more likely, tried to get to grips with the technology of the phone she was holding. 'That depends,' she said judiciously.

'On what?'

'What it is. I've had a few very odd requests from you in the past.'

'This one is easy.'

'Go on.'

'Have you had a chance to look at Leslie Petersen's body yet?'

'The PM isn't scheduled until tomorrow. Congratulations, by the way, on managing to get the name right this time.'

'I'm doing my best. I was just wondering if you had made a preliminary inspection.'

There was another pause. 'Dan washed the body to prepare it for tomorrow. Why?'

'Was there an exit wound? I mean, did the bullet go right through her, or do you think it might still be inside her?'

Another pause. 'There was no exit wound. I expect to find the bullet lodged somewhere inside her abdomen. The trouble with bullets is that they're never where you expect them to be. They can bounce around a lot if they hit bone.'

'But you're sure that it's still lodged inside her somewhere?'

'Yes. Might one ask why?'

'I'll tell you tomorrow. Don't suppose you've managed to check her blood group yet?'

'Yes.'

'And it is?'

Another pause. 'I'll tell you tomorrow.'

'Jane, please. This is important. Rouse is giving me a hard time, and I need some hard facts to throw back at him or I'm up shit creek.'

Jane Catherall was no fan of Alan Rouse either. 'Why do you need to know?'

'I want to know if her blood matches the blood on the doll's dress.'

Silence for a few moments. 'How could the killer have transferred the blood from one crime scene to another? And, more importantly, why?'

'I don't know, and I don't know, but on the face of it, that's what I think has happened.'

'She was AB rhesus negative, if that helps.'

Lapslie was grateful. 'Thanks, Jane.'

Before Catherall had a chance to ask another question, Lapslie hung up. Well, the colonel had been wrong about the bullet. That was something, at least. That said, Lapslie had very little choice but to get Jim Thomson and his team to start searching the church wall for ranging shots.

The Cooke home was a modest but well kept and well presented semi-detached house on a small middle-class estate near Finchingfield. Lapslie made his way along the short path to the front door and rang the bell. A few seconds later a young man answered. His hair was short, his eyes were dark, and he looked drawn. Lapslie presumed that this was Nathan Petersen, the widower. Widower sounded such an old-fashioned term, he thought, but what else was there? He took out his warrant card. 'Chief Inspector Lapslie. I was wondering if Mr Alan Cooke was in.'

After taking a quick look at his card, the man nodded. 'Yes, he is. Please, come in.'

He called up the stairs.

'Alan, it's the police. You need to come down!'

With that he showed Lapslie into the sitting room. The house was filled with framed family photographs on the walls and shelves. Lapslie turned to him. 'May I ask who you are, sir?'

'Nathan. Nathan Petersen. I was married to Leslie. Not for long, but I was.'

Lapslie gave him an understanding nod. 'I'm sorry for your loss, and I hope I can get to the bottom of it for you.'

Petersen shook his head gently. 'Don't take this the wrong way, Mr Lapslie, but I don't think you will. There just seems to be no reason for it.'

'I promise I will get to the bottom of it if I possibly can.'

Lapslie picked up a photograph from the top of the fireplace and looked at it. It was a photograph of a smiling Leslie, together with another boy whom Lapslie didn't recognize. 'Who is the young man with Leslie?'

Petersen looked at the photograph. 'That's her brother, Bob. He's in the Army. He's in Afghanistan at the moment, but I think they're going to fly him home.'

The Army connection interested Lapslie. 'How long has he been serving?'

'Four or five years now, I believe.'

'And you – what do you do, if I may ask?'

'I'm with the local council. Planning department.'

'And was everything okay between Leslie and her brother, and between Bob and you, for that matter?'

'Everything was fine between Leslie and her brother, couldn't have been better – except for the forced distance factor, that is.' Petersen looked to one side for a second, as if considering. 'There was an awkwardness between Bob and me at first, almost as if he resented me. But I put that down to the normal protectiveness of an elder brother. Or perhaps just that we were from totally different backgrounds.'

'And how are things between you and Bob now?'

Petersen shrugged. 'They're good. We got to know each other better on his visits home, and no doubt Leslie also spoke to him, impressed upon him how much we cared for each other. Whatever, the awkwardness faded.'

'And how long had you been seeing Leslie?'

'About eighteen months.'

Lapslie smiled. 'Quite quick, then?'

'I suppose. But there were no reservations on my side, nor on hers – so why hang around?'

'Was she insured?' It was a question Lapslie always hated to ask, so he normally threw it in like a hand-grenade. It was like accusing the victims of being involved in the crime at a moment when they were at their most vulnerable. It was worse when there were small children involved. When the parents, who were normally grief-stricken, had to be treated as prime suspects. That was about as bad as it got. He had seen people's hair turn white with the stress of it all.

'Yes she was: for £200,000. We both were. That was my idea, because I thought I might go before her and I didn't want to worry that she would be left without a penny or any support.'

Lapslie could see no reason why Nathan Petersen

would have been involved in the murder of his wife, but he would remain a suspect until an arrest had been made. Before he could ask another question, Alan Cooke entered the room. Lapslie recognized him from the church hall, although the man looked like he had aged ten years in the intervening days. He put his hand out. 'Chief Inspector Lapslie. I'm in charge of the inquiry into your daughter's murder.'

'Caught anyone yet?'

Lapslie shook his head.

'Then shouldn't you be out there doing that and not bothering us? I've already given a bloody statement!'

Lapslie remained calm. People were never themselves at times like this. 'I have a team of detectives and uniformed officers doing all they can. They'll catch whoever it was.'

Alan Cooke sat down in a large armchair opposite Lapslie. 'Sorry. It's not been a good time. Lost her mum a few years ago, and now Leslie, and Robert's serving in a very dangerous place. We were such a happy family once. Now it's just me and Robert.'

'I know you have already given a statement, but I was wondering if you would mind answering a few more questions.'

He nodded. 'Why not, if it helps? Go ahead.'

'Some of these questions might sound a bit obvious, but I have to ask them.'

Cooke nodded again, and sat up, trying to look as alert as he could.

Lapslie hesitated for a moment, not quite sure how to pose his first question. The grief in the room was something so tangible he could almost touch it. Finally he found the words. 'Murder is always bad, and your daughter's murder, because of the circumstances, is particularly bad. I have dealt with a lot of murders over the years, some of them of young girls like your daughter, but none of them have ever been murdered in such a professional manner. This type of murder is usually reserved for presidents and politicians and soldiers, not normal young ladies who live normal lives. Have you any idea at all who would not only want to kill your daughter but was capable of doing it in such a dramatic way?'

Alan Cooke looked at him for a moment. 'Do you know, I know people say this sort of thing when someone dies, but in her case it's true. She didn't have an enemy in the world. She really didn't. She was like her mother: kind, gentle, thoughtful. Always been popular, never had a problem with anyone. She was a problem *solver*, not a problem *creator*. This is a big mistake, it has to be: someone thought she was someone else.'

Lapslie looked back steadily. 'Now I know that your son Bob is in the Army. But did Leslie at any time have a relationship with anyone in the Army?'

Alan Cooke looked down awkwardly for a second. 'Well, there was someone – but I'm sure it's not connected with this now.'

Lapslie kept his stare steady. 'I think I should be the judge of that.'

This time Alan Cooke looked towards Nathan, as if seeking his approval. 'I'm sorry, Nathan – but Leslie swore me to secrecy.' He took a fresh breath as he met Lapslie's gaze. 'Leslie did in fact have a past boyfriend; a friend of Robert and a fellow soldier serving in Afghanistan.'

'And when did they split up?'

'More or less when she started seeing Nathan.'

'More or less?' Lapslie knitted his brow. 'Why not more specific?'

'Because Mike, Robert's soldier friend, was on a tour of duty in Afghanistan at the time, and it happened four months into that tour.' Alan Cooke sighed and held a hand out. 'That was the main reason for the break-up. All that time away – so hard to keep up a relationship.'

Halfway through, Lapslie noticed Nathan Petersen close his eyes for a second and shake his head. Alan Cooke looked towards Nathan.

'That's why Leslie begged me and Robert not to say anything – thought you might somehow feel guilty and responsible. And that might have put an unnecessary strain on your relationship. But things were already dead in the water between her and Mike before Leslie met you.'

Nathan grimaced awkwardly; a half-acceptance. 'Explains I suppose the initial antipathy from Bob to me – his Army friend being dumped like that.'

'Yes. And Leslie put in a lot of time explaining the situation to Robert, that things had broken down between her and Mike well before she met you. So that her brother didn't hold a grudge against her future husband.'

Or her, Lapslie thought, but didn't voice it. But it was easy to see how Mike might have been less understanding, dumped in the middle of a tour of duty.

'Mike? What's his surname?'

'Stowell. Mike Stowell.'

'And was he a sniper, or at any time had sniper training in the Army?'

'I don't know. Robert would know, I suppose, or you

could check with his regiment.' He pulled his thoughts up short as it struck him where things were headed. 'But I'm sure Mike couldn't have been involved in something as horrific as this. He's such a nice lad.'

Lapslie smiled patiently. If he had a pound for every time he'd heard that said about a murderer by a relative or friend . . . 'We'll know more I dare say after we've spoken to Mike and checked with his regiment. Anything else worthy of note you can think of?'

The two men looked at each other in a telling way. Nathan spoke first. 'Look, there was something. It's probably nothing, but I'll tell you anyway.'

Lapslie looked at him for a moment. 'Go on.'

'Her dress got damaged. Slashed, it was.'

'What dress? Her wedding dress?'

The two men nodded in tandem, and Alan Cooke continued: 'She wanted to get wed in her mother's dress. So she had it taken in a little and cleaned. When it got back it stank of the dry cleaners', so she hung it over the line outside to let the air blow through it a bit, freshen it up.'

Lapslie nodded. 'Okay. So what happened?'

'When she brought it in, someone had cut a big section out of it. Not just slashed it, but cut out a bloody great square . . .'

Lapslie was intrigued. 'What, and took the piece away?'

Both men nodded at once.

'So what did she do?'

Her father continued: 'She was very upset, but, as ever, she sorted it out. Problem-solver, like I said. She took some material from inside the dress and she and her aunt did a sort of invisible mend. You couldn't even see where it had been damaged. It was remarkable, really.'

'And when did this happen?'

'About two weeks before the wedding.'

Remarkable indeed, Lapslie thought; but if Mike Stowell hadn't been around for the past two weeks, then he couldn't have been responsible for that, or for Leslie Petersen's murder. He asked whether Stowell was currently on a tour of duty. 'Either in Afghanistan or elsewhere?'

Alan Cooke answered. 'He's been on leave.'

'For how long?'

'The past five months.'

Lapslie's brow furrowed. 'That's an unusually long leave. What's the reason for that?'

Alan Cooke mulled his mouth for a second, as if the implications of what he was about to say had left a bitter taste.

'Because, according to Robert, he's been suffering combat stress, PTSD. What they used to call battle fatigue.'

Lapslie nodded slowly. PTSD was often Armed Forces shorthand for various psychological disorders.

Emma Bradbury was standing in the small wood that surrounded the secret entrance to the fall-out bunker. She was watching carefully as the Special Operations team did a fingertip search of the ground. They had formed a line at the far side of the wood, and then moved forward slowly on their hands and knees; photographing, picking up and tagging anything that might be of interest. Most of it wasn't, but they still had to do it.

Jim Thomson and his SOCO team were also there, taking samples of the different grasses, plants and soil in case they had to match them against any of the suspects' clothing. If there were suspects.

Bradbury's phone vibrated in her pocket. She pulled it out and checked the screen. Lapslie. Walking away from Jim Thomson and the Special Operations unit, she answered it. 'Sir?'

The signal inside the wood wasn't strong, and Lapslie's voice was weak, but Bradbury could just about hear him.

'How's the search going?'

'Slowly, but I don't mind. They're doing a good job, and rather them than me. They're covering every inch of the ground. We do have a bit of a problem though . . .'

'What's that?'

'Superintendent Rouse has been on the phone. Or rather, his PA has been on the phone. He says that I only have them until the end of the day, and then they have to report back to force HQ for redeployment.'

Lapslie sighed. 'I suspected he'd do that, I just didn't expect him to act quite so quickly. But thankfully we've had a possible breakthrough, so try to at least get the fingertip search finished, plus anything else you think we need, then get yourself over to the following address.' Lapslie read out Mike Stowell's address and explained about him being Leslie's past boyfriend, jilted while on duty in Afghanistan. 'I'll meet up with you there.'

'Sounds promising.'

'Certainly does. We'll haul him in for questioning, search his house for any weapon and run forensics on everything in his house. So take Thomson and his team with you. Later today or first thing tomorrow we also need to be back with Thomson at the church to search the wall around and above the main door where Leslie was shot.'

'How high above the main door?'

'To roof level.'

'And what are we looking for?'

'Bullet holes, bullet fragments. Although she was hit by one bullet, our killer might have made some ranging shots first. If he did, I want to find out where they ended up, and see if we can recover the ammunition. That will help with a match if we find the rifle.'

'I'll wrap up here as quick as I can and see you shortly, sir.'

Lapslie hung up, and Bradbury turned her attention to Inspector Brooke, the commander of the Special Operations Unit. 'Sir, we've only got until the end of the day, and I can only stay here a further half-hour. So can you get your boys to move it along a bit?'

He nodded. 'I can, but it won't be quite so detailed.'

'Can't it be quick *and* detailed?'

Brooke smiled at her. 'I'll have a word.'

As he said it there was a shout from one of the officers at the end of the group. 'Over here!'

Both Bradbury and Brooke moved across quickly to where the officer was kneeling, making sure to remain behind their line. By the time they reached him he had marked the location of the object he had found with a large yellow peg. The object was small, black and square in shape. Bradbury couldn't quite make out what it was.

Brooke handed him a clear plastic exhibit bag, and the officer picked the object up carefully with a pair of tweezers and dropped it inside the bag before sealing it and handing it to Bradbury. She held it up for both herself and Brooke to examine. It was a small but perfectly made teacher's mortar board: the type Bradbury had seen students strutting about in during their graduation at posh schools. It even had a small tassel. It came from one of the dolls: the teacher doll that had been removed from the bunker, almost certainly, if Lapslie was to be believed, by Leslie Petersen's killer. He must have been in a bit of a panic to drop it and not realize. It wasn't much, but at least now she knew that the killer did make mistakes.

Bradbury noticed that the toy mortar board had been found next to a small path that seemed to lead from the edge of the wood to the manhole cover that sat over the bunker. Leaving Brooke with the exhibit, she followed the path to the edge of the wood. She scanned the scene but there was nothing, not even a tyre mark. About two hundred metres in front of the wood was an opening, which she knew led onto the B1053.

She walked up to it and looked each way. As she looked to her left and right she noticed that there were yellow-boxed speed cameras on both sides of the road. She wondered whether, having slipped up the once, the killer might have slipped up for a second time. There might be a picture of his car and his number plate, and with cameras on both sides of the road it wouldn't matter which way he'd gone. It was a shot in the dark, but if they struck gold with this past Army boyfriend and got a plate match with his car, then it closed that particular circle.

'Can you please state your name for the record?'

'Michael Gerald Stowell.'

Bradbury got confirmation of his age, twenty-eight, and address, then informed Stowell that she would be conducting the interview with Chief Inspector Lapslie.

'Also present is solicitor Giles Brent, representing the accused, Michael Stowell, and the purpose of this interview concerns the murder of Leslie Petersen, whom we believe to have been known to the accused.'

They were in an interview room deep in the bowels of Chelmsford HQ, one floor below street level. Lapslie and Brent announced themselves for the benefit of the tape, then Bradbury's opening questions revolved around Stowell's past relationship with Leslie.

'And how did you feel when she dumped you?'

'Cut up, of course.'

'Cut up enough to kill her?'

Brent looked uncomfortable at the comment, but Stowell answered before he could intervene.

'Of course not. I was really hurt at the time – but got over it long ago.'

Lapslie watched Stowell intently. He preferred Bradbury to handle the opening, perfunctory questions, because then the contrast and element of surprise invariably gave more of an edge to his own questions. He leant forward across the interview table.

'Yes. We can see how "hurt" you were from your email at the time.' Lapslie passed across a sheet of paper. 'Is this the email you sent to Leslie Petersen just after she dumped you?'

Stowell's face reddened slightly as he glanced at it. 'Yes, it is.'

'Would you care to read it out for us.' Lapslie held a hand out and smiled tightly. 'And also of course for the benefit of the tape.'

'I . . . I don't know how you could do that to me . . .'

Stowell stumbled on the opening words before getting into his flow, though his face got steadily redder – 'Surrounded here by nothing but desert, dust and bullets, all I could do was think of you and the moment I'd see you again. And meanwhile all you were thinking about was another man. You couldn't have hurt me more if you'd put a bullet through my heart.'

Lapslie waited a second after Stowell had stopped reading. 'Given that email, "hurt" and "cut up" might seem gross understatements of how you felt at the time. Indeed "bullet through my heart" is how you felt – an apt choice of words, given that's exactly how Leslie died on her wedding day.'

'That's how I felt at the time,' Stowell blustered, 'but not now. Like I said, I got over it.'

'Did you now?' Lapslie eyed Stowell keenly. 'So how is it that over four months ago you were given leave due to PTSD?'

Stowell's head slumped a fraction. 'Okay, I've been depressed, but I've been getting treatment for that and—'

'I'm sorry,' Brent cut in. 'My client doesn't need to go into detail about his current PTSD treatment, or indeed how or why it came about.'

'We believe it to be relevant to the investigation.'

'That's as may be. But that doesn't require my client to reveal details of his current PTSD treatment, much of which might not be relevant. Indeed, it is the standard treatment for many a British soldier as a result of conflict and battle stress.'

Lapslie wondered whether there was a compensation claim in the wings, which Stowell's solicitor feared might be compromised. Certainly Giles Brent had appeared at short notice; they hadn't had to summon a duty solicitor. Lapslie looked down, turning a page in his file.

'But certainly your client's leave due to PTSD would have placed him in the UK at the time of Leslie Petersen's murder. Which brings me to your whereabouts on the day in question.' Lapslie looked up from the file, eyes shifting from Brent to rest keenly on Stowell. 'So can you tell me, Mr Stowell, where you were on the twenty-seventh of June between the hours of 11 a.m. and noon?'

Stowell exchanged a glance with Brent before answering. 'I was in the Dundee Café on Stanton Road for most of that time.'

Bradbury consulted her folder with a small map

inside. 'So just over half a mile from where Leslie Petersen was shot.'

'I suppose. If you say so.'

Brent gave his client a sharp look; the first so far. Obviously understanding his client's frustration, but chiding him not to let it show.

Lapslie sensed this was the tensest cat-and-mouse part of the interview, but Stowell had little room to manoeuvre. Their search of his computer earlier had yielded a treasure trove. They knew exactly where he was meant to be and at what time, and because Stowell and Brent were informed of the search, they knew it too, thus the look between them. Lapslie picked up again.

'You say *most* of that time. What time did you leave the Dundee Café?'

'At just before 11.40 a.m.'

'So a good ten to twelve minutes before your ex-girlfriend was shot.'

Lapslie could see that Stowell was tempted to offer another 'If you say so', but with a guarded look from Brent, he bit his lip. Lapslie too held back on his next intended question of whether anyone had seen Stowell leave the café. Since Stowell had admitted leaving in time to do the shooting, the question was redundant.

'And who did you meet at the café?'

'I was *meant* to meet an old Army buddy, Barry Dennell – but he didn't show.'

'Oh. And why's that?'

'I don't know. I tried him a couple of times on his mobile, but he didn't answer.' Stowell shrugged. 'Would have kept trying him if you hadn't hauled me in.'

'Rather convenient. Your Army friend emails you to meet up, but then doesn't show up.' Lapslie raised a brow. 'What did you do? Email yourself posing as your friend so that you had an excuse to be in the area that you could blame on him?'

'That's not how it happened. You can check.'

'Oh, believe me, we will.' Lapslie noticed the tattoo on Stowell's forearm. He nodded towards it. 'So who is Matilda tattooed across the heart and roses? Another past girlfriend?'

'No. That's my mother,' Stowell said flatly. 'She died just over a year ago.'

'Mother dying, girlfriend dumping you. I can quite easily see how that would push many a man over the edge.'

Brent reached across and touched Stowell's forearm. It could have been to console, but it looked too firm for that; a 'Don't rise to it' gesture. Stowell didn't answer, just glared back.

But while Lapslie had him reeling, he didn't feel like letting him off. 'So where do the fireman, the teacher and the others come into it? Did they slight you too – in some way you felt they were also responsible for the split with Leslie? Talk badly about you, did they?'

Stowell looked nonplussed, and, with a quick glance towards his client, Brent's brow furrowed. 'I have no idea what you're talking about, Inspector. And it's clear my client doesn't either. I do hope it's connected with this inquiry now.'

'Yes, very much so. We fear there may be some other connected murders.' Lapslie didn't feel like elaborating – certainly not until he had more proof and some firm connection to the others outside of just a collection of dolls. And Stowell's expression gave little away. He flipped back a page in his file. 'But let's return now to your Army days before your PTSD-related leave. Were you a sniper at any time during your Army service?'

'Yes, I was.'

'For how long?'

'The last two years before my leave.'

No hesitation from Stowell, Lapslie noted; but again these were areas that Brent knew they'd have checked, so he'd have pressed upon his client the importance of answering straightforwardly; with no hedging which might hint at dishonesty.

'And what rifle did you generally use?'

'Two types. An AX50 or L115A3.'

Lapslie exchanged a look with Bradbury. 'And of those two, do you favour any particular one?'

Stowell shrugged. 'They're both good rifles. So it would come down to the type of target – moving or stationary – length of shot and the weather conditions.'

'And do you keep either of these rifles here in the UK?'

'No. They're both kept on the Army compound back in Camp Bastion, Afghanistan.'

'I see. Neither of them at home or in a lock-up somewhere?'

'No.' Stowell met Lapslie's gaze firmly. 'I haven't fired a rifle of any type in over four months.'

'Well, we'll soon know when we've concluded our searches.' Lapslie closed his file and stood up. 'Suspect to be held in custody meanwhile.'

'On what grounds?' Brent quizzed.

'We have motive, MO and opportunity for your client.

And if we find the murder weapon or a witness that can place him at the scene, we'll have a full house.'

Lapslie was already halfway out of the room as Brent continued with some residual protests to Bradbury. But Lapslie knew that if they came up with neither, they'd be hard pushed to hold Stowell more than another forty-eight hours.

Lapslie grabbed a take-out double-shot latte on his way to the church first thing the next morning to revive himself. The previous day had been gruelling and they'd been up until midnight with Thomson and the SOCO team searching Stowell's parents' home where he lived, then finally his dad's allotment shed and a storage unit Mike Stowell had used. Nothing at any of them.

They'd searched every conceivable nook and cranny, the loft, under the stairs, even under some floorboards where they'd eased a fraction underfoot and could have been loosened; then Stowell's fourteen-year-old Ford Mondeo parked in his parents' driveway. Nothing.

Lapslie sipped at his coffee as he approached the church. Bradbury, Thomson and the SOCO team were already there. Thomson was busy supervising ladders being placed up against the church walls and white-suited

SOCOs ready to climb up them. Crawling across the ground at the foot of the wall and the grass bank beyond were six members of the Special Operations Unit Bradbury had been working with in the woods.

Thomson looked across at Lapslie. 'You say we're looking for spent ammunition?'

Lapslie nodded. 'Yes, from a high-powered sniper rifle. Might not be anything, might just be marks where the bullets impacted, or if we're lucky we might just find the bullets or parts of them.'

Thomson nodded and moved away without speaking. Lapslie had seen Bradbury's car, but couldn't see her. 'Anyone seen DS Bradbury?'

Without speaking, one of the SOCO officers pointed to the church. Lapslie walked across to the church door, where he encountered one of Thomson's SOCOs putting small pieces of masonry into an exhibit bag. Looking into the darkness of the church, he finally spotted Bradbury searching the far wall with a small torch. He walked across to her.

'Emma.'

She turned quickly. 'Sir.'

'Can I ask what you're doing?'

'Looking for the bullet that killed Leslie Petersen. If it

did go through her as she was standing in the doorway, then with luck it will be embedded in this wall somewhere. Thought I'd have a quick check before the SOCOs get to work.'

Lapslie smiled. 'Although I like your thinking, according to Doctor Catherall there was no exit wound, so the bullet should still be inside her.'

Bradbury looked at him, crestfallen. 'Oh, I didn't know.'

'That's okay: I'd have done the same. Why is the place so quiet?'

'It's a church.'

'Funny girl. Apart from that.'

'I asked everyone to keep the noise down. Didn't want your head full of fruit salad or runner beans.'

'Ever thoughtful.' Lapslie smiled, looking around. 'How are they getting on?'

'Nothing yet, but they've only been at it twenty minutes.' She straightened up. 'Oh, and there was one thing I forgot to show you with all the commotion yesterday. Some of Thomson's team stayed in the woods finishing up when we met up at Stowell's, so it was left with them.'

Lapslie looked up at her, intrigued. 'What is it?'

'Jim Thomson's got it. Come and see.'

Lapslie followed Bradbury out of the church and towards Thomson.

'Have you still got that exhibit, Jim?' she asked. 'Like to show it to the Chief Inspector?'

Without a word, Thomson reached into a black, leather, box-shaped bag and produced the transparent plastic exhibit bag, which he handed over to Lapslie. Holding it up to the light, Lapslie realized straight away what it was.

'Where the hell did you find that?'

'Just off the pathway leading between the tunnel exit and the edge of the wood,' Thomson said in his petrol-flavoured voice.

Lapslie studied the mortar-board hat. So while Stowell might have been careful to conceal his rifle or get rid of it, he'd slipped up with this. He handed it back to Thomson. 'When are you going to have it analysed?'

He looked at Bradbury, but before she had time to reply there was a shout from one of the SOCOs examining the outside of the church. He was halfway up a ladder and holding up an exhibit bag.

'I've got what I think you were looking for, sir.'

Lapslie, Bradbury and Thomson moved across to the ladder.

'Drop it,' Lapslie said. 'I'll catch it, don't worry.'

The SOCO dropped it and Lapslie snatched it from the air. It was a fragment of a bullet, the front of it flattened out.

'May I have a look at that, Chief Inspector?'

Lapslie's mouth was suddenly filled with the taste of strong peaty whisky. Colonel Parr was standing behind the group. By the expressions on the faces of Emma Bradbury and Jim Thomson, they hadn't heard him approach either. Obviously he was following up on his earlier inspection. Lapslie handed the exhibit bag over and Parr began his examination.

After only a few seconds he handed it back to Lapslie. 'An AX50 .50 bullet, as we suspected.'

Before he could say any more, a member of the SOCO team called out. 'Over here!'

As the four of them approached he pushed a yellow marker post into the ground. Parr and Lapslie looked down at the small metal fragment that lay on the ground beside the marker. This time the bullet was too damaged to identify its type.

Thomson stepped in between the two men, quickly scooping the fragment up in a gloved hand and dropping it into an exhibit bag before handing it to Lapslie.

Parr put his hand out and Lapslie handed it over. The colonel examined it.

'Heavily damaged, but I'm guessing it's a .50 as well. The question now is: where did he get the gun, and, for that matter, the ammunition? This isn't like the USA, where you can just pop down to the local supermarket and pick a rifle up, along with a two-for-one deal on ammunition.'

Lapslie filled him in on the latest developments: that since they'd last met, they'd hauled in a possible suspect. 'A past boyfriend of Leslie Petersen. A British Army man with two years' sniper training under his belt. Thing is, he says his rifles have been left at his Army compound in Afghanistan.'

Parr nodded thoughtfully. 'That's an accurate account. Rifles of this nature are strictly monitored and are signed out for each assignment. You might be able to sneak a standard rifle from a stricken comrade or an insurgent, but specialist sniper rifles are another kettle of fish. And getting any sort of rifle through British customs would be virtually impossible.'

Lapslie looked at the bullet fragment in the bag. 'And the ammunition?'

'Easier to sneak through customs, but still a hell of a

risk with metal detectors and the distinctive shape of bullets. I have one idea, but it will depend on what the bullets are made of.'

Lapslie was intrigued. 'What difference would that make?'

'If the ammunition wasn't factory-made, he might have made it himself.'

'I see. And the rifle?'

'Given customs restrictions, more likely that he got it on the black market within the UK.' Parr held a palm out. 'But then an Army man might well have an idea where to source that, along with the ammunition.'

Lapslie held up the polythene bag with the two bullet fragments. 'And I dare say if the bullet extracted from Leslie Petersen's body isn't too damaged, that will help further determine that.'

'Yes. But you'll still need to find the rifle for a complete match. Barrel grooves and marks are rifle-specific.'

Lapslie nodded sombrely. So close and yet so far.

Lapslie's next stop for the day was the forensic science laboratories. He needed to see the dolls again. They'd focused almost exclusively on Stowell for the last couple of days and on how Leslie Petersen's death might link to the other victims, yet it might be that they had to approach the case the other way round: look at the other possible victims and how they might link back to the killer.

It was only a short drive to the labs, which were situated deep within a wood, surrounded by a high barbed-wire fence and more security than Lapslie was accustomed to dealing with. He was stopped four times before he even reached the main foyer. After that he was accompanied to the area that he wanted and handed over to a senior scientist.

Lapslie remembered the days when the labs were still under the control of the Home Office. Life was far more relaxed in those days. Everyone knew you, and you knew everyone. A smile and a nod was all you needed to get in. Once everything had been privatized, things had changed.

Maybe it had to change, he reflected. The close relationship some of the scientists had with the police force hadn't always been a good idea. He remembered some high-profile cases where a particular scientist had been 'helpful' to the senior investigating officer in interpreting evidence, and a number of people had gone to prison for crimes they might but might not have committed. That said, the close relationship had also produced some very positive and legitimate results. But the world moved on, and this was the world he had to deal with now, like it or not.

Lapslie arrived at the section he needed to be greeted by a tall slender woman in her mid-thirties with a spiky crop of natural blonde hair, and green eyes. She was wearing a white lab coat and smart designer glasses. She introduced herself: 'Gillian Holmes. I'm the senior scientist here . . .'

'Detective Chief Inspector Lapslie.'

She smiled broadly at him. 'We've had a very strange request about you, DCI Lapslie. It came from a Detective Sergeant Bradbury.'

'To keep everything as quiet as possible and not to let too many people talk to me.'

Holmes nodded. 'Yes, that was about it.'

'I have synaesthesia. You might not—'

Holmes cut him off. 'My father had the same condition. He saw people's names as colours. Days of the week too. How does yours manifest?'

'My brain converts sounds into tastes. Sometimes it jumbles them all up.'

Her smile continued. 'And what do I taste of? I'm sure that's the first question that everyone asks you.'

'Something subtle. Mozzarella, I think.'

'Well that's not too bad then. I can imagine some of the tastes are not quite so pleasant.'

Lapslie nodded ruefully.

'I understand you're here to see the dolls?'

Lapslie nodded. 'Yes.'

'I'll take you to them.' She led Lapslie into the laboratory whose door she had emerged from and directed him to the far side of the lab, where ten dolls were aligned, each with its coffin laid behind it. Lapslie pulled out his notebook and began to make notes on each of the dolls.

'We've already done a preliminary assessment – basic descriptive stuff, if it will help.'

Lapslie nodded. 'Yes, it would, thanks.'

Holmes walked across to a desk as Lapslie watched her. She picked up an assortment of papers and brought them over to him. 'That's all we have for now. Would you like to go through each of the dolls with me and discuss what we've discovered?'

'That would be very helpful.'

They moved across to the first doll, the one dressed as a nurse. 'First, although they were found in an orderly line, and we kept that line the same, I can't tell you if that's significant or just random. All the dolls we examined were very well made. Papier-mâché bodies with wax heads. Although the bodies had been made recently, the heads are different. They all came from Victorian dolls. The clothes were made from authentic materials. The nurse's clothes in particular were made from sections of what must have been a real nurse's uniform – the material is precisely the same. Even her small shoes are made from leather, and beautifully made.'

Lapslie indicated the damage around the doll's throat. 'How's that been done?'

'Crushed and damaged by hand. Every one of the dolls is damaged in some way.'

They moved down the table to the next doll, the fireman.

'Once again the clothes are authentic, made from the very same material as a real fireman's clothes.'

'And the damage?'

'The doll has been burnt quite badly. By which I mean that the damage is bad, not that whoever damaged it *did* it badly.'

The next doll was a garage mechanic, his chest crushed flat.

'Stamped on by a foot,' Holmes noted. 'No trace of a pattern on the sole, unfortunately.'

The next doll was a fisherman, dressed in long rubber boots and holding a fishing rod and a keep net. The damage on this one wasn't so obvious. 'What's wrong with this one?'

Holmes looked at it. 'Water damage. The doll has been submerged in water for some time. As with all bodies that have been in water for a while, if you pull it too hard it will fall apart very easily.'

They continued along the table until they finally reached the bridal doll.

'Made any progress on this one?'

Holmes glanced at it. 'The doll of the moment. Not much progress so far. The stains are real blood, not a substitute. We've had it grouped as AB rhesus negative, and we're currently running a DNA analysis. I understand you requested that?'

Lapslie nodded.

'Your boss,' she asked. 'Chief Superintendent Rouse, is it?'

Lapslie nodded.

'Yes, he tried to get the test stopped. Said there wasn't the budget for it. I approved the test anyway. I'll sweep up the cost in something else – I have several under-spent projects that could do with more time being booked to them – legitimately, of course.'

'Of course. I appreciate the help.' He paused, wondering whether to tell her about the blood or not. Deciding that he would, he added: 'The girl who was murdered at her wedding – you're probably seen the evidence coming in?'

'I have.'

'She was AB rhesus negative as well. I'm sure this is her blood.'

Holmes blinked: the only sign that Lapslie had caught her attention. 'How would the killer get hold of her blood?'

Lapslie shrugged. 'There are lots of questions like that. Why would he make dolls of his victims, if indeed they were his victims? There's so much I don't know, so much more I need to discover, and very quickly.'

'You think he might strike again?'

'There's a strong possibility.' He didn't feel inclined to go into Stowell's custody details, unless or until he could find a connection from Stowell to the rest of the possible victims. 'When I first saw the bridal doll her dress was white and she was standing outside her coffin with two others. The next time I saw her, the dress had turned red with blood and she was inside her coffin.'

'And you say there were two more dolls standing outside their coffins?'

'Yes. One was a teacher in a gown and cap, the other was a soldier. From the small crowns on his shoulders I'm guessing a major.' He paused momentarily. 'There is one thing you might be able to help me with.'

'Name it.'

'I'd like to take the dress with me to the PM.'

'Might I ask why?'

'The dress she got married in was damaged shortly before the wedding. It was slashed, and a large section removed. I am guessing that the dress that the bride doll is wearing is made from the stolen section. I'd like to take it and see if I can match the missing bit with the damaged section on the dress.'

Holmes thought about the request for a moment. 'Let's compromise. I won't let you take it with you, but I will meet you at the mortuary with it. Continuity in the chain of evidence is important. Are you okay with that?'

'Fine. When's the post-mortem?'

'First thing tomorrow morning.'

*

Lapslie arranged the meeting as late as possible in the day. He knew that after the post-mortem they'd be running out of time to hold Mike Stowell much longer. At present what they had was mostly circumstantial; they didn't have nearly enough to press charges. So earlier he'd run through a list with Bradbury of what they needed urgently to pursue, then they'd meet at the end of the day and compare notes.

Lapslie would have held the meeting in his office, but a crucial element was input from their computer forensics man, Brad Morton, so they were down in the tech room where both PCs were plugged in, Leslie Petersen's and Stowell's, and Morton had spent the last few hours trawling through them for anything he might have missed before.

Emma Bradbury was last into the room. As she took a seat and opened her notes, Lapslie nodded towards her.

'So how did you get on?'

'Not much luck, I'm afraid. The internet café where the message was sent from only had a security camera covering the cash desk. It didn't cover the entrance and everyone in and out.'

Lapslie held out a palm. 'But surely it would catch him or her as they paid for their time?'

'Unfortunately not. A lot of people just get pointed to a computer as they come in, then pay where they're sat – particularly if they order a coffee too. The receipt gets brought to them and they settle up with the waitress.'

'How many pay that way?'

'Forty per cent or so.'

'So what you're saying is that there's no footage of Stowell or his friend Barry who was meant to send him the email?' They'd earlier got hold of a photo of Barry Dennell as well, for Bradbury to show the internet café staff.

'Unfortunately not.'

Lapslie was thoughtful for a second. 'So that either means one of them did send it, but they didn't come to the cash desk, or it was someone else yet to be identified. You took a lift from the cam tapes for the time the email was sent?'

Bradbury held up a memory stick. 'Half an hour each side.'

Lapslie nodded and looked towards Brad Morton. 'And you're sure that the message Stowell received was sent from that internet café?'

'Hundred per cent. They had twenty IPCs listed, and they were vastly different to the IPC number for Stowell's home computer. Even if he used some hide-my-ass software, they'd have shifted him to some remote server in Phoenix or Berlin. Swansea might have been the nearest, and we pretty well know the IPC groupings they use.'

'Any sightings of Stowell close to where the shots were fired from?' Lapslie asked Bradbury.

'No. Nothing so far. Oh, and I checked his Ford Mondeo plate number on the B1053 road cameras near the bunker I mentioned the other day. It didn't come up on that either – at least not in the past month.'

Lapslie nodded slowly. 'Any better luck with the like or hate lists for the other possible victims?' They'd earlier each got a list from Morton of any contacts from Leslie Petersen's and Stowell's emails who might be nurses, firemen, teachers, mechanics or majors.

'Afraid not. Leslie only had one teacher contact I could find, and when I checked she was very much alive, as was Leslie's regular mechanic. No email contact with other mechanics. And no nurses or firemen – except perhaps in her dreams.' Bradbury smiled wanly. 'And while her father might have known a major or two, he couldn't think of any that had died recently, or indeed that both Leslie or Stowell might have had contact with. You?'

Lapslie shook his head. 'No, nothing. No teachers or nurses. And I didn't think Stowell would be forthcoming with names of majors he'd recently killed, so I checked with his regiment. The majors he had contact with are still alive. Well, one died four years ago – but I think that's out of this particular time-frame, and it was natural causes.' Lapslie took a fresh breath. 'And while I was on to his regiment, I discovered that one of his buddies used to be a fireman before joining up – but again he's still alive and indeed still serving in Afghanistan.'

'And Stowell's mechanic friend?' Bradbury quizzed. 'Because you planned to pay him a visit today.'

'Yes. Well he'd have needed to still be alive for me to visit him.' Lapslie forced a smile. When the mechanic's name had come up earlier, Lapslie had raised the point that with a number of lock-up railway arch units for his garage business and having been friends with Stowell for several years, it might be the ideal place to hide a rifle. 'But as for a stashed rifle: I went with a couple of constables because it was a large premises to search, but we found nothing. In any case we're looking for Stowell's enemies rather than his friends – who would be more likely to be found amongst Leslie Petersen's friends. People whom Stowell feels might have influenced her against him.'

'Yes, of course, sir. But like I say, nothing among her emails on that front.'

'Maybe we simply haven't been able to uncover them yet.' Lapslie ran one hand through his hair and turned to Morton. 'How far were you able to check back on their emails?'

'Three years for Leslie Petersen, just over a year for Stowell. He cleaned his files more regularly.'

Lapslie nodded. That might hint at due caution, or perhaps the fact that he was away for such long spells at a time.

'But some friends you wouldn't email, you'd simply phone them,' Morton offered. 'Do you want me to trawl through phone records – home and mobiles?'

'Yes, yes, good idea,' Lapslie said after a second. 'How long before you'd have a list for me?'

Morton checked his watch. Less than an hour left of his evening shift. 'Late tomorrow morning. Certainly before lunch.'

'Okay. No later than midday tomorrow.' Not long after the Leslie Petersen post-mortem finished, Lapslie considered; only three hours then left before they had to release Stowell.

*

Although he'd gone to bed early, taking a herbal sleeping pill and a small glass of brandy with him, Lapslie hadn't slept well. When he was younger he had developed a taste for listening to plays on BBC Radio 4 if he couldn't sleep, but nowadays, thanks to the synaesthesia, there were too many different voices and sound effects causing too many flashes of taste in his mouth. It was like eating a big mixture of several international cuisines just when you were trying to sleep. After much experimentation he had discovered that one person reading from a book was an acceptable compromise. He had his favourite voices too. They had been selected over a few years of painstaking experimentation. One in particular had a voice like soothing chamomile tea with honey, and he enjoyed listening to anything she read, regardless of the subject or genre. But tonight, even with her reading a recent thriller, Lapslie still couldn't sleep.

Finally, he gave up. He looked at his bedside clock: 4.45. He fell back on his pillow, trying to get the day's events out of his head, but it was hopeless. There were too many unanswered questions.

Finally he decided to go for a walk and watch the sun come up, then cook himself a substantial breakfast and head off to the mortuary for the PM on Leslie Petersen.

The time passed quickly and, despite still feeling a little the worse for wear, Lapslie arrived at the mortuary at 9.45, fifteen minutes early. Despite that, however, everyone who was supposed to be there was present, including Gillian Holmes and Colonel Andrew Parr. He could see that they were both keen to talk to him, but he didn't have the time or the inclination.

Jane Catherall was still in her office, going through some last-minute notes, when Lapslie knocked and entered.

'Morning, Jane.'

She looked up. 'Good morning, Mark. You look worse than some diseased organs I've found during particularly gruelling post-mortems.'

He gave her a half-smile. 'Well, that's still a lot better than I feel. Are we all ready?'

She nodded. 'As ready as we will ever be. I confess that I haven't had a shooting for a while – every other kind of death you might think of, and several you might not, but not a shooting. I am just reminding myself of what exactly to look for.'

'Is the DNA from the blood back yet?'

Catherall shook her head. 'No, not yet. I shall give them a call after the PM. I know they're up to their eyes in work, but I will try to chivvy them along a bit.'

Lapslie smiled at her. Although she was the ultimate professional, she had also been a great friend, and without her help he would never have cracked half the cases he was credited with.

'So who is she?' Jane asked.

Lapslie stared back at her, perplexed for a moment. 'Who is who?'

'*Who* is the very beautiful woman who informs me that she is here at your invitation? Gillian, is it?'

'She's a senior scientist at the forensic lab. I asked her to bring the wedding dress the bride doll was wearing. I think it might match a section of Leslie Petersen's dress that was damaged shortly before she was murdered.'

The PM began precisely at 10 a.m. Leslie's body was gently undressed, and the gown placed into an exhibit bag, as was each item of her clothing as it was removed. Lapslie was glad to see that Leslie's remains were being treated with care and respect, despite the awful things they were going to endure. Her body was touched with sticky tape all over, to recover samples of hair, dirt or contaminants, and her hair was carefully brushed into an evidence bag.

As Doctor Catherall made her first incision, Lapslie

noticed Gillian Holmes leave the room in a hurry. He signalled to Bradbury, who had arrived as late as usual, to go and see if the scientist was all right. She returned a few minutes later and nodded.

The PM took several hours to complete, during which time it was established that the shot had entered her heart, bounced off several ribs and ended up in her liver. The bullet was removed, bagged up and placed on a table at the far side of the room with the other exhibits. Lapslie could see Parr straining to see what kind of bullet it was, but he didn't push it, and waited patiently with the rest of them.

Jane Catherall left her assistant Dan to tidy up while she stripped off her blood-splattered coveralls and returned to her office.

Lapslie and Parr followed, impatient for news.

'So what can you tell us?' Lapslie asked.

Catherall shrugged. 'Not much, really. She was a very fit and healthy twenty-four-year-old. She was free from any diseases or other medical problems, and she was a girl who looked after herself in every sense of the word. She was killed as a result of a single rifle shot to the chest, which smashed through her heart before bouncing off several bones and coming to rest in her liver.

Even if the bullet had missed her heart, by some miracle, it caused so much other damage as it tore through her abdomen that she would have died of blood loss anyway. The hepatic portal vein was completely severed. What can I say? She was shot to death.'

'Would you mind if I took a look at the bullet, Doctor Catherall?' Parr was keen to get to work.

Catherall shook her head. 'No, not at all, as long as you leave it inside the exhibit bag.'

He thanked her and stood, looking down at Lapslie. 'Would you care to come and have a look?'

Lapslie shook his head. 'I'll be along in a moment. Just need a few more words with Doctor Catherall.'

Parr nodded and left.

'Jane, I need to have a look at the wedding dress, which means I'll need to take it out of the exhibit bag for a few moments. Are you okay with that?'

'Well, you have one of the forensic laboratory scientists with you. If she can't see a problem, I don't see why I should. Wear gloves and make sure you put it on the table, so that when you've finished Dan can sweep the table for fibres that might have fallen out while you examined it.'

Lapslie stood. 'Not a problem.'

As he began to leave the room she called after him. 'One more thing.'

Lapslie stopped and turned to her. 'What?'

'Keep me informed. I don't normally like to get too involved with my bodies, but I'd like to know a bit more about this one.'

Colonel Andrew Parr had the bullet held up to the light and was examining it carefully.

Lapslie looked across at him. 'Anything interesting?'

'No, not really. It's the same calibre as the ones up at the church. Enough of the bullet left to match it to the rifle – other than that, it's all terribly disappointing. No luck in finding the rifle, I suppose?'

'No.'

'And how are you getting on with this past squaddie boyfriend you're holding?'

Lapslie sighed. 'Equally disappointing. Nothing else to link him in apart from motive and the general MO of him having sniper training. If we don't find more before close of play today, we'll have to release him.'

Parr grimaced and looked down for a second before changing the subject. 'Are you doing anything on Thursday?'

Lapslie shrugged. 'Nothing definite. Have to see where the inquiry leads. Why?'

'I'm arranging for some of our best snipers to try and copy the shooting. See what kind of problems our killer would have had, how hard the shot was, and whether it might have needed two people to make it. We can't make it one hundred per cent accurate, of course – different wind speeds, atmospheric conditions and so on – but we can get pretty close to it. It might help throw some extra light on whether this Army chap you're holding could have been responsible – so if you can, meanwhile, give me more on his background . . . I was wondering if you would like to come and take a gander?'

Lapslie was interested. 'I'd like that very much. Where do I have to go?'

'Head for Hereford, then head for Credonhill, then look for Stirling Lines. I'll have you booked in. Make sure you have your ID with you.'

'I always do.'

'Good. I'll see you then.'

Parr put out his hand and Lapslie shook it. After that he turned and disappeared towards the car park.

After watching Parr go Lapslie turned his attention back to Gillian Holmes and the wedding dress. He hadn't seen Holmes since she had left the PM, and was inter-ested to see if she was okay. He walked into the mortuary waiting room to see Emma Bradbury talking to her.

'Everything okay?'

Bradbury looked up at him. 'She had a bit of a turn. I thought she was okay but I found her lying on the floor in a faint.'

'What?'

Holmes looked up at him, the colour slowly begin-ning to force its way back into her face. 'I'm so sorry: I thought I would be fine. It wasn't so much the sight, as the smell. I thought I could cope with it. I'm so sorry.'

Lapslie crouched down and looked into her face. 'This kind of thing isn't for everyone, and it's harder than you think. Sergeant Bradbury and I have been doing it for quite a while, and we're still not used to it, so there's no shame in being upset.'

She nodded and gave Lapslie a forced half-smile. 'Thank you.'

'Now, do you still have the wedding dress you took off the doll?'

She nodded. 'Yes, it's in an exhibit bag over there.' She pointed to her handbag, which lay on a chair at the other end of the room.

Lapslie got up and walked over. The exhibit bag was sticking out of the top of the handbag. He pulled it out and checked that the red tape seal was intact, then walked back towards Holmes and Bradbury. 'Emma is going to take you outside for some air. I'm just going to check the doll's dress against the damage to the real one. If they match, we'll be a little bit closer to catching the person who has done this. I'll come out as soon as I have finished and tell you what I have discovered.'

Holmes looked up at him again. 'I really do think I should be helping,' she said in a small voice.

Lapslie shook his head. 'The body is still in there, and so is the smell. I'm not sure it would be a good idea right now. Are you?'

Holmes shook her head. Lapslie nodded to Bradbury, who led her outside and into the car park.

Lapslie returned to the mortuary with the doll-sized dress. Upon opening the exhibit bag containing the real dress, he began to examine it for any marks, tears or damage, but couldn't see a thing.

'Do you require assistance, perchance?'

Lapslie turned. It was Jane Catherall. She was hobbling into the mortuary with a walking stick in each hand.

'You know, you're the only person I've ever met who uses words like "perchance"?'

Putting her sticks to one side, Jane Catherall dropped into a seat. 'You'll have to bring it over here. I can't examine something and stand, not after that post-mortem. I find it drains the life out of me.' She winced. 'Sorry – that was a bad choice of words.'

Lapslie did as he was told, and handed the dress over to her. 'What if something drops out of the dress and we lose it?'

She took a magnifying glass from her pocket and began to inspect the garment. Without looking up, she replied: 'I understand that you are in a hurry. I'll get Dan to give the floor the once-over before he leaves. Here, here's what you are looking for!'

Lapslie walked over to her and she showed him a near-invisible mend in the dress. 'Whoever did this knew what they were doing. I am a good seamstress in my own right – you have to be if you sew enough bodies back up – and I can tell you that this is very good. Very professional. However, if you look carefully, you can see the outline of the damage in the stitching.'

Lapslie looked as she ran her finger over the damaged section.

'Can you bring the doll's dress over?' she asked.

Lapslie collected the exhibit bag, broke the red tape seal, opened it and handed her the contents. Catherall opened the dress as wide as she could and then placed it over the invisible mend. It was almost a perfect match. Just a small section in the top right-hand corner of the doll's dress didn't quite seem to fit. A section was missing.

'Did the doll have a veil?'

Lapslie nodded. 'Yes.'

'Is it in the bag?'

Lapslie shook his head.

Catherall looked up at him. 'Well I think you'll find that the missing bit has been turned into the veil. I'll get everything photographed before you leave, then at least you can compare the outline of the veil with the missing section. If that doesn't work, then bring the veil in and we'll do another match. But there's no doubt in my mind that the doll's dress and the original dress are one and the same. Your lady with the delicate stomach will need to get the fabrics under a micro-scope to check, but I'm sure she will come to the same conclusion.'

*

Struggling to her feet, Doctor Catherall began to make her difficult way back to her office. 'Don't forget to bag the two dresses up again, Mark.'

Lapslie watched her as she hobbled away, then he pushed the two dresses back into their respective exhibit bags. Leaving Leslie Petersen's dress in the mortuary, he took the doll's dress with him to the car park. When he got there, Gillian Holmes was sitting inside her car with the window rolled all the way down. The colour had returned to her face.

Leaning into the car, he handed the doll's dress back to her.

'Here you go. It was almost an exact match.'

She looked at him quizzically. 'Almost?'

'There's a small section missing which we think was used to make the veil. I'll have the dress sent up to your lab today, so you can check it out when it arrives. How do you feel?'

She gave an embarrassed smile. 'My stomach is intact, but my pride is bruised.'

'No need. When I attended my first PM I was as sick as a dog. Hopefully you won't have to go through that again.'

'I hope not.'

*

Lapslie cradled his head in one hand as Bradbury at the other end of the line informed him that she'd found nothing useful from Stowell's or Leslie Petersen's phone lists – 'No teachers, mechanics, nurses or majors. And certainly not any recently deceased.'

Morton had finished his list at just before 11 a.m., and when Lapslie had phoned shortly after the post-mortem, Bradbury had been halfway through working on it; she said she'd phone back as soon as she'd finished. Lapslie had pulled into a lay-by to take the call, the wind rush of passing lorries buffeting his car.

Lapslie sighed. 'I suppose with nothing else coming to light, we've got no choice but to release Stowell. Apparently Brent has already been on to the station first thing this morning, pressing.'

Silence on the line for a moment before Bradbury offered: 'One consolation – with Stowell out there, we'll be able to keep tabs on him – see where he goes.'

'Yes, there is that. If we haven't been able to find any links so far, Stowell might lead us to them.'

'Also while we're watching his movements, it will clip his wings on future murders.'

'Yes, it certainly will.' But Lapslie wondered whether Bradbury was pointing to that silver lining simply to make him feel better, when in reality it was a decided setback. 'But you know how these things work. With resources already stretched, it could be forty-eight hours before we get Rouse to rubber-stamp a permanent tail on Stowell.'

Bradbury fell silent again, then remarked, 'Hopefully Stowell won't be aware of that, so won't make use of the time gap.'

'Hopefully.' But as Lapslie said it, he was struck with another dilemma. 'But we'll have to carefully consider our tactics here, because one aim will work against the other.'

'In what way?'

'We have to decide whether we want Stowell to be aware of our presence tailing him, so as to avoid future murders, or whether we don't want him to be aware, so that he leads us to the next murder – makes the links in the chain that we haven't been able to find.'

PART FOUR

10 March 2009

Gordon Campbell had always been a fisherman. He used to go to the local rivers with his father every weekend when they lived in Scotland. The rivers made their way down from the Highlands, where they had begun their long journey as freshly melted snow. The water always seemed so much more pure and crystal-clear than anything you could get from a tap. You could see right through it to the gravel floor beneath. He had drunk from those rivers on many occasions, and it had been the sweetest-tasting water he had ever sipped.

The rivers were full of fish too: healthy, big fish that always put up the most ferocious fight when they were hooked. Only the most experienced fisherman would have any chance of landing these beauties. When you cooked them they melted on the tongue, and the taste was better than anything you could find in the supermarkets, no matter how fresh they said they were.

When his father was forced to move to England with his job, all that changed. They still went fishing, but it wasn't the same. The banks were littered with rubbish, mostly left by other fishermen who should have known better. The water was murky, and to drink from it meant a couple of days of gut-rot. The fish were never very good either: stunted and misshapen. Pollution had made sure of that. There were a few rivers and ponds that weren't so bad, but it was more and more difficult to find them. Nobody seemed to care, down in the South. He still fished – he couldn't help himself – but it wasn't the same.

He had come down to the River Erk, on the day that he died. It was the best fishing within easy driving distance. He always tried to get at least one day's fishing a week. He found it relaxed him, blew away the stresses of work. Parking up in the nature reserve, he had walked the half-mile along the riverbank to his favourite spot. His only concern was that someone might have got there before him. On arrival he set up his equipment, unfolded his stool, got his rod and line ready and started to fish. If he was lucky enough to catch anything half decent, he would take it home to Mary and cook her a fish supper fit for the Queen.

There had been heavy rain over the last few days, and the water was running quickly. He looked up to the sky as dark clouds rolled over, heavy with another prospective downpour.

Still, he didn't mind the weather. That was half the pleasure. As long as you were warm and had your waterproofs with you, nothing could harm you.

A distant flash of lightning illuminated the sky for a brief moment. He began to count in the way his father had taught him when he was a kid, the old Lincolnshire shepherd's way. 'Yan, tan, tethera, pethera, pimp, sethera, lethera . . .'

He had reach 'tan-a-dic' before the sound of thunder rolled over him.

'Twelve miles,' he mumbled to himself. Still a while to go before it reached him, if it was indeed coming in this direction.

As he watched, his line suddenly dipped. It was a good sign. As he stood to start pulling it in he felt a sudden blow in his back, as if he had been kicked hard. The blow was powerful enough to push him off the bank and into the water. He was only under for a matter of moments before he was pushing his way back to the surface. His first instinct was to gasp for air and spit out the small amount of water he had swallowed, but before he could do this, something was looped over his neck. He grabbed at it. It felt metallic, like some sort of thick wire.

He twisted his head to see over his shoulder. Although his eyes were still full of water, he could see the blurred outline of a figure. Whoever it was seemed to be holding some kind of a pole – or was it a fishing rod? He was holding it out so that

Gordon could grab it. Thank God, at least someone had seen him fall into the water and was trying to help him.

He felt himself being pushed back down under the water, and realized with a cold shock that whoever it was on the bank wasn't trying to help him; he was trying to kill him, trying to hold him under the water and drown him. He grabbed the wire around his neck and tried to push it off, but it was digging into his skin, and the more he struggled the tighter it seemed to get. Blood was spurting out around the wire, which seemed to be held on the end of the pole that the figure on the river bank was holding out, like the kind of thing pet rescuers used to immobilize dogs and cats. Push and struggle as he might, he couldn't get to the surface. He felt his strength ebbing away with his blood. Exhaustion set in, and the water rushed down Gordon Campbell's throat. His last emotion was surprise at the fact that his life wasn't flashing before his eyes. In fact, it was just receding into the dark and the shadows. What was his wife's name? What were his kids' names?

He died quietly in the end, his body surrounded by the fish he had enjoyed for so many years. They, for their part, just ignored him.

Lapslie called for a team briefing at six o'clock the following day, twenty-seven hours after Stowell had been released. He would have called it earlier, but that was the first moment he could be sure that Rouse was going to approve a permanent tail on Stowell. And since that would pull two men out of his squad and essentially change the dynamics of how the investigation was handled, it was important he got that information first. So, two men out of his planned squad of twenty; but eighteen should be more than enough to handle the rest of the investigation, even with such a disparate collection of possible victims with no apparent links between them.

The main task for the team would be to try and determine the names of the other victims, the ones represented by the dolls that had been damaged and left in their coffins. Lapslie knew that each of them represented a person, and if he was to have any chance at all of saving the final two he needed to identify the nine remaining dolls. Lapslie held up one hand to quell a residual murmur in the squad room.

'Now as most of you are already aware, our main suspect in Leslie Petersen's murder, Mike Stowell, was released yesterday. We've got approval to put a permanent tail on him from first thing tomorrow, so that duty falls to Ken Barrett and Pete Kempsey.' Lapslie nodded towards the detectives before lifting his eyes. 'As for the rest of you, your task of tracking down the remaining victims – some past, some still to come – won't be so easy. Unlike Leslie Petersen, none of them were shot by a sniper, so they won't have been front-page news. So we're looking for less overt murders, or in some cases even accidents, that wouldn't necessarily have come to our attention. At least, not linked to this case.'

He called the detectives forward in groups of two, assigning each pair a doll with instructions to concentrate on the means of death – assuming it was mirrored by the damage inflicted on the dolls – and reasserting that they should look at accidents as well as unsolved murders. Time wasn't on his side, and the problem was that there was no evidence that the deaths were only confined to the Essex area. They could cover the whole of the UK. He instructed each pair of detectives to go back at least twenty years. He knew it was a long time, but as he had no idea how long the killer had been active he had to draw a cut-off line somewhere, and he wanted to put it back as far as was practicable. Each pair of detectives was issued with a folder containing photographs and as much information as they had – which made them very thin folders.

At the end of the briefing, Lapslie said a few words to

hopefully fire up the assembly. 'Right: it's up to you now. I feel pretty sure that the lives of at least two more victims are in your hands. If we can discover the real identities of any of these dolls, then maybe we can start making links. If we can do that then we will, with luck, have our motive, and once we have that, well, the rest, as they say, will be child's play. Any questions?'

The room remained silent. Bradbury then stood.

'If there are any now or in the future, can you filter them through me, or email the boss with them?'

A general nod of understanding circled the room. Lapslie finished with: 'Remember, we don't have long. As long as none of you take the piss, I'll sign any overtime claims you have. Good luck and please remember that time is not our friend.'

As the teams filed out, Lapslie took Bradbury to one side. He'd woken early again that morning, suddenly hit with a fresh thought; something of a revelation as he considered it more deeply. Something that could change the whole nature of the investigation. And as the day progressed, he'd further developed that chain of thought.

'You know what I mentioned about the sniper murder being markedly different to the other victims. I think it goes far deeper than that. I think we may have been looking at the investigation the wrong way round.'

'In what way?'

'The main clue is when the sniper killing took place. When was that in terms of our investigation?'

It took a second for Bradbury to latch on to his chain of thought. 'Uh, just after we discovered the bunker and the dolls.'

'Exactly. Until that moment there was no set investigation, because the other victims had been dispensed of in such a way that they fell under our radar. Murders that had gone unnoticed, or accidents. Then suddenly comes an overt murder that couldn't fail to come to our attention, and lo and behold the first thing that comes to light is a past jilted boyfriend who has previous sniper training.'

Bradbury's brow knitted. 'You think it was some sort of set-up. Stowell might have been put in the frame?'

'Could well be the case. The MO with Stowell fits almost too conveniently, and why make that murder so overt and in our face when the others had been so discreet? Then knowing that Stowell was on leave in the UK, all that would have been needed was something to put him in the area at the time.'

This time it took Bradbury a second longer to follow the thread. 'You think that our killer might have sent Stowell the email posing as his friend?'

'I do. Certainly if he'd gone to the trouble of setting up the sniper shooting, that would have been the final component required.'

Bradbury nodded slowly. 'Unless it was Stowell himself, so that he had a cover for being in the area at the time.'

'Yes, we can't completely discount Stowell. But that would still mean coming up with rational explanations for the other victims – why the stark contrast with their deaths?' Lapslie took a fresh breath. 'Unless of course Stowell had an accomplice, and *they* link to those other victims.'

'Is that a realistic possibility?'

'Certainly one worth exploring. We already have the suggestion that the sniper shot was so complex that an accomplice might have been required to measure wind speed and direction.' He'd know more, he supposed, once Parr's team had re-enacted the shot fired. 'But if Stowell does have an accomplice, then putting a tail on him isn't necessarily going to stop further murders.'

Bradbury nodded thoughtfully. 'And what set this in motion, you think, was our involvement in the investigation?'

'Yes. Though I suspect our killer expected that to occur at some stage. I can't help thinking that the proximity of the bunker to that lavender field wasn't a complete accident.'

Bradbury was incredulous. 'You think the killer might know you?'

'Certainly know *of* me and that I have synaesthesia. Or simply that he's very thorough with researching backgrounds. Look at the trouble he'd have gone to delving into Stowell's and Leslie Petersen's background in order to set this up right.'

Bradbury sighed. 'Not only thorough, but quite a level of ingenuity too.'

'Yes. Certainly someone we shouldn't underestimate.' Lapslie was thoughtful for a second. 'And talking about ingenuity, there's something else I'd like you to look at. Find out if Leslie Petersen had been involved in any major accidents over the last, oh, say, a year, that might have required a blood transfusion. Failing that, see if she gave blood on a regular basis, and, if so, where.'

Bradbury quickly saw his reasoning. 'Our killer might

have got her blood from the blood bank. It would certainly explain a lot.'

'That's what I thought.'

'Okay, sir, I'll have the answers by tomorrow.'

As Bradbury turned to leave, one of the team phones started to ring. Bradbury stopped and made her way back to answer it. 'Inquiry Team – DS Bradbury speaking.' A pause, then she said, 'He's here with me. I can pass on a message, if you like.'

Lapslie waited while she listened intently to whatever was being said.

'Okay,' she said eventually, 'I understand. Tell her thanks for letting me know. I'll convey the message. Okay, thanks again.'

She put the phone down and looked across at Lapslie. 'That was Doctor Catherall. The blood on the doll's dress is an exact DNA match for Leslie Petersen.'

The trip next day to Hereford was a long one, pretty much crossing the whole of England, east to west, skirting around London, Oxford and Cheltenham, so he decided to take Bradbury along with him. She was good at clearing the way, making sure that he wasn't distracted by his neurological condition any more than was necessary. And besides, one of the perks of being a detective chief inspector was that he could be driven around by the junior ranks whenever he wanted.

They didn't speak much for the first twenty miles.

'By the way,' Lapslie said eventually, 'any news on Leslie Petersen?'

'Yes: she did give blood, and was a regular donor. Funnily enough, it was at the hall of the church where she was shot. That might be where our clever killer got her blood from.'

'He would have had to have some inside knowledge, wouldn't he?'

Bradbury shook her head. 'Not necessarily, sir. He could have followed her. Stolen the blood after it was taken. It's not guarded like gold bullion – just stored in an ambulance in a cold box. All he had to do was keep it cold after that. Just look on Google: there's bound to be a page telling you how to store blood.'

Lapslie nodded. 'I can't see how else he could have done it.'

'Shall I stick a couple of lads on it? See if they can turn anything up?'

Lapslie shook his head. 'Leave it for now. It's a loose end we can tie up later.'

Lapslie was about to ask another question when Bradbury's mobile rang. She tapped the side of her ear, where a Bluetooth receiver sat like a high-tech earring.

'Bradbury,' she said, and then paused to listen. 'Really? That's a good start, I think . . . You say you couldn't trace any other nurses that fit the bill . . .? Okay, well, that sounds hopeful . . . As long as you're sure . . . I'm sure you are . . . Hang on, I need to make a note of that.'

Lapslie pulled his notebook and a pen from his jacket pocket, and signalled his readiness. Bradbury nodded her appreciation.

'Okay, go ahead. Jane Ann Summers, when was she murdered? First of July 2007. Where? 176 Rutland Road, Chylesmore, Coventry. Okay, got that. Have you got a time and method? Afternoon, and strangled. Okay, we need a full report on the boss's desk by the time we get back.'

Before Bradbury had time to finish the call, Lapslie cut in. 'Who was the senior investigating officer?'

'Who was in charge of the inquiry?' She flicked a glance at Lapslie. 'Chief Inspector Alan Day, and he's retired . . . Yes, and you . . . Goodbye.'

She put the phone down and turned to Lapslie. 'That was PC Parkin. He and Pearce think they've discovered who the first victim was.'

'So I heard.'

'The senior investigating officer was Chief Inspector . . .' she frowned, trying to remember.

' "Arfur" Day.'

Bradbury shook her head. 'No, sir, not Arthur: Alan. Chief Inspector Alan Day.'

'I know. We used to call him "Arfur".'

Bradbury looked confused.

' "Arfur" Day, as in "half-a-day". That's all you could ever get out of him. Always playing golf; got his handicap down to eight on the force's time. Either that or at his allotment. He had a shed there that he used to call his office.'

Bradbury just looked at Lapslie blankly.

'He was still a good detective,' Lapslie added. 'Get hold of him when we stop for coffee and a slash, which had better be soon. It sounds like I need to have a chat with him.'

He could never have realized when he started how difficult it was going to be to kill the Major. He'd never known a more careful man. The Major had left the Army only a couple of years before, as part of the ongoing round of voluntary Army redundancies aimed to reduce military spending, and until his retirement he had been serving with the Intelligence Corps in Northern Ireland. Given the amount of security that always surrounded serving officers, getting to the man was impossible, and that's why he had left him until now.

As a result of his work in Northern Ireland, the Major was very careful. He never used the same route when visiting somewhere on a regular basis, he always checked beneath his car before he drove off, even if it had only been parked in a supermarket car park for five minutes, and he was always on the watch for faces he recognized as having seen before in a different context.

On one occasion he was convinced that the Major had spotted him. They had been in the Major's local high street. He had been idling along, looking in shop windows, catching reflected glimpses of the Major every minute or so, when a pair of women walked past. They were having an animated conversation, but as they passed him the only words he heard were '. . . Be careful: he's watching you!' The words were a clear warning from a higher power, and he started to walk away rapidly. He risked a quick glance over his shoulder, and indeed the Major was looking in his direction. That had been a close call. Had he not been on a mission from God, or at least approved by God, then he might have failed right then. It just proved to him that although God endorsed his plans, it was up to him to make sure *he got the details right. God, after all, helps those who help themselves.*

After that he changed his car every time he followed the Major, and wore an array of disguises, pulled together from a number of charity shops. Getting close enough to kill him was going to be harder than all the others combined. He supposed he could have shot him, just like the bride, but he didn't want two similar murders so close together. Lapslie was no fool, and he might start making the connections that would eventually give him the leads he needed. No, it had to be another accident.

His break came when he noticed the Major buying camping equipment. The man was obviously considering a holiday, but where and when? If it was too far there would be no chance of following: he couldn't afford to go missing from work for too long without things being said. He would have to wait.

Fortunately the normally careful Major made a mistake. He followed the Major's highly visible red open-topped sports car to a small cottage, miles from any town, and watched as he was greeted at the front door by an attractive blonde in her late twenties. They kissed in a manner that showed they were more than just friends. She had to be his mistress, because Major John Alexander Thomas was married. After that he changed tactics. He realized that the key to getting to the Major was her, the mistress. There was no point in following the Major any further. Besides, it would be safer, because the mistress wouldn't be quite so careful.

Finally, he got his lucky break. He got a lot of those, and had become convinced as a result that God was on his side and supported the stand he was making. He noticed a message in one of the milk bottles sitting outside her front door: 'No milk until Monday'. So they were away this weekend.

He decided that he would have to keep watch on the cottage on the Friday night and over to the Saturday morning.

He was in luck. Major Thomas picked his mistress up on Friday evening, and he followed them at a safe distance. He had already decided that if they went further than fifty miles he would have to stop following, go back home and wait for another opportunity. Once again he was in luck. After just under twenty miles they pulled into a campsite.

The site, on the outskirts of some woods near a river, was almost deserted. As he watched, they set up a large modern tent close to the woods. Sleeping bags and other equipment were removed from the boot of the Major's car and put in the tent. The Major then returned to the boot and removed a large gas bottle, which he fixed up just outside the tent. It was clearly intended to be used not only for cooking, but also, he was glad to say, for the small heater that he saw the Major take into the tent. Now he knew how he was going to kill him, and how to make it look just like a tragic accident.

Though he had to wait over an hour for them to head to a local pub before sneaking into the tent to make the necessary adjustments to the heater. Then forty minutes after their return he once again moved through the woods and emerged by the Major's tent. It wasn't as straightforward as he'd hoped. From the sounds coming from the tent the couple were clearly making love, and it went on for some time. He had to admire the Major's stamina.

It was a shame, he thought, as he listened to the sounds of passion, that the girl had to die too. It was the first time this had happened, but needs must when the Devil drives, and he wasn't sure when he was going to get an opportunity like this again. The fact that they were dying together would also help mask the fact that he had got his eleventh victim.

After a couple of hours the lovemaking stopped and was replaced by the sound of heavy breathing and the odd snore. He knew it was safe. All he had to do now was adjust the gas bottle so that it filled the tent with toxic vapours. It would all be over very fast and painlessly. Another tragic accident.

It only took him a few minutes. Afterwards he crept back into the woods and waited for events to come to their inevitable *conclusion. He was sure he would read about it all in the papers over the following days.*

Eleven down, two to go.

Despite Colonel Parr's directions, Lapslie got lost trying to work out which way Bradbury should go once they got past Ledbury. He ended up having to call Colonel Parr to talk him in. The camp lay on the outskirts of the town, and they made it just about on time. He was, as Parr had told him, expected. After going through various checks and having his and Bradbury's ID confirmed and the car searched, they were directed to Parr's office.

The normal, day-to-day business of a military base caused a wash of flavour across Lapslie's mouth that tasted of old, dried blood. He tried to ignore it and keep going.

Parr was waiting for them outside his office. He still wasn't wearing uniform, but this time he was wearing cargo trousers, a polo shirt and a waterproof jacket. Lapslie assumed that the dress code among Special Forces was designed not to attract any attention.

'Morning, Chief Inspector. Sorry about the delay, but I didn't realize until you mentioned it on the phone earlier that your sergeant would be travelling with you.'

Parr first shook Lapslie's hand and then Bradbury's. 'Sergeant Bradbury, good to meet you.'

'Sorry,' Lapslie apologized, 'bit of stupidity on my part.'

Parr looked at him for a moment. 'Yes. Anyway, come in. I've arranged for some tea and biscuits.'

Lapslie and Bradbury followed. It wasn't a good start.

Once they were settled around the table, Parr began to question them. He was more direct, more officious, now that he was on home territory. 'Made any progress?'

Lapslie nodded. 'A bit.'

Parr looked at him expectantly.

'We know that the wedding dress and veil the bridal doll was wearing both came from Leslie Petersen's dress. They'd been cut off a few weeks before she was killed, but we don't know by whom – apart from the suspect I mentioned before, her past boyfriend, Mike Stowell, ex-Army and with two years' sniper experience.' Lapslie grimaced tautly. 'But part of that whole scenario doesn't sit comfortably with me.'

'Oh. Why's that?'

'It's altogether too convenient, fits too perfectly. She's shot by a sniper and lo and behold it turns out her ex-jilted-boyfriend was an Army sniper.' Lapslie sighed. 'Also none of the other likely murders were so overt – indeed many might have been staged as accidents – and no connection thus far from Stowell to any other victims.'

'So your thinking has shifted somewhat on Stowell since we last met.' Parr raised an eyebrow. 'And any other suspects in sight?'

'Nobody in particular. But we now also know that the blood on the bridal doll was definitely Leslie Petersen's: the DNA matches.'

Parr shook his head. 'Forgive me, but how is that possible, unless the killer managed to somehow get hold of her blood *before* he killed her? Surely there was no chance after the event – too many people milling around.'

'We've discovered she gave blood regularly. So that appears the most likely option.'

'I see. Makes sense, I suppose.' Parr took a fresh breath. 'Now, I have prepared a bit of a demonstration to let you see how the old sniper thing works. We normally don't do it here: it's normally done at the sniper school – an old RAF base – but I've booked an area over at PATA.'

'PATA?' Bradbury inquired.

'The Pontrilas Army Training Area. It's a little way up the road from here.'

Lapslie was appreciative. 'Thanks. Not sure how much it will help, but it should be interesting at the very least.'

Parr leaned back in his seat. 'I've taken the liberty of getting a little more involved in the inquiry than I would normally. I got some of our friends within the security industry to see if they can trace any .5 sniper rifles that might have gone astray . . .'

'You mentioned previously an Accuracy International AX50 .50 BMG, which Stowell in our interview has mentioned as one of his favoured weapons. The other was an L115A3.'

Parr nodded thoughtfully. 'Either of those would have been ideal for this range of shot. Might be worth checking Stowell's Army mates to see where he might get either of those rifles in the UK. Meanwhile I can get my contacts to see if there are any INTREPs on similar rifles coming into the country legally or illegally.'

'INTREPs?' Bradbury asked.

'Intelligence Reports,' Parr said without missing a beat or looking at her. 'If we can track guns of that type through those two sources, then we meet in the middle with some success. There aren't many of those guns beyond the boundary fence of this and two other UK compounds, and practically zero in private hands.'

'It's very good of you. We appreciate it.'

Parr smiled. 'I'm also looking at who the best shots in the Armed Forces were, going back twenty-five years. Aside from your chap Stowell, that is.' Parr smiled primly and braced his hands on his thighs with a firm pat. 'Well, if you're both ready, I'll introduce you to our snipers.'

The three of them stood together and left the room. They followed Parr to a LandRover that was parked directly outside. Once in, he drove them out of the camp, along a short section of common road and then up and around a long, twisting track to where a stretch of high-security fencing paralleled the road. A little way along the fence was a parking area and a gate that was operated by a keypad. Parr glanced around and checked his mirrors – checking that nobody else was trying to creep in alongside them, Lapslie assumed – and then typed a code into the keypad. The gate swung smoothly and quietly open. Parr drove in, and waited for it to close before he continued on, past earth bunkers and fifties-style barracks blocks, past strange concrete shapes, until they reached an open area of grass.

'And here we are.' He stepped out of the LandRover and gestured to Lapslie and Bradbury to join him. 'Legs, Spike, are you there?'

Lapslie and Bradbury looked around, and then looked at each other. There was nobody around: the place was empty.

Bradbury raised an eyebrow. 'I think I've seen this film,' she whispered.

The grass just in front of them moved and two figures stood up. Where there had been no one only moments before, suddenly there were two people, and they weren't small either. Not only that, but one of them was holding a rifle that had been part-disguised with bits of greenery. It was remarkable. Lapslie couldn't help feeling that if their killer had these skills then it was no wonder he had no trouble getting in and out of the bunker.

Parr introduced the two men. 'Legs, Spike, this is Detective Chief Inspector Lapslie and Detective Sergeant Bradbury.'

They all shook hands. Neither man spoke. They were dressed in what Lapslie recognized as 'ghillie suits' – outdoor clothing patterned in camouflage and covered in a net of fine twine through which leaves and twigs had been woven. He noticed with interest that he still had no idea of the snipers' real names. That, presumably, was deliberate on Parr's part.

'The boys are going to use the same rifle as we think our killer used, the Accuracy International AX50 .50 BMG. The range won't be quite so far, neither will the elevation, but it's far enough and should make the point.' He pointed. 'You should just about be able to see the target against the sandbank over there.'

Lapslie strained his eyes. He could just about make out what looked like the outline of a human being, silhouetted against the sandbank.

'The aim is to hit the target in the heart.' He smiled at Bradbury. 'With a chest shot, if you're a couple of inches out then there is still damage done. With a head shot, a couple of inches could be the difference between hitting and missing.'

'Are they normally a few inches out?' Bradbury asked.

'Talent and training are only two parts of the equation. A gust of wind could change the situation, as could target movement.' He turned back to the snipers. 'Gentlemen, in your own time.'

The two men lay back in the grass. This time Lapslie could see them quite clearly, but then this time he knew what he was looking for.

One of the men murmured information to the other, barely distinguishable over the noise of the wind. The other man – Lapslie realized with a jolt that he didn't even know which one was Legs and which one was Spike – ranged the shot by adjusting his position, and turning a dial on the side of the sniper scope. After a few moments, he fired a ranging shot. There was a lot less noise than Lapslie expected, but it flooded his mouth with the syrupy, sugary taste of tinned peaches, and he winced. He hoped they wouldn't have to do much of that.

After a few moments the two men conferred again, and a second shot was fired. Once again, only slightly stronger this time, Lapslie's mouth was awash with tinned peaches, but this time the taste was bizarrely overlaid with sea salt.

Bradbury saw his discomfort. 'You okay, sir?'

Lapslie nodded, and put his hand up, indicating to her to stop fussing. Parr glanced over at them curiously.

The sniper fired his final shot. Lapslie resisted the temptation to spit: it would make little difference to what he was tasting, and wouldn't look too good.

Legs and Spike stood, and made their way towards the sandbank and the target. Parr, Lapslie and Bradbury followed.

The final shot had certainly hit the target, but only

on the outer edge. A kill shot for sure, but whoever had shot Leslie Petersen had hit dead centre, and from a longer range.

Parr turned to Lapslie. 'Whether our shooter is this chap Stowell or someone else – he's a remarkable shot. A highly dangerous man.'

Lapslie, looking at the target like a rabbit hypnotized by the lights of a car, said nothing, but had to agree. And if it was someone able to put Stowell in the frame and mask any link to the other victims so successfully, more remarkable still. A killer to be reckoned with.

PART FIVE

2 September 2010

Clair Brett dropped down in her armchair, exhausted. It had been a very long day. People never really appreciated how hard modelling was. It really took it out of you, especially if the photographer hadn't a clue what he was doing, and this one didn't. She knew much more about the process than he did. He didn't seem to understand that maintaining an unnatural position for minutes on end while he fiddled with his focus and his exposure was hell on the muscles.

She was used to a broad range of photographers. There were the professionals who were normally fine, and the semi-professionals, who were also pretty good. After that there were the clubs, who varied dramatically, and then there were the rank amateurs. Some were okay and took it very seriously; some just liked the idea of photographing attractive girls naked; and some regarded it as something like a dating agency for creeps. What she had to beware of was the occasional nutter whose entire aim in life was to try and get her naked somewhere private and chance his arm, or some other part of his anatomy.

Picking up her diary, she leafed through the pages, trying to work her week out. She was booked every day, mostly with professionals, but she also had one club and one life art class, and one amateur, but she'd worked with the man twice before, and she trusted him – well, trusted him as much as she trusted anyone.

She totted up her fees. Just shy of two grand for a week's work, and most of that tax-free. She always declared a bit in order to stop the taxman becoming suspicious, but not all of it. She wasn't stupid. Still, eighteen hundred quid for a girl without a GCSE to her name wasn't bad going. She never told her dad about the details – he would have gone loopy – but she did tell her mum. She told her mum everything. Her mum's attitude was: 'Well, if they can only see and can't touch, that's fine by me. Girl's got to make a living, ain't she?' Clair had laughed. She loved her mum.

Stripping off her clothes and leaving them where they fell, she made her way out into the garden, to where Richard had set up the hot tub jacuzzi. She had turned on the heater as soon as she got into the house, and she was looking forward to a good hot soak. As she made her way into the garden she stopped by the full-length mirror on the wall and looked at herself. She was a little less than six feet tall, with what she knew was a perfect body. She knew because everybody said so. Flat stomach, high breasts, long legs, long dark hair, green eyes and a perfect mouth that didn't need any work done on it to make it pout.

She really would have to start charging more for her shoots, she thought.

Walking out into the garden, she made her way over to the hot tub and dipped her hand into the water to check the temperature. It was perfect. Climbing the few steps into the tub, she slowly slid under the warm waters. It was the most relaxing experience possible. She felt the tensions of the day just melt away into the water. She ducked her head under, staying there for a few seconds and rubbing her hair between her fingers before she emerged and wiped the hair away from her face.

Leaning back, she decided to switch on the jacuzzi and let the bubbles massage away the aches and pains and frustrations of the day. The hand control was only a few feet away, and she could reach it easily. There were three levels: gentle, medium and full-on. She wanted full-on: she wanted the water to pummel her body, smashing out the knots and the twists. She could turn it back to gentle after that, and drift the rest of her time away.

She turned the dial hard to the right. The giant electrical surge filled the hot tub at once: thousands of volts crackling through Clair Brett's perfect body. She only felt the pain for a second. It wasn't even long enough to scream, never mind try and get out. Death was almost instantaneous, and as the charge continued to flow through the water and along her nerves, the hot tub which had been Clair Brett's sanctuary slowly began to cook her from the inside out.

On the way back from Hereford Lapslie had decided that his next stop would be the senior chief investigating officer for the nurse's murder in 2007. Fortunately he was an old friend: former Chief Inspector Alan Day. Bradbury had managed to get him after just a couple of calls. The Chief Inspector had retired two years before after thirty-two years' service, and now spent most of his time gardening and working in his allotment. He had arranged to see Lapslie there at 2 p.m. the day after the Hereford trip. Lapslie left Bradbury behind at force HQ, checking on the progress of the team. Also, he had it in the back of his mind that Alan was a very old-fashioned copper and investigator and the force had been glad when he finally went. He'd had little time for female officers, saying that they were only good for two things: sex, and bringing the coal in on a cold winter's night. That kind of attitude was not only wrong, it was unsupportable in the current political climate. However, Lapslie reminded himself, it wasn't Alan's politics he was interested in, but his opinions on the Jane Summers case. He found Day in a small greenhouse behind his house, cutting away some very red-looking tomatoes.

'Hello, Alan.'

He turned. 'Mark: how good to see you.' His voice was dry grass and clover. 'Just cutting you a few tomatoes. Seem to remember you were quite fond of them.'

'I am, and they are beautiful. Thanks a lot.'

'I've picked you half a dozen. Cherokee Purples, they are. They go great with a bit of cheese. Come over to the shed: I've got the kettle on.'

Lapslie followed him out to his garden shed where an old kettle was boiling on a small gas burner. Day mashed the tea and added a dash of milk from a thermos flask before the two of them sat down in a couple of old deck-chairs just outside the shed.

Day's allotment was quite wonderful, Lapslie reflected. Full of a variety of vegetables and fruit: a real green haven away from the rigours of the city. And Lapslie would lay money on the chance that not only could Day name all the varieties, but that they were rare or heirloom varieties as well. Day had a thing about generic, tasteless fruit and vegetables becoming the only kind that consumers knew about, because of the pernicious cost-saving manoeuvrings of the big supermarket chains.

After sipping quietly at their tea for a while, and discussing long-dead colleagues they had known – a popular subject when old officers got together, like an ongoing competition to see who could live the longest – Lapslie brought Day back to the point. 'Do you remember the murder of a nurse called Jane Anne Summers in 2007?'

Day put his tea down. 'First of July 2007, to be precise. Mother found her dead on her bed, strangled. Never did get anyone for it.'

'Why not?'

'Usual reason: no evidence, no witnesses. She was a nice girl, well thought of by her friends and work colleagues. She was engaged to be married: nice lad with a cast-iron alibi. She never played around, not that we were aware of, anyway. No jealous former boyfriends in the background. She was a beautiful girl too, and yet there'd been no sexual assault. Whoever killed her got in through an open window. It was a warm summer – everyone was leaving their windows open. Manual strangulation, it was, so in the end the only thing we were sure about was that it must have been a man, based on the size of the bruises on her neck.'

He sipped his tea again. 'She lived on a busy estate, lot of people about, yet he still got into her bedroom in the middle of the afternoon, strangled her, and then left without a single person seeing a thing. We had half the bloody force doing door-to-door, appeals on local radio and TV; even got that Nick Ross bloke to make an appeal on *Crimewatch*. We did a reconstruction and everything. Not a bloody thing.'

'Forensics?'

'Not a jot. No fibres, no hair, prints, shoe marks, nothing. He was like a bloody ghost.' He sighed. 'Most frustrating case I've ever worked on. Thanks for reminding me of it.'

The description of a ghost seemed to fit Lapslie's man perfectly, he considered. 'So there was nothing out of the ordinary about the case?'

Day shook his head. 'Other than it was the only murder case I never solved, no. Why the renewed interest after so many years?' He fixed his gaze on Lapslie. 'Got a fresh lead, have you?'

Lapslie looked across at Day. He certainly wasn't going to go over everything about the dolls again; besides, a copper of Day's generation would think he'd gone mad. But the link to Leslie Petersen's murder might be worth a spin, now that they had a possible suspect.

'Maybe. Did the names Leslie Petersen or Mike Stowell ever come up while you were investigating?'

Day sank into thought for a moment. 'No. Can't say that they did.'

'And there were no other nurses murdered during your time, were there?'

He shook his head. 'No. Well, not that I heard of, and I am sure I would have.'

'What about her parents?'

'Both dead now. I swear it was the shock of losing her that helped them along the way. I kept in touch, seemed to be the decent thing to do. If anything came up I let them know at once. Not that much did, and what did turned out to be rubbish. They only lasted a few years after her murder. They seemed to age rapidly, every year like ten. I've seen it before. It's like the shock closes the body down.'

Lapslie had seen that too, far too many times.

Day continued. 'She was an only child, you see. Her mother had her later in life. Both parents were a bit surprised, but delighted. She was the apple of their eye and from all accounts a wonderful girl.' He sighed again. 'Then I let them down by not catching the bastard. Pity, really, because her old man was foreman on a jury I once gave evidence to, managed to steer the jury towards the right verdict. I recognized him. Would have been nice to have returned the favour.'

'You didn't have a bad hit rate, Alan.'

Day sipped at his tea again. 'It's funny, really: it's not the nicks you remember in the end, but the ones that got away. I've always remembered Jane Summers, and it bothers me. It rankles. If you get anywhere, you will let me know, won't you?'

Lapslie nodded. 'Of course I will.'

Finishing off his tea, Lapslie picked up the bag of tomatoes and stood. 'I'd better be getting off.'

They shook hands. 'Heard you'd gone doolally tap,' Day said with a question mark in his voice. 'Everything okay, is it?'

Lapslie smiled. 'Everything's fine. You've been very helpful.'

As Lapslie turned to go Day called out to him: 'There was one thing, now I come to think of it.' Lapslie turned, his interest sparked. 'Our killer, he cut her nurse's uniform up. Took a large section of the dress and the hat away with him. We never found it. Some sort of trophy, I guess. The rest of the uniform was bagged up: might still be in the exhibits cupboard. Might not be, of course. You know how things are. Of interest?'

Lapslie nodded. 'Yes, Alan, could well be.'

Lapslie knew he had to remain calm, but his stomach was turning over. From everything that Day had said, he had strongly suspected that Jane Summers had been killed by his man – but the damage to the uniform was a clincher, and that opened all sorts of doors. The nurse's had been the first doll in the line, so, given the meticulous nature of the killer, she had almost certainly been the first victim. That would then give him a starting point. He could look into both the nurse's life and the bride's, and see if there were any links. People, places, events . . . Stowell, or, as he increasingly suspected, an ingenious killer who'd been murdering undetected for seven years, and as his team had become involved, had put Stowell in the frame.

As soon as he got to the car he called the Essex Constabulary's exhibits officer and gave him what information he had. The amount of evidence that got lost or was disposed of, especially when it looked like a case had gone cold, was a scandal, and the exhibits officer had been put in place to try and stop it. He had, by all reports, done a good job, and quickly discovered that most things that were supposed to have been lost had actually just been mislabelled or misfiled, or not labelled at all. He came back to Lapslie after about five minutes. 'Yes, the clothing is still here, sir. Still in its bag. What do you want me to do with it?'

'Call Detective Sergeant Bradbury, tell her what you've got, and get her to pick it up at once and take it to Gillian Holmes at the forensics lab. She will know what to do with it.'

Bradbury had reached the lab with the nurse's uniform ahead of Lapslie. By the time he had managed to get through the various security checks, Bradbury and Holmes already had it open on a table and were examining it. The clothes smelled musty. The doll, which had been undressed, lay naked beside them.

'Afternoon.' Both women turned to acknowledge his arrival. 'Afternoon, sir. Hope you didn't mind us starting without you?'

Holmes smiled. 'We knew time was important, so we thought we would get on with it.'

'That's fine. How are you doing?'

Gillian Holmes beckoned him over. 'Come and see.'

Lapslie walked over to the table. The two women were comparing the damage to the nurse's uniform with that of the doll's uniform. With the exception of a few sections which had clearly been removed so that it fitted the doll neatly, it was a perfect match: much the same as the bridal doll's dress had been to the real thing.

Lapslie walked over to where the other dolls were lined up, still inside their exhibit bags, and looked at them. Picking one up at random, he gazed at it. It was a female doll, dressed in a red bikini. Bizarrely, a song lyric began to unspool in his brain: 'She wore an . . . itsy-bitsy, teeny-weenie, yellow polka-dot bikini . . .'

Holmes joined him.

'How was this one damaged?' he asked.

Holmes shook her head. 'It wasn't. Bit of a mystery, that one. The only odd thing about it is her hair.'

Lapslie looked at it again. The doll's hair seemed to be sticking straight upwards, and its face had a look of surprise. He replaced it in the bag. 'Perhaps she had seen what was coming.'

Lapslie considered. He now knew who his first victim was, and who his last, or latest, victim was. What he needed to know now were the names of the other ten.

More important, he needed to know who the next two were going to be – the last two. Maybe now he would have a chance of stopping this doll-maker before he killed anyone else.

Lapslie dreamed about the dolls again that night; and, as before, there was a thirteenth doll that remained obscured, its image blurred, however hard he strove to bring it into focus. It was as if he knew it was significant, but couldn't work out how or why.

If he could just see it more clearly – he saw part of a dark uniform on the lower part of the doll, but as he moved up and towards the face . . .

He awoke sharply, catching at his breath. Had he seen the face in that final second, or had it remained obstinately out of reach, out of focus? Certainly he couldn't recall any clarity to that image now – though another significance suddenly struck him about the number thirteen.

He looked over at his bedside clock: 5.18 a.m. Too early to make the call, so he brushed his teeth, freshened up and made some fresh coffee to kill the time while his thoughts gelled. Finally, he picked up the phone and made the call.

*

Emma Bradbury looked at her phone through bleary eyes and checked the time as she picked it up: 6.04 a.m.

'Yes . . . ?'

'Emma. We've got a trip to make, and I've called early because we should move sharpish. How long before you could meet me at King's Cross Station?'

She noticed her partner, Dom McGinley, stirring at her side. Thirty-forty minutes to get ready, she calculated, then getting into central London. 'Uh, I suppose just under two hours.'

'Fine. Meet me by the entrance gate for the train to Edinburgh. I'll have already bought your ticket for you. Oh, and pack a small overnight bag, in case we don't make it back tonight.'

'Okay, sir. I'll see you then.'

But Lapslie had already cut off his end halfway through the sentence. Dom was now sitting up beside her, brow arched.

'Who the hell was that calling at this time?'

She smiled wanly. 'My boss, of course. Who else would it be?'

Something fleeting crossed his face, as if whatever alternative might have sprung to mind he'd quickly discarded. She felt his eyes on her back as she padded to the bathroom.

'I've got to go with him to Edinburgh,' she called over her shoulder. 'And he's asked me to pack a bag in case we have to stay overnight.'

'What, you and Lapslie?'

Was there a hint of doubt in his voice, or was she just imagining it? She felt tempted to respond, 'Who else?', but that might just make matters worse. She shut the bathroom door softly behind her without comment-ing, and when she came out Dom was lying on his side facing away from her, either already back asleep or feigning it.

Ten minutes later when she was dressed and on her way out, she risked a hushed, 'See you later, Dom. Either late tonight or tomorrow morning.'

No response.

Lapslie explained his thinking on the train to Edin-burgh. 'I've had a couple of dreams now about the dolls, and each time there have been thirteen – though in each dream I haven't been able to see that thirteenth doll clearly. I wondered whether it might be significant, even if only the religion–superstition factor – and suddenly that triggered something from a while back.'

'What, something religious or superstitious?'

'Well, both played a part – superstition due to suspected witchcraft, and religion due to Christian burial rites. Both were apparently suspected, along with links to the Burke and Hare murder case, when seventeen dolls were found in miniature coffins in Arthur's Seat, Edinburgh.'

'Burke and Hare?' Bradbury smiled. 'So not one of your own past cases then, sir?'

'Somewhat before my time.' Lapslie returned the smile thinly. 'Which no doubt is why so many of the details are lost on me, and we're now on our way to see a curator at the National Museum in Edinburgh, Jeffrey Lydall, to fill in the details.'

Three hours later, after checking into their hotel and when Lapslie had run through the introductions and the purpose of their visit, Lydall was indeed able to provide more details on the historic mystery.

'You're right in mentioning both possible witchcraft and Christian burial rites – *both* were suspected, though only the latter had any possible link to the Burke and Hare murders case.' As Lydall observed Lapslie's brow furrow, he elaborated. 'You see, witchcraft was suspected at first because of the bizarre nature of the discovery, and miniature symbols used in other areas of witchcraft and black magic. But the main reason the dolls were linked to Burke and Hare was that their number, seventeen, matched exactly the number of murders in that case.' He shrugged as he corrected himself, 'Well, sixteen murders, because the first body they sold to medical practitioners had in fact died from natural causes. But this was also reflected in the way the coffins were arranged.'

'Yes, I understand they were arranged in three different layers,' Lapslie commented – one of the few online details he'd been able to source meanwhile.

Lydall nodded. 'One coffin on its own at the top – perhaps representing the first natural-cause death – then two layers of eight coffins.'

'Why not one coffin on top, then a single row of sixteen?' Bradbury questioned.

'That's never been adequately explained,' Lydall said, 'beyond simple space restrictions. Laying out sixteen in a row would have required a broader flat area. Where they were found, there simply wasn't the room for that.'

'So why would the witchcraft theory have necessarily fallen by the wayside with the advent of the connection to Burke and Hare?' Lapslie asked.

'It was still a possibility, but a slimmer one, because no firm reason was propounded for witchcraft connected with those murders. Whereas a religious connection was another matter, because they'd been murdered for the purpose of autopsy, with the bodies immediately dissected.' Lydall held out a palm. 'You see there was a strongly held belief in Christianity at the time that the body had to be whole in order to ascend to heaven. So these poor dissected victims would not have been able to achieve that – thus the theory arose that whoever was behind this was trying to effect that ascension to heaven at least in doll-effigy form.' Lydall shrugged. 'I suppose at a push some black magic connection could be argued, along the lines of some modern-day Christian religions, such as the Umbanda in Brazil, which blends Catholicism with symbolism and effigies more akin to black magic.'

Lapslie nodded thoughtfully. 'And I understand you have a number of the dolls here on display?'

'Yes, indeed all those that survived intact: eight in all.'

'What happened with the others?'

'Too severely rotted and degraded to display, I'm afraid. Only parts remained.' In the lull as Lapslie appeared momentarily lost in thought, Lydall prompted, 'Would you like to see them?'

'Yes, very much so. If we may?'

Lydall smiled tightly and led the way down the corridor towards a grand hall, then guided them towards one side.

'Here we are.' Lydall indicated a large glass cabinet with miniature coffins arranged on two plinths.

The first thing Lapslie noticed was the absence of clothing on most of the dolls. Only two were fully clothed, and their dress was quite drab, didn't hint at any particular profession or social status. The coffins too looked far older, their wood darker.

'You say the other coffins rotted somewhat?' Lapslie said. 'Was that also a factor with the clothing? Were the other six dolls originally clothed?'

'Yes, we believe they were. There was quite a gap between the dolls being placed in the cave and their discovery, and in that time damp affected both the wooden coffins and the dolls' clothing.'

'Quite a gap?' Bradbury said. 'How many years are we talking about?'

'The murders took place in 1828 and the coffins were discovered in 1836 – so eight years in total.'

Lapslie leaned closer towards the display cabinet, trying to pick up finer detail. 'And was there any suggestion that the clothing betrayed any particular profession?'

'I'm afraid not.' Lydall held a palm out. 'What you see here is all we have. On one the dress is just a full-length cloth and the other chequered. The closest might be prison garb, but none of the Burke and Hare victims were prisoners. On another that was partially clothed we see a mostly rotted working man's jacket, but that's about it.' He looked at Lapslie. 'Why, is that a feature with the case you have now?'

'Possibly.' Lapslie had mentioned in his introduction that they had a current case involving dolls in coffins, but he didn't feel inclined to go into more detail with Lydall. 'So do you get many visitors these days interested in the possible religious significance of the dolls?'

'A few. But we get more than our fair share of medical students too.'

Lapslie arched a brow. 'Oh, why is that?

'While most were rightly horrified by what Burke and Hare did, to the medical establishment they were seen as something of a boon. Before that time, medical research was floundering because of the lack of dissectable corpses. Burke and Hare changed that, and not long after their trial came the Anatomy Act of 1832.' Lydall nodded towards the dolls. 'So rightly or wrongly, the Burke and Hare case still holds something of a fascination among those who've taken the Hippocratic Oath.'

Upon their return from Edinburgh, they made their way to force headquarters. Lapslie grabbed a quick coffee from the corridor machine, so Bradbury was ahead of him, looking through the glass doors to the Incident Room.

'Are the team all here?' Lapslie asked. He'd made his calls to convene the meeting just before leaving their Edinburgh hotel.

Bradbury nodded. 'Yes, looks like everyone's present.'

Lapslie walked into the briefing room, followed by Bradbury. Bradbury spoke first.

'Okay, usual rules apply. Unless it's urgent, any questions to be filtered through me after the briefing. Until then, head and hand gestures will be all you need. When I say "hand gestures", keep them decent: that especially applies to you, DC Parkin.'

Parkin put his hands up and tried to look innocent. Lapslie stepped forward and began the briefing.

'First, the good news, and believe it or not we have to give a big pat on the back to Parkin and Pearce here. I can now confirm that Jane Anne Summers was our first victim. The killer cut her uniform up and took part of it away to make one of his macabre dolls with, just like he did with the bridal dress of our recent shooting victim. So we all owe Parkin and Pearce a very large drink.'

The two detectives looked delighted.

'However,' Lapslie went on, 'they won't be touching a drop until this case is solved. One swallow doesn't make a summer. They had better keep up the good work or they are going to be thirsty for a very long time.'

The two detectives looked less delighted.

'Okay, back to the point. The first victim of our killer was a nurse called Jane Anne Summers. She was strangled in 2007. The reason we know this, as I just outlined, is because her uniform was damaged at the time of the murder and sections were taken away by our killer. Those sections were used to make the uniform on the nurse doll found in the bunker. From now on we are searching for victims between the first of July 2007 and the murder of Leslie Petersen a few days ago. We have a seven-year window now, rather than an open-ended one. We also know that our killer is a deadly shot, among the best. So whether that's Mike Stowell or somebody else, we've yet to determine. On which front, has Stowell been anywhere interesting in the past forty-eight hours?' Lapslie's gaze shifted to Ken Barrett and Pete Kempsey, who'd been given the duty of tailing Stowell.

They looked at each other and Barrett shrugged before speaking. 'Nowhere ground-breaking: home, launderette, pub. Oh, and he met an old Army mate while at the pub.'

'And did you in turn follow this Army mate?' Lapslie asked.

They looked at each other again briefly. 'No, that would have meant splitting up, which we were told not to do.'

Lapslie could have launched into a speech about 'initiative' and how Stowell having an accomplice had been a possible factor – not only to commit murders Stowell wasn't present for, but with AMOS wind-speed assistance on Leslie Petersen's long-range shot – yet the truth was he had told them to stay together; and besides, getting approval to split the team or to assign another tail would have required consulting Rouse and eaten up another twenty-four hours.

Perhaps sensing Lapslie's disapproval from his lingering gaze, Kempsey offered, 'We did check him out, though: Bill Ewan, same regiment as Stowell's and still active in Afghanistan. He's on a one-month leave in the UK.'

Lapslie's eyes narrowed. 'And, like Stowell, does he have any sniper experience?'

'Don't know. But we can check.'

'Good idea – if you can.' Lapslie shifted his gaze to the room at large and took a fresh breath. 'So, what else do we know about our killer? We know that he makes dolls and doll costumes, or knows someone who does. It's an odd combination, but one that might help us track him down. Also, looking recently at possible links with the dolls, our man might have a medical connection, or at least an interest in medical history. Now, it's your turn. Anyone discover anything about any other possible victim?'

Nobody moved. No hands went up.

Lapslie was disappointed. 'What, nothing?'

A few of the team shook their heads; the others just looked ahead blankly. Eventually, DC Pearce put his hand up. Bradbury looked at Lapslie, who nodded. 'Okay, Carl, what do you have to say?'

'I think I can speak for all of us, boss. With the obvious exception of Jane Summers, the team have checked and double-checked. Not only in this force area but every force area. There are no records of firemen, fishermen or mechanics being murdered over the last ten years, let alone the rest. It's just a blank. Are we sure these other dolls aren't there just to try and throw us off the trail?'

Lapslie shrugged. 'Maybe, but I don't think so. Following the line of a possible medical link might explain how our killer has disguised a number of murders as accidents. That's an avenue which needs exploring further.'

A murmur arose from the room, but didn't spill over into open comments or questions. Lapslie took a fresh breath, scanning the room keenly.

'We're missing something. I'm not sure what it is, but something's wrong. We're not looking close enough, deep enough. We are missing the bloody obvious. We know there are two more dolls so far untouched, and I am sure they are the next two victims. One is a major in the Army, the other a teacher. If we don't get it right, and quickly, they are going to be murdered, and it's going to be, in part, our fault. No matter how far-fetched an idea you might have, I want you to go for it. I'll back you all the way. Does everyone understand?'

A more muted murmur, a number of eager nods.

'Okay: do your best. That's all any of us can do. If we crack this I'll pay for the biggest party you've ever been to, and that's a promise. That's it – now get out there and find me something I can work with.'

The team filed out of the office.

Lapslie looked across at Bradbury. 'Do you know what?' he said quietly.

'What?'

'With no leads or links to other murders, we're floundering with this case. Totally lost.'

After the briefing, Lapslie went home. He was just coming out of the shower when his mobile rang.

'Hello, Mark?' It was Jane Catherall. 'I think I have found something. I may be wrong, but I don't think so. That is your call. I'll be in the mortuary until ten if you want to come over.'

She hung up. He dressed back in his suit, making sure he had a fresh shirt, and climbed back into his Saab.

There was, a wise man had once observed, no rest for the wicked.

He got to the mortuary in less than half an hour, which, he was pleased to say, was something of a record. The traffic lights had been friendly, and for Essex there was a marked lack of idiots on the road.

Catherall was in her office typing out a report when he knocked and entered.

'Evening.'

She looked up at him. 'Hello, Mark. I hope I haven't spoiled any plans you had for the evening?'

Lapslie shook his head. 'No, not at all. What have you discovered?'

'It might be something, or it might be nothing, but given what you said about the two dolls not in their coffins and one of them being a major in the Army . . .'

Lapslie could feel himself getting excited. 'Yes, what of it?'

As Catherall pulled herself to her feet using her sticks, Lapslie moved to help her. 'Can I—'

'No, thank you. I am quite capable.' Finally getting up, she walked out of the office and down the corridor. Lapslie followed her towards the fridges in the mortuary.

She finally reached a fridge whose label read: *Mr John Alexander Thomas*. Catherall looked up at Lapslie. 'I think he might be your man.'

Lapslie was confused. 'I haven't heard of any new murders, and I'm sure I would. I've been on the lookout specifically. He's not a major, either.'

Catherall contradicted him. 'Actually, he is. Pull the drawer out, would you?'

Lapslie did as he was bid. The drawer slid out easily, and Catherall pulled back the white sheet that was covering his body. 'I give you Major Thomas.'

Lapslie looked at her for a moment. 'If he is a major then why doesn't it say so on his label?'

'Because when the label was made out we had no idea that he was.'

'Not like the Army to slip up over something like that.'

'The Army weren't involved . . .'

Lapslie could feel himself become frustrated. 'Then how can he be a major?'

Catherall smiled. 'He's retired, and not too long ago either. When soldiers of a certain rank retire, they retain their rank.'

'How did you find out?'

'Two of his friends came to see him in the Chapel

of Rest. They were both in uniform. They asked if his name tag could be changed from *Mr* to *Major*. When I asked why, they explained. I haven't had time to do it yet, or rather, I haven't had time to get Dan to do it, but I will.'

'How did he die?'

'Gas fumes while he was camping with his mistress. She's in the drawer below him.'

'How apt.' Lapslie grimaced. 'So he wasn't murdered, then?'

'You are looking for murder victims, such as the nurse and Leslie Petersen?'

Lapslie nodded.

'You tell me that this murderer is clever. Well, perhaps he's clever enough to have made all his murders look like accidents. Maybe that's why he has got away with it for so long.'

Lapslie looked at her levelly. 'Yes, we had started working on that theory – but interesting to see support for that line of thinking from pathology also.' He sighed. 'Have you got an address for him?'

'You want to see if any of his uniforms have been damaged, obviously.'

'I do. There's no point running around like a

headless chicken until after I've checked the obvious. Having spent days *missing* the obvious, I don't want to do it again.'

'You might want to start with the wife.' Catherall passed him a sheet of A4 paper. 'That has all the contact details.'

He glanced at the words on the paper. 'I'll do it tomorrow. It's late now, and she won't welcome a call at this hour, not from the police.' He glanced up and met Jane Catherall's eyes. 'Thanks, Jane. I appreciate this.'

Lapslie had no idea what time it was when his phone suddenly started to play Beethoven's *Egmont Overture*. Gently moving the naked Charlotte from her position sprawled across his chest, he picked up his mobile, glancing at the time as he did. Five thirty-five.

It was Bradbury, so something had happened. He tried to speak quietly. 'Yes, Emma, what is it? Don't you ever sleep?'

'I'm out at the bunker, sir. I think you had better come down: there's been an incident.'

The bunker again. He was spending more time there than he was at home. 'What do you mean, an incident?'

'Think you had better come down, boss. It's difficult

to explain on the phone. Are you at home? Shall I send a car for you?'

That was the last thing Lapslie wanted. 'No, it's okay. I'll be there as quick as I can.'

Hanging up, he looked across at Charlotte's naked body. The night before had been the first time they'd been able to spend any time together since their disastrous weekend sailing; the hectic investigation and Charlotte's schedule had swallowed up every other opportunity. He watched her for a moment as she slept: her beautifully shaped breasts moving gently up and down with every breath.

He edged himself to the side of the bed and lightly stood, hoping not to wake her.

'Where are you going?'

Lapslie looked down at her. 'I've had a call. I'm so sorry, but I think it's urgent.'

She smiled up at him, her eyes still full of sleep. 'Don't worry. I've had plenty of emergency calls at the hospital, although I'm usually kipping in a supply room, so I don't have as far to go. It's what you do. I understand that.'

'I have to get dressed.'

Her smile broadened. 'Okay. I *had* planned a few surprises for you this morning, but they can wait.'

After dressing, he made his now familiar way to the bunker. Bradbury was waiting. The place was alive with activity again. Detectives, SOCOs, lights everywhere.

'So now what's happened?'

'The young policeman on last night's duty shift here was assaulted and knocked unconscious. They found him about an hour ago.'

Lapslie was genuinely concerned. 'Is he badly hurt?'

Bradbury shrugged. 'They don't know yet. He hasn't come round. They're doing all the tests, so we'll know soon enough.'

'So do we know why he was attacked?'

Bradbury nodded. 'We think he disturbed someone inside the bunker. The door's been opened with a key . . .'

'A *key*? Where the hell did our intruder get *that* from?'

'Good question. We think the copper must have heard someone inside and gone in to try to catch them, rather than call it in.'

'Everybody wants to be a hero.'

'I think you need to come inside: there's something you should see.'

Lapslie was intrigued. 'Should we be suited up?'

Bradbury shook her head. 'Thomson said no.'

'Is he around?'

Bradbury shook her head. 'I asked him to keep out of the way until you had gone.'

'Good thinking.'

The bunker was saturated in light, and it was easy to find their way to the area where the dolls had been stored. As they entered, Lapslie was amazed to see that there were two more dolls set up on the shelves that were supposed to have been empty, following the removal of all the dolls and the coffins. Or, to be more accurate, there was one coffin with its lid closed and one doll beside it with a coffin propped up behind it. The doll in the open was dressed in a dark blue uniform, but he ignored it for the moment. He was more concerned with the closed coffin. If he was right, he knew what was inside.

He pulled the lid open.

Inside the toy coffin was the Army doll, the one in the major's uniform. Its face had been coloured red, mimicking the effects of gas poisoning. It was, of course, meant to be Major John Alexander Thomas, whose body was even now lying in a drawer in Jane Catherall's mortuary. Now the timing made more sense; obviously the major had been killed days ago, but due to their watching the bunker, this had been the killer's first opportunity to break in and get to the dolls.

Lapslie turned his attention to the other one – the thirteenth coffin, the thirteenth doll. He felt a shiver run down his back as he recognized the uniform. It was a police officer's uniform. On its chest was a small oak leaf denoting the Queen's Commendation for Gallantry. Lapslie had one of those. The doll even had a collar number. Lapslie leaned as close to the doll as possible without disturbing it, so he could see the numbers on its lapel.

245.

His heard began to thump within his chest. Two hundred and forty-five had been *his* collar number, in those far-off days when he had been pounding the beat in Brixton and elsewhere, with Alan Rouse.

He looked across at Bradbury, but saw in her expression that she already knew the truth.

The doll he was looking at was meant to be him.

He was to be the occupant of the thirteenth coffin.

PART SIX

15 March 2011

Alex Mitchell had wanted to become an actor since before he knew what the words 'job' or 'vocation' actually meant. Even as a young boy he would dress up in his mother's clothes – never his father's, for some reason – and put on small shows for his friends, his sisters or sometimes just his pets. He would also wear his mother's make-up, which didn't please his father much.

Alex was in every school production there was during his time at school. He played Joseph in the junior school nativity play, and later had more important roles in his senior school's adaptations of Shakespeare and Oscar Wilde. He joined an amateur dramatics group, The Essex Players, and was cast in at least four different plays a year. He couldn't help noticing, however, as time went on, that they were careful never to give him a lead role. When he talked to his mother about it, she said that he would just have to get used to people being jealous of his talent.

After a stint at LAMDA and several years touring the provinces, he got his big TV break on a forensic science show called The Citadel. He had already changed his name to Rick Mitchell, on his agent's advice some time before. At first he was concerned that the change had made him almost unknown again. He needn't have worried; the name went down well, and it looked great on the opening credits.

Standing on the edge of the set of The Citadel: Series 4, episode 9, he prepared himself for the next shot. He was to run from a specially constructed hut five seconds after the word 'Action'. There was then to be a small explosion, lots of smoke and a very loud bang. It would look and sound great, but there would be no real explosion, just a puff of smoke. Perspective would make it look like he was closer than he actually was. That's why on this occasion there would be no need for a stuntman. By the time the computer graphics wizards and the editors had finished with it, it would look like he had survived a massive explosion. It was the wonder of film.

The he heard it: 'Action!'

He pushed the handle of the door down and outwards in the same movement, as he had rehearsed several times, but it didn't open. He tried again once again. Nothing! The door was either locked or jammed. Realizing that the bang and smoke were *only seconds away, he called out, 'Can you stop the explosion and get me out of here please?'*

He put his hands over his ears. He wasn't scared; he just didn't want to be deafened by the bang. 'Excuse me!' he yelled, 'can you please get me—'

He never finished his sentence. The explosion, when it happened, was enormous. Much bigger than planned. It blasted the hut apart and blew Alex Mitchell over thirty feet in the air. He was already dead, burning and in several pieces before he hit the ground.

All Lapslie wanted to do was get home and see his uniform, used now only for official occasions. Most of the time it just hung in the back of his closet. But despite the overwhelming desire to jump into a car and race the distance back to his house, he knew there were things he must do first. Jim Thomson and his team were already on the scene. They must know every inch of the area by now, Lapslie pondered. He knew the chances of their finding anything were almost nil – their killer was far too careful for that – but he'd already made one mistake in dropping the teacher's mortar board, and there was always the chance he'd make another.

He looked around for Bradbury. 'Emma?' She walked

over to him. 'I want you to arrange for minicams to be put inside the bunker. Make sure they have some infrared facility so we can get a look at the bastard if he comes back again.'

'Do you think he will?'

'I'm sure of it. This place is like catnip to him.' He felt the skin between his shoulder blades crawling, and he glanced around involuntarily. 'The only thing I'm not sure about is whether I will still be here to see it. He's a bloody good shot. He could have me in his sights right now.'

Bradbury glanced around uneasily. She returned her attention to Lapslie. 'You need to be careful.'

Lapslie nodded his head. 'I know.'

'Protective detail assigned to you at all times, I think.'

'Not a chance.'

'At the very least, you need to tell Rouse.'

Lapslie shook his head. 'Not a chance. He'd have me off the inquiry so fast—'

Bradbury cut in. 'That might be for the best. At least we could protect you until he is caught.'

Lapslie appreciated the sentiment but remained adamant. 'No. Definitely not. Unless I catch him, he won't get caught.' Noticing Bradbury's raised eyebrow, he went on: 'Do you really think I'm going to entrust my life to Alan Shaw? I'd be dead and buried, and they'd still be filling out a health and safety risk matrix. No, we need to get this nailed ourselves. We only let Rouse know when it's all done.'

She was still staring at him, uncertainty and concern in her eyes. He was touched, but he had to convince her to let him get on with the case. If she went behind his back to Rouse then the game would be up, and he'd find himself in a safe house for the rest of the year with only pizzas and daytime TV for company.

'Look,' he said, more calmly, 'the doll with my police number is the last one. The killer is working in order, for some strange obsessive-compulsive reason. So our first priority is to try and find the teacher and keep him safe. If we can find the killer before then, I'm safe too.'

'And if we fail and the teacher does get killed?'

Lapslie shrugged, but his face was heavy with that prospect. 'Then we rethink our strategy.'

'And if *you* get killed?'

Lapslie looked at her for a moment. 'Like they say in the movies: "Avenge my death." '

'Chief Inspector?'

Over to one side, Jim Thomson gestured to Bradbury to join him.

'We haven't finished with this,' she said to Lapslie before crossing the storage room to Thomson. They talked for a few moments, then she returned to Lapslie's side.

While she was gone, he found that he couldn't take his gaze off the doll in the police uniform. *His* uniform.

'He wanted to know if you needed the dolls removed to the lab for examination,' Bradbury said.

'Yes, tell him to get them over as soon as he can. Don't mention the number of the police doll's collar to anyone. As far as they are concerned it's just a generic police doll. Not identified. Did you mention the cameras to him?'

Bradbury nodded. 'Yes: he's going to get that done. He also suggested having some hidden in the woods as well. That way they can monitor the pathways in and out of the wood and the entrance to the escape exit.'

Lapslie nodded. 'Good idea. Any other reason I still need to be here?'

Bradbury shook her head. 'No, sir.'

'Right, I'm going to head off. I'll be at home, checking my uniform, if I'm needed. Let me know if anything turns up and also keep me updated on the condition of the young probationer.'

'I will. I'll call you later.'

As Lapslie turned away, Bradbury cleared her throat. He turned back. 'What is it?'

'I'm not trying to be funny, sir, but check under your car before you drive off. Look for suspicious packages. And drive defensively: make sure you're aware of what all the other drivers are doing. And when you get home—'

'It's okay – I get the idea. Thanks.'

Taking Bradbury's advice, Lapslie made his way home slowly and carefully. He normally had a thing about time and distance, and was always trying to beat his own personal best, but on this occasion he felt he could give it a rest. Jumping out of his car, locking it and scanning the shrubbery around his cottage for signs that someone might be hiding, he made his way inside, first checking each of his security systems as he went. He'd had them installed a couple of years back, after a psychotic killer, the son of a forensic psychiatrist, had broken into his cottage and tried to kill him. Burglar alarm, lights, video cameras. They all seemed intact and to be working well. He would get the security company in to give them the once-over later, check that all the batteries were charged and the sensors unobstructed by foliage or cobwebs.

He took the stairs two at a time to his bedroom. Opening his wardrobe doors, he flicked though his various jackets and suits until he came to his dress uniform. It was still in its clear plastic bag, as it had been the day he'd brought it back from the cleaner's months before. Laying it on the bed, he pulled the bag clear and began to examine it.

He first examined the front of the uniform, which seemed fine, up to and including the medal ribbons which were situated in a short line over the left-hand tunic pocket. Unbuttoning the jacket, he looked inside at the lining. It was all there, not ripped and not damaged.

He was just beginning to feel optimistic when he turned the jacket over to examine the back. The entire centre of the jacket had been cut away and was missing. It had been sliced across the shoulders, down both sides and across the bottom, just missing the back vent.

Lapslie looked at it for a moment, hardly able to take it in. How the hell had someone got past his security, got into his house, and managed to do this without being detected? More importantly, how did the killer know when he would be out? Either he'd taken a hell of a chance or he'd been watching Lapslie.

Or, a little voice whispered in the back of his mind, *the murderer was already part of the inquiry.*

He tried to silence the thought, but it kept coming back. What if the killer was someone known to him? Someone he was working alongside? What would that mean?

It meant he needed evidence before anything else, he told himself firmly. Evidence. Everything else was just wishful thinking or scaremongering.

He put his uniform back into the plastic bag. He had initially thought to take it down to the forensic laboratory and get it matched, but there was no point. The doll was dressed in cloth cut from his original uniform: there was no doubt about that. There would be no forensic evidence: the killer was too good for that. Getting the lab technicians to analyse the uniform jacket and the doll's costume would only take them away from other duties that were more likely to yield a result.

He looked about him. Nothing else seemed to have been touched. He considered calling Thomson and his team in, but knew he would be wasting their time, and for the same reason. If the killer could get in and out of his home quite so easily without tripping the alarms or showing himself on the video cameras, what would be the point of Thomson and his team raking over everything?

Emma Bradbury looked across the table at her partner, Dom, as they started eating dinner.

'Everything okay?'

'Yes . . . fine. Fine.'

Her eyes stayed on him for a second. She sensed that something was troubling him. He'd been thoughtful for a while before dinner, and his response now had been a second slow, his accompanying smile strained. They also knew each other well enough now for him to read that it wasn't just a casual enquiry about whether the dinner she'd served was okay.

Finally: 'So how was Edinburgh?'

'Okay.' She shrugged. 'Might be something, might end up a total wild goose chase. We won't know for a little while.'

He nodded thoughtfully, picking at his food. 'I know sometimes it can be awkward opening up fully about your investigations.' Again that strained smile. 'Especially with someone like me.'

So that was it, she considered. Dom, the villain. Lapslie had strongly advised her against the relationship, and perhaps Dom too was now facing the stark reality of what made it an awkward association. Or could it be that the precept of 'opposites attract' only had so much shelf life? Though she knew from past Criminal Psychology lectures that that was far from the truth; indeed, nobody knew a villain better than a copper, and vice versa, given the nature of their cat-and-mouse game either side of an often transparent divide.

Or perhaps now it was simply the fact that with work keeping her late and her hours irregular, their mealtimes were often delayed and rushed, which indeed had been the case recently. Forcing their relationship and quality time together more and more into a corner. Or could it be that he'd become keener on probing about her late hours and her trip to Edinburgh for other reasons? She pushed the thought hastily away.

'I daresay I could say the same about you,' she said, waggling her own fork back in challenge. 'I don't ask you how the latest bank heist has gone.'

'You know I don't do that sort of thing any more.'

He feigned a hurt expression, then after a second an easy smile surfaced; reminded her of what had endeared her to Dom McGinley in the first place. 'But, yes, touché.'

The tension eased between them then, became more mellow; and mellower still when they'd downed a bottle of red wine between them.

So when later that night in bed she saw the same dark shadows in Dom's eyes, it caught her by surprise.

'You'd never leave me, would you?' he muttered.

'No . . . of course not.'

But she'd answered on the back of a fractured breath, the timing of the question catching her equally by surprise.

It was a game they'd play regularly in bed. As Dom felt her passion rising, he'd lightly clasp her throat, but in a loving way, softly stroking her neck. The gentle pressure had the effect of making her breath fall even shorter, her excitement seem more intense. Dom had started gently squeezing, but as the question came she felt him grip harder – harder than she'd ever experienced before – as if, if the answer was wrong, he might just continue squeezing. And unsettled by that thought, she'd been a second slow in responding, making her answer, combined with her caught breath, seem more uncertain than it should have.

And in turn that pressure stayed there a second longer as Dom's eyes searched hers, until at last he reverted to more gentle stroking and regained his rhythm.

It took her a moment to catch her breath, but for her the rhythm and sensations had gone – so she faked it. Something she couldn't recall doing before in their love-making. Eyes gently fluttering closed, she returned to her fevered gasps, so that he wouldn't guess his question was nearer the mark than he feared.

After having a quick shower, changing and grabbing some breakfast, Lapslie made his way down to the forensic labs. Once she had realized that it was Major, not Mr, Thomas who had been gassed, and what that meant, Jane Catherall had had the presence of mind to send the lethal gas bottle to Technical II, which was part of the forensic science labs. Tech II, as it was more commonly called, dealt with all things mechanical and technical. Lapslie had to go through all the normal security checks, but this time, instead of going into the main labs, he drove around to the back of the laboratories, to where Tech II was situated, and parked.

The inside of Tech II looked like the inside of Q's hangar in the James Bond films. All sorts of bizarre activity seemed to be going on. There was only one man that Lapslie wanted to speak to, however, and that was Peter Edwards. Edwards had been a police officer once upon a time, and for many years had worked for Lapslie as a detective sergeant, and a bloody good one too. The continual liberalization of the police force hadn't suited him, however, so he had left the force and somehow managed to get himself into Cambridge to read Mechanical Engineering before returning to work with the FSS and establishing Tech II. It was the only department like it in the entire country, with the possible exception of MI5 and Special Forces. With everything gradually being privatized, Lapslie knew Edwards was going to make a fortune, and as far as he was concerned it couldn't have happened to a better bloke.

Edwards, as ever, was in his office. It was an unconventional place, and resembled the inside of a garage or garden shed more than it did a workspace belonging to the head of a department. As usual, Edwards had his head down over some odd-looking contraption on his bench, trying to pry out its secrets or work out a method of using it to best advantage. Occasionally something would spark, and Edwards would swear quietly under his breath, but he always kept going, focused as ever.

'Morning, Peter.'

Edwards didn't move. 'Just a moment, Mark. Remind me, what were we talking about?'

'I haven't seen you for about a year. I can't remember.'

Edwards straightened up. He was a big, bulky, shambling man with a short crop of blond hair. 'I think it was rugby. Or maybe cricket. Similar things.'

'In what way?'

'I don't like either of them.' He extended a meaty hand. 'Good to see you, as always.'

'And you. Had a look at the gas bottle?'

'What, no small talk? No catching up on old times? No *conversation*?'

'No, sorry. Too much to do.'

Edwards thought for a moment, flicking through the filing cabinet that he called his brain. 'Ah yes, over here.' He directed Lapslie to an old wooden bench at the far side of his office. Pulling off an old sheet, he exposed an off-green gas canister. 'Well, here it is: the killer of your major and his beautiful mistress.'

'So what can you tell me? Innocent victim or premeditated murder?'

He placed a hand on top of the gas bottle. 'Guilty as charged. A premeditated killer. However, although important, this particular perpetrator had a partner in crime.'

Lapslie was beginning to feel confused. Edwards always had spoken in riddles, but Lapslie could have done without it now.

'Who was it?'

'Not a "who"; more an "it".' Edwards produced a small heater from another bench. 'This belonged to the major, and it was because this was tampered with that he and his lady friend died. You see, no matter how hard you turn the knob, it never quite closes off. Let me show you.'

Connecting the heater to the large blue gas cylinder, he slowly turned the gas on by twisting the handle at the top of the gas cylinder. He then opened the valve on the heater. He lit it with a match. After a few moments he turned the heater off, but though he twisted as hard as he could the flame stayed on.

Edwards continued: 'So you see, it is physically impossible to turn the gas heater off completely.'

Lapslie could see that, but something was bothering him: 'Wouldn't the major have noticed the flame, or at least the sound or the smell?'

Edwards nodded. 'Indeed he would, and that's where your killer has been very clever and taken a bit of a risk.'

'How so?'

'He waited outside the tent. As soon as the major turned off the heater, he cut off the gas supply from the bottle by turning the valve. So as far as the major was concerned, the gas had been shut down.'

'I wonder what would have happened if the major had stepped outside for a piss or something?'

'Edwards smiled. 'With the lengths this killer has gone to, I'm sure he'll have had a back-up plan of some sort. Anyway, as soon as our loving couple were asleep he turned the gas bottle back on again and left. Look, I'll show you something.'

As Lapslie watched, Edwards took the small heater apart and showed him the on/off valve mechanism inside the burner. Using a pair of tweezers, he removed a small black washer. 'This is the thing that stopped the valve closing, and it was put there on purpose. If you notice, it's broken at one end. It should fit at the top of the valve. To an untrained eye it looks like it has just worn out.'

'But surely any half-decent examiner would have

spotted that? With the greatest respect to your own good self.'

Edwards smiled. 'People see what they want to see, and often they don't think the problem through. The police would have said it was a tragic accident; it looks like the rubber bung has worn out and stopped the gas being turned off. Combine that with an overworked, underpaid, underappreciated lab technician who is looking for the obvious and finds it. Happens all the time: you should know that by now, Mark.'

'I should, you're right.'

Edwards continued: 'So what now, you announce you have another murder?'

Lapslie shook his head. 'No, not yet. The Coroner has opened and adjourned the inquest for further inquiries to be made, so I have time before we have to give an official cause of death. Let's let our killer think he's got away with it.'

'You think that might help?'

Lapslie shrugged. 'No idea. I get the impression that he is trying to finish the job he started quickly. I'm not sure why, but he is. If he thinks we are on to him he might disappear for a few years and I'll miss catching him. If he thinks he's got away with it, he just might aim to kill the next one on the list: the teacher. That means there is a chance I can get him.'

'And put the teacher's life in danger?' Edwards asked shrewdly.

Lapslie looked at him. 'No more than it is right now. I have no idea who the killer or the next victim is. If my instincts are right then I need to find one or the other or both quickly. If he does get to our teacher before me, I want to make sure it is his last murder.'

Failing to plan is planning to fail. It was a now clichéd SAS and regiment motto, but it happened to be true. It was the main reason he had been killing for so long and getting away with it. Meticulous planning, and some divine assistance, had lured the police up many false trails, all leading nowhere.

But now Lapslie was beginning to worry him. He was good, and instead of his synaesthesia debilitating him as it should have, it seemed to have increased his deductive powers. He had known that Lapslie might become involved at some stage, which was why he'd chosen the bunker close to the lavender field to hide the dolls; but its overpowering scent would only go so far in throwing Lapslie off. The other thing which might throw Lapslie would be finding that he was the thirteenth doll in the thirteenth coffin – though that wasn't the reason for its choice;

Lapslie's presence as a doll was for the same reason that all the others had to die.

He'd had to change the order of things because of some obstacles, but while Lapslie and the police knew at least the profession of his next intended victim, they didn't know specifically whom. There were hundreds, possibly thousands, of teachers in the area. How on earth were they going to watch all of them? All he needed to do was to come up with another unusual but not uncommon accident. One that would be tragic, but not obvious. They had focused on the sniper at the church and the links to Stowell, as he suspected they would. That had left him free to arrange his accidents.

It sometimes felt like he had been killing for most of his life. He was tired of it. Sometimes he wanted to stop, but he knew that God wouldn't want him to do that. God wanted him to stay the course, complete the set of murders. He knew that because earlier on, when he had returned from another fruitless reconnaissance of the Teacher's house, he had turned on the radio. A heartbeat later he had heard the beautiful warm voice of a young woman, singing 'Don't give up!' It was the chorus of a pop song, but it was as if she was singing to him, just to him. Nobody else out of the thousands or hundreds of thousands of people listening to that radio station was the object of that message. Only him.

He couldn't give up now. Not when God was expecting him to see it through to the end.

Lapslie's next stop was Major Thomas's widow, Jill Thomas. Bradbury had contacted her to arrange the meeting.

Lapslie had learned early on in his career to always try and take someone with you when you were dealing with bereavement. If it was a woman you were breaking the news to, try and take another woman – a friend or relative if possible, or, failing that, a WPC.

He met Bradbury outside the house. It was like a small mansion. Sitting back from the road, its sweeping, circular driveway led to a double-fronted house with a large porch and door. It must be several hundred years old, and Lapslie's guess was that it had been in the same family just as long.

The two detectives walked up to the imposing oak door and pulled the bell handle. They both heard it ring inside. This set off the sound of what seemed to be at least a hundred dogs barking, causing a cascade of vegetable flavours inside Lapslie's mouth. He could taste every type of vegetable he had ever eaten and a few he hadn't.

Bradbury looked across at him. She could see from the look on his face what was happening. 'You okay, sir?'

Lapslie nodded. 'Yes, fine. Dogs. Very noisy. That's why I don't have one.'

After a few moments a voice penetrated though the great door. 'Can you hang on for a moment while I put the dogs away?'

Bradbury replied: 'Yes, not a problem. Is that Jill Thomas?'

'Yes, I'll only be a mo'.' Her voice was cultured, refined, and flavoured with mint and cardamom.

After a few moments the two detectives heard the metallic sounds of bolts being pulled back and a large key being turned. The door opened. Standing before them was a tall, slender woman in her late thirties. She had an attractive face, green eyes and a crop of brown hair tied tightly into a bun at the back. She was wearing jeans, a red checked shirt and a green hacking jacket. Her feet were encased in tall leather boots which extended to her knees. She looked every inch the upper-class lady.

'Sorry about that. Meant to put them away before, but got busy. You know how it is.'

She put out her hand to Bradbury. 'I'm Jill Thomas, and you must be Detective Sergeant Bradbury?'

The formality felt stilted, of a bygone age. 'Yes,'

Bradbury replied. 'And this is my boss: Detective Chief Inspector Lapslie.'

Jill pushed her hand out towards and he took it. She had a very firm grip, probably the strongest he had ever experienced from a woman. She continued: 'Please come inside; the dogs are in the kitchen. They won't bother you again.'

The two detectives followed her into the house, once she had closed and locked the thick oak door. She led them into a large sitting room with a huge stone open fireplace and directed them to a large sofa, while she sat in a comfortable armchair opposite. Without asking if anyone minded, she lit a long black cigarette. It was her house, after all, Lapslie supposed. After drawing in a large mouthful of smoke and blowing it out with a heavy sigh, she looked across at her visitors. 'I take it you are here to talk about poor John?'

Lapslie nodded. She didn't seem that cut up about her husband's death. 'Yes. If you don't mind me saying, you don't seem to be too upset about it.'

She smiled. 'I'm not. Well, that's not quite true – I'm sorry he's dead. I wouldn't have wished any harm to come to him, but, you see, John was a total bastard, and had been for most of our married life. He had *weaknesses*, you see . . .'

Lapslie was intrigued. 'Such as?'

'The usual: gambling, drink and women. Shagged my bridesmaids on our wedding day. Both of them – separately, not together, of course. He wasn't a total cad.'

Bradbury couldn't quite understand. 'So why did you stay with him?'

She smiled. 'Nowhere else to go, to be honest, and besides, I'm a lesbian. He tolerated my other women and I tolerated his. Sometimes we even shared. Divorce is an expensive business and I wanted to keep the money in the family, not give it to some University of Paddington lawyer, if you know what I mean?'

'So it was really a marriage of convenience?'

She nodded. 'Yes. We considered making the effort and having children, but it never really worked. I think his plumbing was up the spout. The bloody lot will go to my nephew when I join John in the great unknown.'

Lapslie was intrigued. 'Was he insured?'

'Oh God, yes: we both are. Or were. We knew that if one of us popped off then the other would need a pretty penny to keep this place going.' She straightened up in the armchair. 'If you think I killed John to get my hands on his money, you can think again. He was good to me, in his own way. There are more marriages like ours than you would believe, Chief Inspector. They're odd, but in their own way they work. Like Vita and Harold.'

'Neighbours?' Bradbury ventured.

'The Sackville-Wests,' Lapslie murmured.

'Oh,' Bradbury acknowledged. She paused, thinking. 'Neighbours?'

Jill nodded. 'Distantly related.'

'So who had the money in the family?' Lapslie asked.

'Well, such as it was, me. Not that there was a whole lot left. Death duties cripple us, like so many other families.'

'If I told you that we thought your late husband's death wasn't an accident and might have been murder, would you be surprised?'

She shook her head. 'No, not really.'

'Why?' Lapslie asked, intrigued at her brazenness.

'Because I am reasonably sure that a detective chief inspector and his sergeant wouldn't be coming around to see me and asking me questions about money and insurance if it had been an accident.' She frowned, and glanced into the fireplace. 'To be honest, I did wonder. Johnny was pretty careful about things like gas bottles and the like. Years in the Army taught him that at least.'

'I don't suppose you do any camping yourself?' Bradbury asked pointedly.

Jill shuddered. 'Certainly *not*. I refuse to holiday anywhere that doesn't have air conditioning and those two essentials of life, a spa and a bar.'

'When did Major Thomas leave the Army?' Lapslie asked her.

Jill Thomas leaned back in her chair thoughtfully. 'Mmm, now let me think. August 2012? No, no, I tell a lie, it was September. I remember because he had only been out a short while and we were just getting stuck into the work on the house when I was called away for jury service and was gone for two weeks. Bloody jury service, there seems to be no way to get out of it except for feigning madness. Just what we needed. He's away for years and then I have to go away.' The smile slipped from her face, and her eyes suddenly became very bright and wet. 'I make it sound like I wanted us to spend some time together. Which I did. He was a bastard, but he *was* charming.'

'Why did he leave the Army?' Lapslie asked softly.

'To help me. I was finding it difficult to cope on my own. House was too much, needed a hand. Couldn't afford servants, and, to be honest, couldn't afford workmen

too often. Johnny was a dab hand at DIY. Saved us a fortune in the long run and made a good job too.'

'Do you shoot?' Bradbury asked.

She threw her head back and laughed. 'Of course I do.
The bloody rodents you get around here, you have to. My
father taught me.'

'What kind of weapons do you use?'

'Shotguns. They're in the cabinet in the gun room.
Want to see them? I have a licence and all that.'

Lapslie put up his hand. 'No, that won't be necessary.
Tell me, when Major Thomas was in the Army, did he
have any enemies? Other soldiers he perhaps fell out
with?'

Jill shrugged. 'I'm bloody sure he did. The Army is a
place where you can make enemies very easily, just by
doing your job. But do I think they would have murdered him? No, I don't.'

'And does the name Michael Stowell ring any
bells? A fellow Army man, until recently stationed in
Afghanistan.'

Jill reflected for a moment. 'I'm afraid not. But then I
knew only a handful of John's Army friends, so I'm probably not the best person to ask about his broader circle
of contacts in the ranks.'

Lapslie nodded. 'Now this might sound like an odd question, but it *is* important. Were any of his uniforms damaged?'

She smiled broadly. 'All of them. It's a soldier's lot. If they're not crawling about on the earth then they're wrestling each other and riding motorcycles in the officers' mess. That's one of the main expenditures we had in this household: repair bills for his bloody uniforms.'

Lapslie realized he wasn't explaining himself very well. 'Sorry, I didn't quite mean that. Were any of his uniforms deliberately cut up or slashed? Bits of them ripped away and taken?'

She thought for a moment. 'Well now you come to mention it, one of his sets of fatigues was damaged when it was out on the washing line. Thought it was kids, or maybe peace protesters.'

'When was this?'

'Eight years ago. Is it important?'

Lapslie nodded. 'Yes, very. Are you sure of the date?'

'Pretty much. It was when I was called to do jury service. Alex was bloody furious.'

'Why?'

She laughed loudly. In fact Lapslie had never heard a woman laugh quite so loudly before. 'He was jealous!'

'Jealous?'

'He had always wanted to do jury service and was never called. His father did it a couple of times: sent one poor sod to the gallows, apparently. I think Alex had ideas of doing the same.'

Bradbury cut in. 'I think capital punishment was abolished in the sixties.'

She laughed again, her voice echoing around the room. 'I know, I know, but try telling him that!' Suddenly realizing what she had said, she calmed down. 'You know what I mean.'

Lapslie looked at her and nodded sympathetically. 'Sorry – the mutilated uniform?'

She coughed awkwardly. 'Yes, sorry. Anyway, I came home to get the stuff of the line and there was his uniform in tatters.'

'Which part of the uniform?'

'Jacket. Great chunk at the back missing, just cut out. Felt sure it had to be bloody kids.'

'Did you report it?'

She shook her head. 'What was the point? I wouldn't want policemen traipsing around the house and grounds for the sake of some damaged clothing.'

Bradbury cut in. 'Do you still have it?'

She shook her head. 'No, sorry. Only good for rags, so I burnt it.'

It didn't really matter, Lapslie thought. Everything was now confirmed. The reason their killer had been getting away with it for so long was that he was making the murders look like accidents.

'Well, I hope that's all been of help?'

Lapslie nodded, and stood. 'Thank you.'

'I can show you the rest of his uniforms if you like. They're in the bedroom.' Jill made eye contact with Bradbury. 'If you're busy, Chief Inspector, then perhaps your sergeant would like to come and have a look.'

Bradbury's eyes widened, and for a moment Lapslie was tempted to say yes, but he couldn't do it to her. Not even in jest.

'No, that's perfectly fine. We have what we need.'

Thomas smiled broadly at Bradbury. 'Well, come back any time.'

Lapslie was surprised to see his detective sergeant go bright red.

Lapslie noticed that Bradbury seemed preoccupied for much of the drive back to the station.

'You haven't let the major's wife trying to get a bit fresh get to you, have you?'

It took a second for Bradbury to detach from her thoughts. She pushed a smile in return.

'No, it's not that at all. Just Dom being a bit moody of late, giving me a hard time.'

'Well, I did warn you about these ex-villains.' He kept the teasing smile there for a second before becoming more serious. 'In what way?'

She didn't want to go into detail about the possibly implied threat of their love games taking a wrong turn, so chose the recent trip away.

'He was asking all sorts of questions about the trip to Edinburgh – who was I with, why the need to stay overnight, et cetera.' She laughed nervously. 'Almost as if he suspects I'm seeing someone else.'

Lapslie nodded, looked at the passing traffic for a moment. He noticed she'd said the last part flatly, hadn't added 'ridiculously' or 'unbelievably', so he asked equally flatly:

'And are you?'

Stone silence for a second, then she eased out a long breath. 'Yes, I am.' Perhaps she'd wanted to share this with someone all along, ease the burden; perhaps get some advice too on how to handle the situation. And who might know better how to handle an ex-con like Dom McGinley than Lapslie? 'Been seeing this other guy, Peter Wilkinson, for five months on and off now. He's an academic, a lecturer in genetic engineering. They couldn't be more different – chalk and cheese.'

'Oh, Jesus, Emma. Not a good move.'

She arched an eyebrow as she glanced across. 'Thanks for the support. It was you that always said Dom was a bad idea. A bad match for me. And now that I try to move on ...'

'Yes, I did. And I still hold to that. But that doesn't mean I'd want to see you in any sort of danger. Leaving someone like Dom needs a clean break for a start, and handling with kid gloves. All sorts of hurt-macho-pride, old-school-villain factors there.' He shook his head. 'But cheating on him, you're playing with fire.'

'Thanks.' She stared blankly ahead at the road. 'I was hoping you might offer some useful advice.'

'And I have. Make a clean break from Dom or dump the other guy – however much I might think he'd be the better match for you. But don't keep seeing both at once.'

She nodded. What else had she expected from Lapslie but sheer bluntness? And while in her head she knew he was perfectly right, could she get her heart and emotions to agree? Right now both men were answering different needs in her that were difficult to shed. She sighed.

'You're right. I'll have to do something.' But she knew that might be weeks or months away, unless something else forced her hand. Meanwhile she'd keep walking the tightrope of seeing both; but then maybe that tightrope was part of the excitement.

PART SEVEN

27 January 2012

Keith Sampson shouldn't have been working on his birthday. He should have been out with his mates, celebrating. He'd had plenty of invitations, but here he was in the dark, in the pissing rain, waiting for his next call, a flask of just bearable tea and a few stale sandwiches by his side.

The truth was, he needed the money. He liked playing poker at home, online, late into the night. He knew it was draining his bank accounts the way a punctured bucket drained water, but he couldn't help himself. It made him feel . . . special. Part of something big.

He poured himself a cup of tea and gulped it down. Not only was it stewed, but it was cold. If he'd had somewhere to spit it, then he would have. As it was, he was forced to gulp it down and wince.

He opened the driver's-side window and poured the remainder of the flask onto the grass outside his taxi. Two cheese-and-something sandwiches followed.

Suddenly his radio burst into life. 'Tango Golf Twenty-three, come in, over!'

He didn't want to respond, but a job was still a job. He picked up the mike. 'Tango Golf Twenty-three, go ahead, over.'

'Are you available for a call, over?'

'Yes, over.'

'Can you go to Old Quarry, off Mill Road? There's a Mr Brond in need of your services. He's at the end of the old dirt-track road, if you know where that is, over.'

'What's he doing down there? Over.'

'He's been fishing, over.'

'Brilliant. Stinking carp in the back of the cab, and maggots all over the floor. I'm on my way. Over.'

'Good boy. Out.'

Old Quarry Road was about three miles from his location. It was ten o'clock at night and there was very little traffic around. He did find himself wondering why a fisherman would still be at the Old Quarry at this time of night, but then fishermen were funny people. They seemed to love roughing it, and revelled in discomfort. Each to their own, he supposed.

He reached Old Quarry Road and turned left onto it. After half a mile of avoiding potholes, he finally reached the end of the road. His headlights shone out across a few metres of ground and then into the darkness of the quarry.

He looked around. No sign of anyone. He flashed his lights and beeped his horn several times, but still there was no response. If this was someone's idea of a joke on his birthday then he wasn't amused.

He got back onto the radio. 'Tango Golf Twenty-three to control: I'm at the location but no sign of our fisherman. Could you give him a call and see where he is, over?'

'Wait one, over.'

Keith waited, looking around to see if he could spot anyone. He did consider getting out of the car and having a look around, doing a bit of shouting, but it was still raining hard. There was only so far you could go for a punter.

The radio burst into life again. 'Tango Golf Twenty-three, over.'

He picked up the microphone. 'Go ahead, over.'

'Sorry, but he isn't replying. I think it must be a hoax. Sorry about that. Return to standby. Over.'

'Ten four. Over.'

He wasn't sure whether to reverse back down the track or do a three-point turn. Given the number of deep potholes he had encountered on the way down the track, he decided on a three-point turn. Turning his wheel hard to the right, he pulled the car forward and to the right, then put it into reverse. Pulling hard to the right, he managed to get halfway through his manoeuvre when he suddenly noticed a set of headlights racing towards him from the side. Before he had a chance to react, the other vehicle hit the side of the car.

Because he was wearing his seat belt, the inertial reel belt kept him fixed in place and his body took the full impact of the collision. Semi-conscious and shocked, he realized that his car was being pushed towards the edge of the quarry. He tried to take his seat belt off, but it was stuck. Press as he might, nothing happened.

Moments later he was rolling over and over in mid-air. Before he could tell which way was up, the taxi crashed into the murky waters below.

Water rushed in through the broken windows. Still fighting against his locked seat belt, Keith tried to hold his breath, but his ribs had been crushed by the impact and agony was flooding him like fire. Eventually, he had to take a breath, but by that time there was no air left in the car. He choked.

Up above, on the edge of the quarry, a figure emerged from the car that had pushed Keith's cab over the edge. He stood there for a full fifteen minutes, watching for some sign of movement. When he was sure that nobody was going to emerge from the dark waters, he stepped back in his car and drove away.

Given the now proven accident – victim link, Lapslie knew his next step would be to call a briefing of the squad and inform them of developments. Now that they had several new lines of inquiry, a breakthrough might be on the cards.

He called the briefing for 10 a.m. For once, everyone was on time. Bradbury did the pre-briefing, reminding them all of the rules and summing up the situation. Once that had been done she beckoned to Lapslie, who entered a very quiet briefing room.

He stood in front of them with an assortment of stickers in his hand.

'Okay, we have a little more information for you, but it's information that should help a lot, hopefully widen the case and bring it to a quick resolution.' Looking around and making eye contact with everyone in the room, he continued: 'I now believe our killer has disguised many killings to make them look like accidents. He took a chance with one of them, a nurse, Jane Summers, whom he strangled, and my gut instinct with Leslie Petersen – given that it was such a showcase killing, unlike the others – is that it was staged to put her past boyfriend, Mike Stowell, in the frame. On which front, anything new on Stowell?' Lapslie's gaze homed in on Barrett and Kempsey. Kempsey answered.

'Nothing out of the ordinary: routine trips to his local

bank, post office, some shopping. But he hasn't met anyone else since seeing his old Army mate Bill Ewan a few days back.'

As if sensing the pending question, Barrett cut in, 'And we checked Ewan out, as you requested: no sniper experience.'

Lapslie nodded. 'Okay. So far everything points to that killing being set up, a one-off. The rest, I am now convinced, were overlooked by the police because they were seen as accidents. We already know that the late Major John Alexander Thomas, who at first we thought had died as a result of a leaking gas bottle a few days ago, was, in fact, murdered. As you know, the next-to-last doll was dressed as a major. We also know that his uniform was damaged and a large section cut away, and that the gas bottle was tampered with . . .'

One of the DCs, Rebecca Graves, put her hand up. Bradbury looked at Lapslie. He nodded. She nodded to Graves to ask her question.

'As I remember from the papers the major died with a woman. Was she one of the dolls?'

'No, she was just unlucky. Wrong man, wrong place, wrong time.' Glancing around the room again, he continued with his briefing. 'We have now checked the damaged uniform against the material on the doll, and they are a match, which I feel makes it conclusive.'

DC Parkin put his hand up this time. Lapslie nodded to Bradbury, and she gave him the okay to speak. 'How did you get on to the major, sir?'

'The police pathologist made the connection for us.'

The squad were clearly impressed.

'Now, as a result of that, I have tasks for all of you. The tasks will be put up on the board *thus*.'

Lapslie stuck a photograph of the fireman doll onto the board. Under the photo, he wrote *DC Parkin & DC Pearce*. He then stuck a photograph of the mechanic doll, under which he wrote *DC Graves & DC Putter*. This went on until the eight unknown dolls had each been given to a team of two detectives.

'Now I want each team to find out if any members of these professions have been killed in an accident since July first, 2007. Those detailed to non-professional dolls like the fisherman and the girl in the bikini will have to use their wits a bit more, but you're all clever people, or you wouldn't be here . . .'

The ones detailed to those dolls all looked at each other dubiously.

Lapslie continued: 'I don't have to tell you how

important speed is in this inquiry. The major is already dead and there was nothing we could have done about that. However, because the teacher doll hasn't appeared inside its coffin yet, I am hoping that means our teacher, whoever he or she might be, is still alive. We need to get to them before our killer does. I am also assuming that our killer is aware of that, and will do his best to finish the job before we have a chance to get our hands on his latest potential victim and keep him out of harm's way. So I'm sorry, but no leave is to be taken, under any circumstances. We are on sixteen-hour days – so work, eat, sleep a bit, and then work again. All I can say is, think of the overtime. You'll all be in clover by the end of this. Now, do we all understand what we have to do and how quickly we have to do it?'

There was a general nodding of heads.

'Okay, then let's get on with it, and good luck. Remember: a teacher's life is in your hands.'

If he had said it once, he had said it a thousand times: failing to plan was planning to fail.

The Teacher was the last one, and he had to be sure of the kill. After that he just had Lapslie to deal with and then he was free to live his life normally again. So far, he had established where the Teacher, Tony Turner, lived, what school he worked at, his hours of business and which way he went to school and back, as well as which nights he tended to go out socially, where he shopped and where he played rugby on weekends. The Teacher also liked old sports cars, and ran a 1980 MG GT which always drew admiring glances in the school playground on the rare occasions he drove in rather than taking the bus.

He liked victims with a routine. It made his life so much easier.

He had parked his car a little way down the road from the nineteenth-century artisan cottage where Tony Turner lived, deliberately facing away from it. From here he could see all the man's comings and goings quite easily without being seen himself. He kept a newspaper held up over his face, as if he was reading it, while at the same time watching the cottage through his wing mirror.

A little after 8 a.m., Tony Turner left the house, turned left out of his gate and made his way towards the bus stop at the top of his road. Ten minutes later, his wife, Elizabeth, followed the same route. An attractive woman in her mid- to late twenties, she was a chemist. The fact that she was both clever and attractive meant she wouldn't be a widow for long, and he was pleased about that. The nurse he had murdered all those years ago had been very beautiful as well; so beautiful that it had almost been a crime to kill her.

Once Elizabeth Turner had disappeared he left ten minutes to be sure and then stepped out of his car and made his way to their cottage. He needed to have a good look around, see what opportunities there were to rig something up. Maybe discover something about Turner that he didn't already know that might help him.

He didn't go to the front door but took a small path that led to the back of the house. He'd already checked the locality out on the land registry plots in the council offices, so he knew the shape and size and orientation of the house.

The path was a bit like an old-fashioned alley with high walls, so people walking along it couldn't be seen. That was useful. The back gate was locked but he had expected that. After a glance around he climbed over quickly and dropped down on the other side. He looked at the back door. Yale and a Chubb; not an easy pick, but then he'd been trained by the best.

Once inside, he looked around. The cottage was neat and tidy, and, he had to admit, quite cosy. There were photos of Tony and Elizabeth on the walls, as well as a number of others, whom he assumed were family and friends. There was even one of Tony's father. He felt his heart rate increase as he recognized the man's face. The arteries in his neck began to pulse hard, and he could feel the blood pressure building up behind his eyes. He had a sudden and dramatic urge to smash the photograph, but he kept his urges under control. He always did. That was how he had got this far.

The cottage was made up of one very big room that served as both a sitting room and dining room. There was a small but well equipped kitchen off to one side. There was also a surprisingly long hallway, off which were the stairs to the top half of the house. He climbed them two at a time. Upstairs there were two bedrooms: one large master bedroom and a small guest room which they clearly used as an office, although there was a double futon for guests should they want to stay over. There was also a small bathroom with a shower toilet and sink, but no bath. How anyone could live without a bath he wasn't sure, but it seemed to be the modern way. He'd heard that apartments in New York were being built with no kitchens, because people mostly either ate out or brought back takeaways. What was the world coming to?

His eyes scanned across the bookshelves, and he felt his breath suddenly catch in his throat. The way four of the books lined up, the initial words of their titles formed a short but panic-inducing message in four different fonts: You Are Not Alone!

He froze where he stood, straining to hear any other movement in the house. For a long ten seconds there was nothing, and he was just about to relax and continue when he heard a key turning in the front-door lock. Someone had returned to the house, or maybe the couple had a cleaner that he didn't know about. Whoever it was, they might have heard him moving around and called the police.

He waited to see what they would do; not moving an inch, keeping his breathing under control. Unfortunately whoever had entered the house was now climbing up the stairs.

Picking up a tall scent bottle from the dresser table, he moved slowly and deliberately to take up a position behind the bedroom door. If it was the Teacher, he decided, he might as well kill him here and now. Get it over with. Not what he had planned, but occasionally it was best to go with the flow and take the chance when it presented itself. He was sure it would work out okay. So the police had another murder to investigate; they hadn't done too well so far.

As the unknown person entered the bedroom he jumped out quickly and caught them a heavy blow on the back of the head. As he felt the skull fracture under the blow, as blood squashed, jelly-like, into the hair, and as the figure crumpled to the carpet, he realized that it wasn't Tony Turner who had entered the room. It was his wife, Elizabeth.

She moaned and tried to get up, arms moving spasmodically. He had to be quick. He pulled her up by her hair and, before she had a chance to scream, he pushed her face into a pillow on the bed, holding her arms behind her back with one *hand. She struggled frantically, but he was too strong, and she was too stunned to put up too much resistance. Quickly, her body went limp. He pulled her face away from the pillow and felt for a pulse. She still had one. He didn't want her dead. The murder of a teacher's wife would mean that his next and final victim would be surrounded by police and family for a good while, and he didn't want that to happen. It would constrain his options. He also knew there had been too much contact between them. Fibres from his clothes would be all over hers, and over the bedspread.*

Turning her over, he stripped the clothes from her body, leaving her unconscious and naked on the bed. As he looked down at her he couldn't help but admire her body. She really was in good shape, but he didn't touch her, just spread her legs wide and put her hands above her head in a sort of rape position. He also inspected the wounds at the back of her head. Fortunately, although bleeding, they were not as far as he could tell life-threatening.

Taking her clothes and the bedspread down to the kitchen, he searched through the cupboards for a plastic bag, finally finding an ASDA Bag for Life, which seemed curiously apt. Stuffing the clothes and bedspread into the bag, he made his way back the way he came. He would burn the lot later.

When he considered he was far enough away he would call

the police from a phone box, disguising his voice, and tell them that he had seen someone breaking into the house and heard a woman screaming. She should get the help she needed then.

He hoped so. He was a compassionate man, and he didn't want her to suffer unnecessarily. And neither, of course, did God.

Emma Bradbury would never have thought that an evening in with her cat, Purdy, would have ended so productively. It was a lesson she'd learned from Lapslie: switch your brain off, don't think analytically about things, but let your subconscious pick up on odd coincidences and apparently unrelated events.

An evening by herself was something of a luxury. Dom had gone out to see an old mate at a pub, and she had no plans to see Peter; in fact hadn't seen him since returning from Edinburgh.

It was an item on the six-thirty local news that broke into her thoughts. A woman had been attacked and sexually assaulted locally. It wasn't the woman that caught Emma's subconscious attention, however, but her husband. He was a local teacher. Emma knew it was a shot in the dark, but it was worth checking out. What the hell, it would just take an hour or so in the morning. She wouldn't tell Lapslie just in case she was wrong: no point giving him the opportunity to gloat. On the other hand, if she was right she would be doing all the gloating.

She contacted DS Stuart Lewins, the senior investigating officer, early the following morning. She had worked with Lewins before, and while he was certainly a good detective, he was also a good friend. She needed to discover what had happened and also where the woman was now.

Lewins was helpful. She learned that the woman, Elizabeth Turner, had been physically assaulted, but although she had been stripped naked she hadn't been touched sexually. Nothing had been stolen either. Lewins could only conclude that whoever had been in the cottage had been disturbed in some way before he could carry out an assault or turn the place over. The assailant had already been in the house when she entered. She had forgotten her bus pass and had to go back for it. The odd thing was that there was no sign of a break-in. Either the door had been left open, which the woman denied, or the intruder had a key or had picked the lock.

The more Lewins explained, the more Bradbury felt it could be their man.

Lewins concluded by telling Bradbury that the woman was now in the Royal Free Hospital and giving her his permission to visit.

An hour and a half later Bradbury was walking along the corridor towards Ward E1 and her meeting with Elizabeth Turner. The woman was in a small private side ward, which was handy, given what Bradbury wanted to talk to her about. Bradbury knocked gently and entered. 'Elizabeth Turner?'

She nodded wearily. 'Yes. You must be Sergeant Bradbury?'

Bradbury nodded. She couldn't help but notice what an attractive woman she was, even with her hair shaved and head bandaged and two swollen and black eyes. She also had a gentle, almost sad, smile.

'Yes, I am. Is your husband around?'

'He's gone to get a cup of tea and have a rest. I insisted that he went. He's been here all night, poor dear.'

'Are you okay to talk, or shall I wait until he comes back?'

She nodded. 'Don't worry – let's talk now. I might fall asleep later – I find I keep dropping off. Please sit down. It's not very comfortable, but it's all there is.' She indicated a small blue hard-seated chair by the side of her bed. Bradbury sat. 'Sergeant Lewins said you would be coming. Is it about the attack?'

Bradbury shook her head gently. 'Not directly. There may be a connection to another case, one that I am working on. Did you get a look at your attacker? Even a glance?'

She shook her head, wincing. 'No, nothing at all. I remember walking back into the cottage, and after that everything is a blank. The next thing I remember is a policeman covering me up with his coat.'

'But your attacker never touched you?'

'Other than hit me over the head and undress me,' she replied bitterly, 'no, nothing. Or so I'm told. I wouldn't have known anything about it if he had. Sergeant Lewins seems to think he was disturbed, but I'm not sure who by. No one ever comes to the house, except the postman, and he'd already been.'

'Unless, of course, lots of visitors come when you are not there.'

She smiled that gentle smile again. 'Maybe. We probably have thousands of visitors every day who stop turning up just before we get home.'

'No ideas at all as to who might have attacked you?'

She shook her head. 'No, none at all.'

'I'm sorry to ask, but any old boyfriends or lovers who might still be jealous?'

She shook her head firmly. 'No. I didn't have that many boyfriends before Tony, and the ones that I did have tended to be the quiet, shy type. I always tried to avoid the axe murderers.'

'Any admirers who have been sending you flowers or letters, or following you about?'

'Not that I noticed, but I suppose there are always people who tell you years later they had a mad crush on you, and you never knew.'

Bradbury nodded. She was right, and with looks like hers it could be a cast of thousands. 'What about at work. Anyone tried to flirt?'

'I didn't even get a Valentine's card this year.'

'This might seem like an odd question, but please, think about it before you answer. Have any of your husband's clothes ever been vandalized, or cut up, or maybe just stolen?'

She shook her head. 'No, sorry, nothing, and as I do all the washing I'm sure I'd remember something like that.'

Bradbury felt crestfallen. She was glad she hadn't mentioned her long shot to Lapslie before she had followed it up. She stood. 'Well thanks very much for seeing me. Especially when you're not a hundred per cent.'

She smiled. 'That's fine. I'm sure I was of absolutely no help at all.'

She hadn't been, but Bradbury wasn't going to tell her that. However, before she had a chance to speak, the door opened and a bunch of red roses appeared, followed by a man who must be Elizabeth's husband, Tony Turner. He walked across to her, gave her the roses, and kissed her gently on the forehead. 'I got these at the shop in the foyer. Thought you might like them. You're looking better; how are you feeling?'

She breathed in deeply, allowing the pungent smell of the flowers to drift through her nose. Even Bradbury could smell them, and she was standing several yards away.

'Much better, now you've given me these.' She noticed her husband looking across at Emma quizzically. 'Oh, I am sorry; this is DS Bradbury, Tony. She's come to ask me a few more questions.' She turned to gaze at Bradbury. 'Why don't you ask Tony that question you asked me?'

Bradbury looked at her for a moment, slightly confused. 'Which one?'

'The one about his clothes.'

Tony Turner was looking confused by the sudden strange turn in the conversation. Bradbury tried to enlighten him. 'Have you ever had any of your clothes vandalized, cut up, or maybe stolen?'

He shrugged. 'Nothing. Was that the wrong answer?'

Bradbury smiled. 'Yes and no. Never mind.' She looked across at Elizabeth. 'Well, get well soon, and don't let it get you down. Remember, they only win if you let them.'

As Bradbury turned to leave, Anthony Turner called after her. 'I did have my gown damaged at school, but that was a few months ago. Does that count?'

Bradbury turned. 'How was it damaged?'

'Kids probably.'

Bradbury nodded. 'Maybe. What happened?'

'Someone took a knife or a pair of scissors to it and cut it up.'

'Did they take part of it away with them?' she asked, feeling her pulse start to race.

Turner looked surprised. 'Well, yes, actually they did. Half the back was missing. How did you know?'

'Just a lucky guess.'

Bradbury felt a wave of triumph wash through her. She'd been right! Her hunch had paid off!

*

Every so often Lapslie would slide into a grey abyss. Normally the moods didn't last long – five or six hours or at most a day – but this one had hit at the worst possible time: at this stage in the investigation, he couldn't afford his thoughts to be addled for even a few hours, let alone possibly an entire day.

When the grey moods hit, all the smells that the thorazitol had subdued and kept at bay over the past days, real or induced by his synaesthesia, would come flooding back in: a bacon and egg roll on the train journey to Edinburgh, the people nearby and passing in the carriage, the recent meetings, interviews and forensics examinations – primrose, asphalt, vinegar, mould overlaid with cologne, sour cream, burnt toffee, formaldehyde – and he'd be gripped by stomach cramps and nausea, his senses reeling.

He'd find himself desperately reaching for the thorazitol bottle again, but the dilemma was the same each time: one pill would calm the effects for half a day or more, and then they might return more intensely. But if he took two pills or more, while that would work for far longer, he risked tipping over the edge and suffering hallucinations, which were equally daunting. Also, with too many pills he'd feel curiously numb to most sensations, not just the smells assaulting his synapses from synaesthesia, and would feel he could hardly function at any level. Not ideal in many a circumstance, but particularly not in the middle of an investigation.

So when the mood gripped Lapslie not long after returning to his home in Saffron Walden to catch up on paperwork, he looked long and hard at the thorazitol bottle before finally taking one pill. And after nearly an hour, just as he was starting to think about preparing dinner – wondering in fact if he'd be able to stomach any – he felt the sharper edges of the multitude of tastes subside. His overall senses felt slightly numbed too, but with luck that effect would also subside over the coming hours. And through that faint haze, he was surprised to hear a car pull up outside his house.

He walked to the front door and opened it. Bradbury was standing there, a broad grin across her face.

'You look like the cat that's got the cream.'

Bradbury looked into his face. 'And you look like you've lost a pound and found sixpence.'

'I always do. It's the way my face naturally falls.' He

didn't feel inclined to go into detail about having just topped up on his thorazitol. 'Come in.'

Lapslie showed Bradbury into the sitting room and sat opposite her. 'So what's up?'

Bradbury pushed herself to the edge of her seat. 'I've found the next victim, the teacher.'

'Alive or dead?' Lapslie asked, incredulous.

'Alive.'

'How did you manage to make that link?'

'From a news story on local TV about a woman who had been attacked in her own home. The report said she was the wife of a local teacher. It just stuck in my mind, so I gave Stuart Lewins a call . . .'

'He still on the job?'

'He retires next year. Anyway, I asked him about it, and he said it was a little odd. The woman was knocked out, stripped naked, but not assaulted. Nothing was stolen from the house and there was no sign of a break-in. He thought the man might have been disturbed and legged it. I wasn't so sure.'

Lapslie fought to shake off the remnants of his thorazitol haze, to focus. 'Why not?'

'Well, Lewins said there was no sign of a break-in,

so my guess is he picked the locks. All the doors were double-locked with the latest Chubb model and a complicated Yale. Your average burglar isn't going to get past them, but chummy did.'

Lapslie nodded. 'Very sharp thinking, but I'm still not clear on how you made the link.'

'I went to see the girl that was assaulted. She wasn't much help and couldn't remember that much. Then her husband turned up—'

'The teacher?'

'Yes, and he told me a gown he had at school had been vandalized and a large section cut out.'

'Has he still got the gown?' Lapslie asked, feeling his heart race.

Bradbury shook her head. 'No, threw it away. Well you would, wouldn't you?'

'I suppose – but a shame. So where is he now?'

'I've sent two of the DCs to keep an eye on him until you decide what you want to do.'

Some clarity finally filtered through. 'The answer is: nothing.' Bradbury looked taken aback. 'Not yet, anyway. I want him watched very closely. I don't want him exposed to unnecessary danger – but this might just be what we needed.'

'Use him as a sort of decoy?'

Lapslie nodded. 'Yes. It might draw our man out, especially if he doesn't know we're on to him.'

'Let's not forget there is a doll of you too.'

'The killer also knows that I know, and that I will be ready for him. Or maybe he's trying to set us on edge, make me think more about my own safety than about the case. We know he's a clever bugger.'

'If he's that clever, wouldn't it be better to put Turner into protective custody for a while?' Bradbury shrugged. 'Or at least forewarn him of our plans, get his approval?'

'Under normal circumstances, yes. But in this case it would just put him on his guard, make him act unnaturally. Put his life more at risk.'

'But he might shoot Turner from a distance, as he did with Leslie Petersen, and how would we prevent him?'

'We'll keep a close eye on him, don't worry. I'll even get Rouse to authorize an armed unit to monitor him twenty-four seven.'

'Some reassurance, I suppose.'

'If we don't do something like this, the killer will get to Turner eventually in any case. We can't keep him in protective custody indefinitely, nor offer this sort of armed back-up long-term. With a short-term concentrated plan, we can.'

Lapslie could tell from Bradbury's expression that she still harboured strong doubts, and he questioned for a moment whether his thorazitol top-up might have skewed his own rational thinking: was he doing the right thing, or in his desperation to catch the killer was he putting an innocent man's life at risk?

How the hell they'd got on to him so fast he didn't know. Perhaps he should have raped the Teacher's wife to create a reason for him having been in the house. Maybe stolen the few things they had that were worth anything. The police didn't have a record of his DNA and were very unlikely ever to get one, so he would have been relatively safe. He could have chucked what he had stolen into the nearest river. As for fibres, well, he could have burnt his clothes as soon as he got back. Failing to plan was all very well until the unexpected happened, then even the best-laid plans turned to shit.

He was getting too old for this. If it wasn't for the constant pressure of knowing that God expected him to complete his mission, he would have given up long ago. For every step forward, there seemed to be a step backwards. He couldn't believe it when he saw Parkin and Pearce parked 'discreetly' outside the school. *Good job he had seen them before they saw him. He knew Lapslie was good, but he'd been hoping that the man's neurological condition would be holding him back, making him careless. That obviously wasn't the case: Lapslie had worked out what he had done with the Major, and now Lapslie had found the Teacher before he had a chance to kill him. Not even seeing his own doll had thrown him.*

Perhaps he should have killed Lapslie first, or certainly earlier; then life would have been a lot easier. But the police always investigated the death of one of their own much more assiduously than with a member of the public. They never would have given up, and even had he faked an accident, that extra vigilance might have unearthed his modus operandi.

Still, he mused, what was done was done, and he had to deal with the situation as it was. First, Lapslie had obviously decided not to hide the Teacher in an effort to try and draw him out. Well that wasn't going to happen. He could try and pick him off from a distance, but his guess was that Lapslie would have an armed unit standing by, and this time he might not get away. Especially if the police had air support ready to move in. No, he would have to be a lot cleverer than that. He already had a plan, and if it worked both Lapslie and the Teacher would come to him and then it would be ended. Finally ended.

PART EIGHT

8 August 2013

Dr Robert Cann wondered whether, at forty-one years of age, he wasn't getting a bit too old for the hard climbs like this.

That said, climbing the Naples Needle had always been his dream. It was, after all, the birthplace of rock climbing, and it should be attempted by every climber worth his salt before they retired to talk of peaks they had climbed and, more importantly, failed to climb. Like fishermen talking about the 'giant ones' that got away.

This had to be his last climb. He dipped his fingers into the chalk bag, grabbed the edge of an overhanging rock and pulled himself upwards. He could feel his entire body strain against the effort as he searched for a foothold. He would remember this climb for the rest of his life, not just because he had wanted to do it for so long, but because he knew that for weeks, if not months, his body would remind him of it in various subtle and not so subtle ways.

He looked up, towards the peak. He still had a good way to go, but another hour or so should see him there. Then he could sit on the top and be master of all he surveyed.

He looked back across the Lakes. If he wasn't going to climb again then he knew he would have to find something to do. Walking would probably be the thing. The Lakes had some wonderful walks, both long and short. He would try some of those out. Forty-one wasn't that old, he knew, not these days, but he also knew he had to keep himself fit. It wasn't that he was scared of dying, but he had three children and he didn't want to put them through the same pain that he had felt when his own father had died too early. Everyone has to go through it in the end, but he would try to put the day off as long as possible. The older you got, the less the hurt seemed to be.

Checking his safety harness, he began to make his final ascent.

A couple of big pushes and he would be there. He had brought a camera and small collapsible tripod with him, to record the extraordinary moment. His father had photographed him, aged ten, after his very first climb; now he was going to photograph his very last. He would have to get them framed together.

Finding a good foothold, he pushed hard. As he did there

was an odd sound, like something hitting the rock with a hammer. All of a sudden his rope went slack. He grabbed wildly at the rock face, searching for something to hold on to, but there was nothing. Suddenly he was falling backwards. He cried out involuntarily and began to flap his arms as if he could somehow slow himself down. The summit of the Needle suddenly seemed to be a long way off, and getting further away with every moment. He didn't think, and he didn't see his life flash before him. The horror of his situation erased everything from his brain except the sheer terror of knowing that in a few moments he was going to be dead.

As his body hit a sloping section of scree, his skull fractured and over half the bones in his body broke. He died at once: a red flash, and then nothing. Nothing ever again.

Lapslie knew his next visit would have to be to his old friend Jane Catherall.

He pulled into the mortuary car park and made his way straight to her office. She knew he was coming, but still he knocked. Her familiar voice came back: 'Come in, Mark.'

He opened the door. Catherall was sitting at her desk, writing some report. Longhand, with a fountain pen, of course. Without a word, she used it to point to the chair on the opposite side of the desk. Lapslie sat, like a well-trained dog.

After a few moments she looked up. 'So the accident-murder theory was proven right then?'

Lapslie nodded. 'Yes. That's what I've come to see you about.'

'I see. So how can I help?'

'There are a number of links yet to fully make,' Lapslie said, 'but we are now positive that a number of murders have been committed, and made to look like accidents. We have eleven dolls already inside their coffins, and two still outside. One is a teacher whom we think we have just identified, still alive, and the other is, well, me.'

Dr Catherall stared at Lapslie, her eyes wide. '*You* are the thirteenth doll? *You* are to go in the thirteenth coffin?'

He nodded. 'The doll has my police number on its uniform, and the uniform's made out of pieces of one of mine. There's no mistake, but I've told Bradbury to keep it to herself. There's no point confusing the issue by telling everyone. We have a murderer to catch, and a teacher to save.' He paused for a moment, collecting his thoughts. 'We also know that three of the people represented by the dolls were definitely murdered. Our task now is to determine whom the rest were.'

Lapslie handed Catherall a large A4 envelope.

'Inside are photos of the remaining dolls. Each doll seems to represent a profession or the hobby the victim was involved in at the time of their deaths . . .'

'And you want me to check through the files of the last so many years to see if anyone within those professions has died unexpectedly or in an accident. Yes?'

Lapslie nodded. 'Yes. And one more thing.'

She looked at him quizzically. 'If we find any of them I'd like you to arrange to have them disinterred and redo post-mortems on them.'

She nodded soberly. 'I don't have a problem with that. Don't forget old Professor Gilbert was here before me. He might well have done the original PMs, and he wasn't one for making mistakes.'

Lapslie shook his head. 'He was, towards the end of his career. We just covered them up.'

Catherall looked surprised. 'Would you do the same for me?'

Lapslie smiled broadly. 'Let's hope I won't have to.'

Catherall threw the envelope Lapslie had given her down on her desk and looked across at him. 'Very well: I'll do the checks as quickly as I can. Probably by the end of the week.'

'Thanks. I appreciate that.'

'I'm not doing it for you. I'd like this twisted maniac caught as well.'

Bradbury was working in the office when DCs Parkin and Pearce came in. They both seemed puffed out with importance.

'You two are back early. Thought you would be on the golf course by now.'

'We've found out who the fireman is.'

Bradbury stood. 'Well, give me a name then.'

'Bloke called Richard Dale, was killed in 2008,' Pearce replied.

'Eighth of August 2008, to be accurate,' added Parkin.

Bradbury walked across to them. 'How was he killed?'

'Fell off his ladder into the fire.'

'So it might just have been an accident?'

Parkin shook his head. 'No. He was the best ladder man they had, there was no need for him to fall.'

Pearce continued: 'There was a PM. He died from smoke inhalation, but that was it. He was otherwise a very fit man. No history of any physical problems. Heart in good condition, as was the rest of him.'

The other half of the double act chipped in. 'So there was no reason for him to fall naturally.'

Bradbury was becoming increasingly interested. 'So how else did he fall?'

Pearce produced an A4 envelope. 'It's all in here: the PM report. They discovered an impression . . . an indentation . . . on the top side of his skull. They wrote it off at the time as having been caused when he fell.'

Bradbury nodded. 'Sounds fair.'

Parkin shook his head. 'Well, maybe, with what they knew then. It would never have occurred to them that he might have been knocked off his ladder. Now we think he was murdered, it takes on a new significance. We think he was hit on the head with something, and that's what made him fall.'

Bradbury took the envelope from them. 'It's a bit thin, and I don't mean the PM report.'

Pearce smiled confidently, giving the impression that he knew something Bradbury didn't. 'It might be, if we hadn't gone to his fire station and discovered that about a month before he was killed his uniform was vandalized and a great piece of material cut out.'

'Who told you that?'

'The station officer,' Pearce glanced at his notebook,

'one Peter Brooking. He remembered it happening because Dale did his nut. He accused everyone in the station of having it in for him. That's fire-station life for you, far as I can tell: they all play tricks on each other all the time. Dale was the first fire officer ever to die from their station, and only the second in the county over the period you asked us to check. That's why Brooking remembered him so well.'

Parkin joined in again. 'The other one was killed in a road-traffic accident on the way to a fire. We've already eliminated him as a possible.'

'The RTA was very well investigated. Caused by too much speed. The driver lost it on a bend and hit a tree.'

Bradbury was impressed, but there were still some remaining hurdles. 'There'll have to be another post-mortem. It will mean digging him up. The family aren't going to be happy about that.'

Pearce shrugged. 'They'll be happy enough if we discover the real reason for his death, and bring the bastard who did it to justice.'

Bradbury nodded decisively.

Parkin cut in: 'I'm okay with it as long as I don't have to do the digging.'

*

Lapslie's mind and body were crying out for more boat time to get away from things. What had turned his mind to it was George phoning an hour ago to tell him that all the repairs had been done – 'Everything's ship-shape again.'

He could do with getting away from all the distractions and noises and just thinking for a while. Let the facts churn and shift in his brain until a pattern emerged. But the problem was that even a short spin out on the boat would eat up half the day, and at this stage in the investigation he just didn't have the time. So all he'd committed to was meeting George at the marina at first light the next morning for a quick spot check.

He went over the current state of the inquiry in his mind. They had thirteen dolls, counting him, but he wasn't one of the originals and he still wasn't sure if that wasn't just a ploy on the part of the killer to throw them off the scent. But what if it wasn't a ploy: what if he *was* linked in some bizarre way to the other twelve dolls? Maybe he'd been blind to that, too quick to convince himself that he was an add-on rather than an active part of the case.

Of the original twelve dolls, he now had the identity of five of them: the nurse, the fireman, the major, the poor bride and the teacher. The teacher was, of course, the only one still alive. These weren't random murders, Lapslie's instincts told him. They were planned. The killer had taken years to execute them; picking his victims off one at a time, carefully hiding the truth and never killing in the same way twice, knowing that patterns were what tipped the police off. He had made one big mistake, however: the dolls. For whatever reason he had needed to commemorate or celebrate his crimes. Or maybe he'd just been keeping score. With luck his warped sense of the dramatic and his arrogance would give Lapslie the link that would lead to his arrest.

The people – the victims – had to be linked. There had to be a common factor that involved them all. Discover that, and he would have his killer, of that he was sure.

Lapslie had arranged to meet Bradbury outside Richard Dale's widow's house. He had to start linking these killings. He needed to know this man better than his wife did. He needed to know everything. Name of his school or college. Sports and pastimes. Any enemies he might have had. And not just him, but his wife and family as well, just in case it was murder by association. He had dealt with quite a few of those in his time, and they were more common than was generally thought. People often tried to hurt other people by killing or hurting the people they loved. Lapslie supposed it was because the pain lasted, and was tinged with guilt as well. Mostly it happened in domestic murders: one party or the other killing the children to harm the other parent. Lapslie had learned early in his career that passion and emotion were the main causes of murder, and probably always would be.

Bradbury was already there when he arrived.

'Morning, Emma. Any more updates?'

She shook her head. 'Nothing since I phoned you yesterday to tell you about this bloke.'

'We'd better go in and see what we can find out.'

'What are we looking for?'

'Links. Anything that linked her husband to any of the other people that we now know have been murdered. Anything at all, no matter how small, insignificant, or even how stupid you might think it is. Got it?'

Bradbury nodded. 'Got it.'

They walked down the path together towards the small neat three-bedroom semi-detached house. Before they had a chance to knock, a little and pretty woman opened the door.

'Hello, Sergeant Bradbury?'

'Yes, sorry I'm a little late, Mrs Dale.' She turned to Lapslie. 'Can I introduce you to my boss: Detective Inspector Lapslie?'

Lapslie put out his hand and Mrs Kate Dale took it. She was shy and pleasant, and despite everything she had been through, her eyes were still full of life.

She stood to one side. 'Come in, please come in.'

Lapslie and Bradbury walked past Kate Dale and into the sitting room. The room was like the house: neat and clean. There was a strong smell of flowers, so thick that Lapslie could feel it on his tongue. He wasn't sure if it was Kate Dale's voice or an air-freshener set on overdrive.

They both sat down on the settee and waited for Kate Dale to join them. After a few moments Lapslie called out to her, 'Mrs Dale, are you okay?'

As he went to stand, she finally entered the room, a tray of tea and biscuits in her hands. She put them down on the small coffee table in front of the two detectives. 'Sorry, I thought you might like some tea. I know I do.'

She poured three cups of tea and handed two of them to the detectives. Lapslie noticed that the cups were made of fine china. He smiled. She reminded him of his aunt, when he went for tea on a Sunday with his parents. They sat in a front room that was never used unless guests were coming round, drank from china cups and ate from china plates. The cups and plates were also only ever used for visitors. It was all to do with respect and place in society. Standards were maintained, no matter what. The vicar might pop round for tea at any moment. He had a sudden flash of memory of watching his grandmother cleaning the front doorstep, which she did every Saturday morning. He remembered her ample backside swaying from side to side as she polished.

He forced himself back to reality. 'Mrs Dale . . .'

She cut in. 'Kate.'

'Kate. I need to know as much as you can remember about your late husband. It is very important.'

She put her cup back down on its saucer and looked disarmingly into Lapslie's eyes. 'Mr Lapslie, is there something you need to tell me? If there is, please do me the respect of getting on with it.'

Lapslie knew she was right. There was no point playing games with her. He might as well just tell her the stark truth and hope the shock became something positive rather than negative. 'We believe your husband was murdered,' he said simply.

Bradbury looked at Lapslie, shocked at his bluntness, and then at Kate Dale to see what the effect on her had been. She was unmoved.

'I thought he must have been,' she said quietly.

Lapslie was intrigued. 'Why?'

'Two things . . .'

'They are?'

'The first one is very practical: there was nobody better on a ladder than Richard. He would never have fallen off – never. Secondly, and I know you're going to laugh at me, but I just had a feeling that something was wrong.'

'I'd never laugh at you, Kate. I'm a big believer in feelings, or at least in things that can't be catalogued and analysed, but I still have to ask the questions.'

She looked at him for a moment, then stood. 'I think I might be able to save you doing that.'

She walked over to a sideboard and pulled out a drawer. Bradbury and Lapslie looked at each other. She pulled a blue A4 file from the drawer and handed it to Lapslie. 'You'll find what you're looking for in here.'

Lapslie opened it, intrigued but wary. A bold claim, somewhat weird; but Kate Dale said it in such a calm, down-to-earth manner.

The file contained a collection of newspaper cuttings

concerning the death and burial of her husband, fireman Richard Dale. After flicking through the file, Lapslie looked up at her, puzzled. 'So where would the name be?'

She shook her head. 'I'm not sure. You'll have to find it, but it is in there.'

Lapslie was confused. 'But how do you know?'

'You said you believe in feelings, Chief Inspector?'

Lapslie nodded. 'Yes. Yes, I do.'

'Then take my word for it, I have a feeling that what you are looking for is in there.'

He had a good idea what Lapslie had in mind, but he had to be sure. He wasn't often wrong but it had happened in the past, with near-disastrous consequences.

Having established routes and transport links on the internet, he parked his car in the second from nearest railway-station car park, took the bus until he was about a mile from the Teacher's cottage, and then walked the rest of the way. He had also disguised himself. Nothing heavy: just enough to smear his identity a bit.

As he turned onto the road he saw that he was right. The dark Transit van parked halfway along the road was carefully anonymous, but it was parked beneath an advertising hoarding, and the beautiful model whose photograph was on the poster was pointing downwards directly at it. Anybody else would have thought she was indicating the words of the advert, but he knew differently. She was communicating with him, and only him.

Further down the road, three men were slowly and painstakingly setting up a plastic barrier around a broadband routing box. Now that he had been alerted, he could see that they were obviously detectives.

The security surrounding Turner impressed him. It would be harder to get to him now. Harder, but still necessary. Time was creeping on. Lapslie would already be trying to establish the links between the victims, and as soon as the policeman did that it would all be over. He had to act fast and decisively, before it was too late.

He carried on walking along the street and past Turner's cottage. He'd put a stone in one of his shoes to change the way that he walked. As he limped along, near to the cottage, he noticed a car approaching, and his heart began to race as he recognized Lapslie in the passenger seat, and Bradbury driving. Lapslie looked him straight in the face but still failed to recognize him. As the car went past he glanced at the number plate. The last three letters were TTW. Something told him that the letters weren't a coincidence. They were a message. They meant something.

TTW.

Of course. TTW. Take The Wife.

Now he knew how he was going to get to both Turner and Lapslie, finish his quest and still get away. All he had to do was to kidnap the Teacher's wife from the hospital. That would bring them both to him.

He walked on, elated. Who would have thought that it would be Lapslie who would give him such inspiration?

Lapslie needed to check on the protection team for Tony Turner, make sure all was well. He had not only arranged for the teacher to receive twenty-four-hour protection, but had made sure there was someone on Elizabeth Turner's private ward at all times. Other officers, including snipers, had been posted at various places, watching all the time for a sniper on the off-chance he decided to follow that method once again. He'd all but given up on it being Mike Stowell, was convinced now that he'd simply been put in the frame, but as belt and braces Barrett and Kempsey remained on Stowell's tail.

Bradbury parked the car behind the surveillance van and Lapslie quickly moved from one to the other while Bradbury stayed where she was.

The inside of the van looked like a control room at NASA. It was manned by four highly trained officers on a rotating three-shift system. They all looked like they had been shelled from the same pea-pod.

'Everything okay, boys?'

They turned as one. 'All fine here, boss.'

'Anything happening?'

They shook their heads together. Lapslie couldn't help feeling they would make a great music-hall act. 'What, nothing at all?'

One of them broke from the anonymity of the trio to say: 'We've had several people with no tax and insurance . . .'

Emboldened, another chipped in: 'And a couple of cars with no MOT.'

'This isn't a traffic detail, guys. This is a major murder inquiry, and you're an important part of it.'

The third man spoke, defensively. 'We have got a couple of outstanding warrants . . .'

The first one again. 'One of those was for shoplifting, theft . . .'

He stopped speaking when he noticed how dark Lapslie's face had become.

'Okay. Right. No more traffic, no more warrants, no

more anything. Just do your job and feed all the information to the control room. They will decide what to do or whether anything needs to be followed up. If it's immediate action you need, there are armed officers pretending to be workmen outside, and several armed patrols in and around the locality. If you do want to transfer to traffic, please let me know, and I will arrange it at once. Clear?'

They all nodded obediently. Satisfied he had made his point, Lapslie jumped back out of the van and drove away.

He was pleased to see that he had been proved correct. Walking past Turner's cottage to see what the police were up to had certainly been a risk, but one he was glad now he had taken. He was sure that similar arrangements had been made at the school, and for close but not obvious protection wherever Turner went. If Lapslie and the police thought they had covered all their angles, they were wrong, and had no idea who they were dealing with.

He had travelled to the hospital by bus, and kept his disguise on. Hospitals these days were rife with CCTV cameras, and it was hard to walk anywhere without being noticed and filmed. He made a mental note of each camera and its position as he passed it by.

From the moment he walked up the hospital steps and into the main foyer, he knew he was under observation. It was nothing serious, they were hardly likely to pick him out as a possible killer by the way he was dressed and looked, but if anything happened they would play the recordings back and look for anything unusual. From the main entrance hall he turned left, walking along a hospital corridor for over a hundred yards before taking the lift to the first floor. Stepping out of the lift, he crossed the corridor into the fire-escape stairwell and took the steps to the third floor. He wanted to see how many cameras, if any, were situated inside the fire escape, monitoring the stairs. As he suspected, there were none. They were on every ward, all the hospital entrances, in the lifts, in the main stairwells, and yet for some reason the fire escape had been forgotten.

Finally reaching the third floor, he walked though Ward DC3. He noticed an empty bed with the bedding stripped down, but still retaining its name plate, with the name 'Mr David Johnson' neatly written across it. Made a mental note of the name. There was, however, no sign of Elizabeth Turner.

He walked through the wards and back out onto the corridor at the far side to where the private single rooms were situated. The moment he walked onto the corridor, he knew she was there. Parked outside the third ward down was an armed police officer reading a newspaper.

A voice from behind interrupted his thoughts. 'Can I help you at all?'

He turned quickly, to be confronted with a blue-uniformed nurse, not unlike the one he had murdered a few years before. Attractive, fresh-faced, yet so earnest.

'Yes, I rather think you can.' He had changed the pitch of his voice to sound weak and rather confused. 'I am looking for my cousin, David Johnson.'

A look of concern flashed across the nurse's face. 'Oh dear. I'm so sorry. You have just missed him: he was discharged just over an hour ago.'

'I thought he was due to be in much longer than that.'

She smiled. 'He was, but he has made a very quick recovery, so the doctors have sent him home.'

He smiled at her. 'Well, I suppose that's very good news.'

He turned and looked at the police officer, still reading his newspaper and apparently unconcerned about events happening a little further down the corridor. 'Well, I had better pop around and see him at home, then.'

The nurse's smiled broadened. 'I'm sure he will be glad to have a visitor, there haven't been too many since he's been here.'

'Well, that's not very nice, is it?' He smiled. 'Thank you very much, you've been a great help.'

He nodded politely and walked back along the corridor and

towards the lift. As he did, his gaze swept across every poster on the walls and every notice attached to the noticeboards. Somewhere there were the words that would tell him what to do next. Somewhere there he would find his instructions.

The latest news from the incident room was good. Two more of the victims had been identified. One was a mechanic, Michael Cohen, murdered in 2008, and the other was a fisherman, Gordon Campbell, killed in 2009, although there was still a little doubt about that latter one and some of the facts still needed to be confirmed.

The killer had been killing at least one person a year for seven years or more. Leaving a gap was almost certainly part of his strategy, in order to try and throw the police, or perhaps the media, off his scent. He was very careful, this one. He took his time, took care. He wasn't your average serial killer. These appeared to be random murders born out of some strange compulsion, but done in a very controlled way.

In Lapslie's time he had dealt with a few cases like these. 'Catch me before I kill again, I dare you.' There was something inside these people that drove them to kill. Some desire that needed to be satisfied; something so strong that it could only be released by killing and torturing. After they had killed once, it was normally enough to satisfy them for a while, sometimes for years. They felt genuine remorse, for a while, but, like wife-beaters who swear they will never do it again, the desire and the provocation returns. And, as time goes on, the intervals grow less between each killing. Bad for the victims, but good for the police, because it's then the killers start to cut corners, take chances and inevitably make the mistake that gets them caught.

Something told Lapslie, however, that this killer wasn't like that. Lapslie knew there was never going to be any panic, no mistakes, just everything planned to perfection right up until the end. This evil bastard had been killing since 2007, and they had only just discovered him, and only then because of a piece of unusual luck. Then on top there was the frame-up with Stowell to throw them off the trail to consider. All in all it pointed to a meticulous, methodical killer, the like of whom he'd rarely seen before.

He finally arrived at police HQ and parked. He made his way up to the incident room and into his office, closing the door behind him and putting the 'Do Not Disturb' sign up. He hoped people would respect it. They didn't always, and that was why he needed Bradbury there when he was working, but he had no idea where she was right now.

He sat down and opened the report waiting for him on his desk. It was from Bradbury. Two sides of A4 explaining in some detail how they had come across the murders of the mechanic and the fisherman, who'd discovered them, and how. He sat back and began to read. Before he'd got halfway, however, there was a gentle knock on his door and Bradbury poked her face around.

'Shall I come back after you've had time to finish it, boss?'

Lapslie shook his head and waved her in. 'No, come in, come in. I'll only be a second.'

After a further ten minutes he closed the report and put it onto his desk. He looked across at Bradbury. 'Good report. I see it was young DC McMurdo who was responsible for identifying the mechanic?'

Bradbury nodded. 'Yes, she's doing well.'

Lapslie nodded. 'Keep a close eye on her. She's going places.' He glanced at his watch. 'It's getting late. Let's call it a day; start afresh tomorrow.'

'I think I'll stick around for a while,' she said, not making eye contact. 'Catch up on some paperwork.'

'Careful,' he teased, 'I wouldn't want Dom McGinley to think I might be this *other* man. He has a way of making a point that involves sharp knives and concrete.' As he saw a shadow cross her face, he became more serious. 'Sorry. How's it going on that front? Made any decisions yet?'

'Yes, actually,' Emma said, the words emerging as reluctantly as pulled teeth, 'as of last night Dom and I are . . . taking a break. Reassessing our relationship.'

'And was this your suggestion, or McGinley's?'

'Mine,' she said, meeting his gaze steadily.

'Ah, I see.' An uncomfortable afterthought struck him. 'Does McGinley actually *know* you're taking a break? I imagine that would be a difficult conversation to have.'

'And one that has yet to occur,' Bradbury said. 'I'm waiting for the right moment.'

The only ideal time for that might be on McGinley's deathbed, Lapslie thought, but left it unsaid. 'So this is a sort of halfway house – until you're decided what to do?'

'Yes, I suppose you could say that. A halfway house.'

Lapslie knew when he'd had enough. He wasn't physically tired, but mentally he felt exhausted. He wasn't thinking straight at a time when he really needed to be at the top of his game. The inquiry was difficult enough, and although he felt he was getting there, albeit ever so slowly, he knew he wasn't getting there fast enough. The killer was a man with a mission: there was a point to his killings to link their otherwise random nature, even though Lapslie had no idea yet what it was. He needed time to think and re-energize himself, so on the way to meet George the next morning at Clacton Marina to check the boat over, he decided to take it out for a quick sail.

'Do you want me with you?' George asked. 'I've got a spare few hours.'

'No, George, thanks. I'm only going to take her out locally – probably won't shift more than a few miles offshore.'

George nodded. 'I took her out myself for an hour yesterday afternoon. But I suppose at least it will give you a chance to test-run yourself that everything's okay.'

'I'm sure it is.' Lapslie smiled tightly.

George said his goodbyes and handed him the keys. 'Don't forget to furl all the sails in fully and lock all the hatches.'

'I won't.'

The weather forecast was for a fine day with medium winds. Lapslie took a fresh breath of the sea air as

George left, but most of all he was breathing in the fresh air of being alone at last. And as minutes later he steered out of the harbour, cut the engine and pulled the sails round, he took another fresh breath. Isolated. Alone. Apart from finally being away from onshore activity and the confusion of thoughts that went with it, the other advantage about being on a boat was, of course, that he was out of the way of the killer. He didn't have to think about looking over his shoulder.

Nevertheless, having already gone round the boat with George to inspect the repairs made, as soon as he weighed anchor in a quiet spot two miles from the shoreline, he again searched from stem to stern so see if anything had been fiddled with, or any unexpected packages hidden away. There was nothing: the uncluttered boat was just as he had left it a few days beforehand. Taking a pair of binoculars, he scanned the shoreline, but nobody appeared to be taking any undue interest in him. There were fishermen and birdwatchers, of course – there always were – but they seemed legitimate.

After making himself a quick tea, he lay back on a bunk and began to flick through the file Kate Dale had given him on her husband. Although she seemed convinced that all the answers Lapslie was searching for were to be found within these pages and clippings, Lapslie wasn't so sure. He would, however, at least give Mrs Dale the courtesy of reading everything and seeing what he could find.

He hadn't slept well the night before, thoughts about the case revolving in his mind. He found himself rubbing his eyes at points as he read now, and after an hour or so, what with the gentle rocking of the boat, he dozed off and started to dream. Lapslie rarely dreamed, or rather he hardly ever remembered his dreams on waking. It was only since he had begun sailing that they had suddenly become so vivid. Things came and disappeared: people, faces, numbers, symbols, all jumbled up and doing odd things. Dancing, pulling strange faces, exploding into a million brightly coloured flowers. Weird items disappeared into caves and called for him to follow. There was no sense to any of it.

Suddenly Lapslie was awake again. How long had passed? Two hours, three? And what was it that had disturbed him, made him reawaken suddenly?

He lay there and listened for a moment, trying to make out any unusual noises. Maybe someone had rowed up and climbed on the boat, setting it rocking. He waited, senses all on alert, but there was nothing.

Just the gentle rocking of the boat and the sound of the water slapping against the hull.

It took a moment or two, but Lapslie realized that what had woken him was not external, but internal. It was something to do with the file; something he'd read and not consciously appreciated.

He reached across and picked up the file again. Something – he couldn't tell what – drew him to the page that contained the report on Richard Dale's funeral. He read through it again. It was a moving account, but there was nothing that might indicate who his killer was. How could there be?

He moved on to the column beneath the report, the one with all the names of the mourners who had attended the funeral. It was then that he noticed it. Four names: Jack and Amelia Summers, Arlene Campbell and Joseph Cohen.

Summers, Campbell and Cohen. They were the surnames of three of the other victims – Anne, Gordon and Michael: the nurse, the fisherman and the mechanic. It couldn't be a coincidence, could it? This had to be what Kate Dale had been talking about.

He had found his link. Now he had to get back, and in a hurry.

PART NINE

4 January 2014

John Robert Lyon was a solicitor, and was proud to be one.

He hadn't always been a solicitor. He had been a police officer for ten years, but a good kicking received during the miners' strike had changed all that. Before then he had been one hundred per cent fit, and could run five miles carrying a riot shield. After that, with a damaged spine to deal with, he couldn't even run for a bus.

The police had done what they could. They had offered a position doing community work, but it wasn't him. He hadn't joined the police to be a social worker.

In the end, he decided to go to university and at least give himself time to think. He applied for and was accepted at Trinity College, Cambridge, to read Geography. After doing summer school in his first year he changed to a Law degree, which had been his aim from the start. It was far easier to move sideways into a Law degree from an existing course than it was to chance getting in cold from the start.

After that, it was easy. He worked hard and did well, getting a good 2:1 degree. On graduation, and because of his police background, he was soon picked up by a firm of solicitors in a small market town in Essex, and from there he went from strength to strength. He was now a partner in his own law firm, and really going places.

One look at the amount of work he had lined up for the week made him sit back at his desk and sigh. It was one of those situations where the work seemed so overwhelming you didn't know where to start, so in the end you did nothing. Finally, in a fit of despair, he did what he always did: went to get a large mug of coffee from Cosmo's Coffee House across the road, and hope all the free newspapers hadn't been taken. He would take an hour out for lunch and sort it out when he got back, refreshed.

Taking the stairs to the ground floor and waving at the receptionist, he crossed the road, ordered his coffee, grabbed the tatty last copy of the Mail and found himself a quiet table with a large easy chair in the corner. There was only one other person at the table, and he was as engrossed in his paper as John Lyon was.

At some stage the man opposite got up and left, but Lyon

didn't really register his disappearance. He was engrossed in
the report of a long-running litigation case at Southwark Crown
Court when he suddenly began to have trouble breathing. It was
as if there was some spiky obstruction in his throat. He tried to
cough it out, but it made no difference. He stood up, staggering,
and headed across to the coffee counter to get a glass of water,
but he never made it. The darkness closed in too fast.

His last thought was that he ought to sue Cosmo's Coffee
House for the poor state of the coffee they provided.

It took Lapslie longer than he had hoped to get back to
force HQ. Bradbury was working at her desk when he
arrived. He knocked loudly on the glass, she looked up
and he beckoned her into his office. He handed her the
scrapbook. 'Read the list of names at the bottom of the
page. That's all the people that went to Richard Dale's
funeral in 2008.'

Bradbury did as she was bid.

Lapslie continued. 'Take a special look at the last few
names.'

Bradbury concentrated, and then realized what she
was reading. 'Bloody hell, that's a bit of a coincidence,
isn't it?' She looked up at Bradbury. 'Do you think they
are related?'

Lapslie shrugged. 'Can't be a hundred per cent sure until you've checked them out, but my gut tells me they are.'

'And *if* they are, then it might give us the link we've been looking for, which should—'

Lapslie cut her short. 'Give us the name of our killer. Right.'

Bradbury read through the list again, just to make sure there was no one else that Lapslie might have missed. There wasn't. 'Okay, I'll get onto it at once.'

'Start with the Cohens. I think the Sampsons are dead. Failing that, have a good look at Campbell.'

Bradbury nodded her understanding. 'Right. I will.'

Lapslie was as impatient as ever. 'How long do you think it will take you?'

Bradbury looked at her watch. 'A couple of hours, maybe less.'

'Maybe less sounds good.' Lapslie nodded. 'Whoever he is, he's nobody's fool, and I'm still worried that no matter how much security I put around Turner our killer will still get through it.'

Bradbury nodded grimly, and Lapslie watched her return to her desk. It was all down to her now, and how quickly she could make the association. She was a bloody good detective, and if anyone could do it, she could.

Lapslie was sure he was close to catching his man. He could almost touch him. He knew it was a race against time. Every second counted. The killer planned, and planned carefully. If he hadn't also been a little theatrical they probably would never have made the connections. But he was human, he made mistakes, and it was up to Lapslie to capitalize on those mistakes and make him pay the price for what he had done.

He looked out at Bradbury once last time. It was all down to her now.

He had finished making his plans. He had discovered over the years that you always had to identify the point where any further planning would just be counter-productive. It was possible to overplan, to make things much more complicated than they should be, to build in layers and layers of contingency that just served to create more points where something could go wrong. Keeping it simple but effective was what he did best and this policy had served him well for years.

He ran through a final mental checklist. Handcuffs: three pairs. Ball gag. Blindfold. Duct tape. Body bag. Taser. Nine mm handgun with hollow-point ammunition and home-made silencer. White coat. Stethoscope. Syringe, two spare needles. That was it.

The car had been hired under a false driver's licence, and there was a gallon of petrol in a jerrycan in the back. He was all set.

Oh yes, one more thing: his Doctor on Emergency Call sign for the front dashboard of the car. After all his careful planning, it would be ridiculous to get clamped.

He laughed to himself. Despite what he was about to do, he could still see the funny side.

He parked his car as planned, right outside the hospital fire escape. Slipping his Doctor on Emergency Call sign on top of the dashboard, he stepped out of the car, leaving it unlocked, and pushed his shoulder against the fire-escape door. If he had planned it correctly, and if his bolt obstructor was still in place, stopping the fire door being locked properly without it being too obvious, it should open.

He was in luck: the door gave way easily, and he stepped inside. Once at the foot of the concrete staircase, he slipped on his white coat, hung his stethoscope around his neck, clipped on his identity badge, slipped his handgun into a small holster attached to the back of his trousers and dropped the silencer into his coat pocket. He then began to climb the stairs.

He knew which floor Elizabeth Turner was on from his previous reconnaissance. This time he would exit the fire escape *from the west wing of the hospital, which would bring him out only yards from her private bedroom and save him having to walk through any of the wards.*

As he reached the door leading out into the main corridor, he looked through the window. It gave him a partial view along the corridor, but he couldn't see who or how many police officers were outside Turner's room. Taking the pistol from its holster, he screwed on the home-made silencer, making sure it was on tightly. Every move he now made had to be done quickly and without thought, but with pure concentration. He had done it a hundred times before, in training. He'd held the record, for a while at least, for the fastest time.

The idea of killing anyone apart from his chosen target nauseated him, but he knew he had no choice. God was willing for there to be some collateral damage on the way to the completion of his quest. That had been the title of a film on at the cinema when he had driven past: Collateral Damage. *A shop in the high street that specialized in cash converting – a pawnshop under a new brand – had a sign in the window that said* All Loans Require Collateral, *while the car-repair shop next door had a sign saying* Damage to Your Motor? Get it Repaired Here! *God was telling him it was all right.*

He breathed in and out deeply several times, and then made his move.

He stepped out from the emergency stairwell and immediately put two shots through the head of the constable who stood outside the room. The 'double tap'.

He caught the constable's body before it fell and manoeuvred it through the door of the side room. A female constable was standing there, talking to Elizabeth Turner. He let the first constable's body slide as he shot the woman, again twice. She went down without a sound with a look of astonishment on her face. Her eyes stayed open, staring blankly back towards him.

He swung the gun around and pointed it at Elizabeth Turner. 'Scream and I'll kill you.' He said it with such fierce determination that it was clear he meant it.

She nodded her understanding, trying hard not to react to the horror she had just witnessed.

'Get up.'

Elizabeth Turner stepped out of bed and faced him. She was wearing pyjamas.

'Put this on.' He threw her dressing gown over to her. She caught it and slipped it on quickly.

'Turn around.'

She turned quickly.

'Put your hands behind your back. Move.'

She did as she was told. He quickly snapped a pair of handcuffs over her wrists. Grabbing her by the hair, he pushed his gun under her chin. 'Do as you are told, my dear, and you will survive this. If you don't, I will blow your head from here to Kingdom Come. Do I make myself clear?'

Elizabeth Turner nodded. He could feel her convulsive trembling.

'Right, then let's go.'

He knew he had to be quick. He couldn't be sure how long it was going to be before someone checked on the room, or wondered where the constables had gone. The last thing he wanted to do was start killing doctors and nurses, but if he had to, he would.

Pushing her ahead of him, he returned to the corridor. The blood from the police officer's head had splashed against the wall: he hadn't noticed that earlier. The corridor was clear. Still pushing her ahead of him, he made his way back onto the fire escape and down the stairs. He had a momentary panic when he wondered if his car had remained unmolested, or whether some fool had either stolen it or clamped it. It's the little things that trip you up.

He pushed the fire door open. The car was still there. He opened the car boot and pushed Elizabeth Turner inside. She tried to say something, but he ignored her, slamming the boot shut and jumping into the driver's seat. Once there he struggled to remove his white coat and stethoscope, turned the ignition key and drove away.

He didn't drive quickly: just nice and steady. He didn't want to draw attention to himself. Within a few minutes he was outside the hospital grounds and on the main road. So far everything had gone well. All he had to do now was drive to the woods where he had left his own car and transfer the woman into its boot, before emptying the petrol over the interior of the hire car and setting it alight. Yet another burned-out car in the Essex woods: they were getting to be more numerous than the badgers.

The first part of his plan was now complete. The next stage now had to be contemplated very seriously indeed.

It had taken Bradbury more than two hours to check out the first two names. Grace and Jack Summers had been the parents of Jane Summers, the nurse strangled in July 2007. Although she had made the link, and it was an important one, it was as far as she could take it for now. Both parents had died within a few years of their daughter's murder. The only chance she had now was to try and locate any surviving family and see if that led anywhere. The problem was it was all going to take time, and that they just didn't have. If the next two inquiries took as long as the Summers' had to complete, their final witness would be dead and buried before they got the lead they needed, and the killer would be stalking Lapslie.

There was only one answer as far as she could see. She walked back into Lapslie's office.

Lapslie looked up. 'You sorted it out?'

'Only up to a point.'

He pointed to the chair that faced his desk. 'Take a seat.'

Bradbury sat. 'Well, the good news is that Grace and Jack Summers are the parents of the murdered nurse Jane Summers . . .'

'And the bad news?'

'They are both dead, and it will take days to track down any remaining family, and even then they might not know anything.'

'What about the other names?'

Bradbury shrugged. 'Still searching. We'll find them but it's going to take time . . .'

'And your solution is?'

'For the sake of time, I think we need to go back and see Kate Dale . . .'

'You think she might know something more?'

'No idea, but she was right about the answer being inside the scrapbook, even though she didn't know what it was.'

'So when we point out what it is, it might stir some memories?'

Bradbury nodded. 'Exactly. We *will* get there the way we are doing it now but it's going to take time . . .'

'Which we don't have.'

'Right. If Kate Dale knows something, anything, then it might get us to our killer that bit quicker. It's got to be worth a chance. The team are still following up on the other names in the book, so that part of the inquiry won't stall. What have we got to lose?'

Lapslie thought for a moment then stood. 'Okay, let's get going. Like you said: not a moment to lose.'

Ignoring the speed limits and the flashing speed cameras, Lapslie and Bradbury arrived outside Kate Dale's house in record time. Bradbury had tried to ring her from the car but there was no reply, which was a worry, though there could be a thousand reasons for that. Pulling up outside her home, both detectives sprinted down the short path to her front door. Before they could knock, however, the door opened and Kate stood before them.

'I was right, then,' she said before they could open their mouths. 'The answer *was* inside the book?'

Lapslie nodded. 'Almost. Let's go inside, and I'll explain.'

The two detectives walked into the sitting room. Without bothering to sit down, Lapslie turned to Kate Dale. 'Kate, you were right about the book. We discovered some names inside that we need your help with.'

She nodded expectantly. 'Anything.'

'Do the names Summers, Cohen and Campbell mean anything to you?' Lapslie searched her face for any sign of recognition. There was none. He tried again. 'They were in your scrapbook. They went to your husband's funeral. Jack and Amelia Sampson, Arlene Campbell and Joseph Cohen.'

'The Campbells, I remember. So sad – they lost their daughter a few years before Richard died.'

'How did you know them?'

She shook her head. 'I didn't really. They were friends of Richard's father. I met them at a barbecue at Richard's parents' house. They were a very nice couple.'

'In what way were they friends with Richard's parents?'

'They were on the same jury as his father.'

'Jury?'

'Yes. It was a murder case that went on for a while, so they all got to know each other quite well. It took them a fortnight to come to a verdict, so they were all stuck in the same hotel together. Some of them kept in touch after that. They used to go on holiday together.'

Bradbury cut in with what she thought was the obvious question. 'Can you remember the name of the defendant?'

Kate shook her head. 'No, sorry, but I think he was found not guilty, if that helps.'

'Not guilty?' Bradbury was surprised. She had already begun to formulate a theory about a vengeance-crazed killer killing off jury members, but Kate's last statement had just blown the theory to hell. 'Can you remember when the trial took place?'

Kate shook her head again. 'No. But it was a while ago.'

'Before 2007?'

Lapslie's mobile rang. With a muffled apology, he answered it, indicating with a wave of his hand that Bradbury should continue the interview.

Kate nodded. 'I think so. Can't you check?'

'We can,' Bradbury said. 'What about Richard's father: do you think he would remember?'

'No, he died last year. He was a strong man, but Richard's death broke him. Bit like the Summerses and their daughter.'

Bradbury nodded sympathetically. She couldn't think of anything else to ask. 'I'm sorry: I'm afraid we have to go. If anything else comes to mind please call us as quickly as you can.'

She nodded. 'I will.' She suddenly looked torn. 'When will I get my scrapbook back?'

Without knowing Lapslie's plans, Bradbury extemporized. 'I'll get one of the team to drop it around to you over the next couple of days.'

'Will you let me know what happens?

Bradbury nodded. 'That's a promise . . .'

Before she could say any more, Lapslie called across. He had his hand over the mobile's microphone. 'We have to get to the hospital. There's been an incident.'

He had taken a leaf out of Lapslie's book when it came to buying his home. It was isolated. His nearest neighbour was over two miles away, and you could only reach the house via a mile-long dirt road at the end of which was an electronic gate and video camera. He had the house surrounded with cameras.

He slowed as he approached the electronic gate, and used his remote control to open it. It swung away from him silently. He drove in, and glanced in his rear-view mirror to check that it was closing properly. Approaching the garage door, he used another remote control to open that door and parked the car inside. The garage was built against the side of his house, with a connecting door allowing him to come and go by car without actually having to step outside. Once he was parked up and the door firmly closed he made his way to the boot and pulled Elizabeth Turner out by her hair, slapping her hard when she struggled. He had to keep her terrified: that way she would remain under his control and was less likely to do anything stupid, like try to escape. He looked into her face.

'There are rules. You speak only when I tell you to. If you do anything I don't like, then I will shoot you like I would shoot a rabid dog. Do I make myself clear?'

She went to speak, 'Ye . . .' but then thought better of it and nodded her head instead.

He smiled. 'Good. We are getting to understand each other.'

With that, and still pulling her by the hair, he dragged her into his kitchen, and from there into the cellar. The cellar was dark and smelled of damp, but it was clean. He prided himself on keeping things clean, neat and tidy.

A single mattress was pushed up against the far wall. Above the mattress was a large metal hoop, which had been fixed into the wall about two feet above the ground. Pulling her over to it, he threw her onto the mattress, pushing her face down. With his knee pushed firmly into her back, he released the handcuffs *from her hands, but it wasn't to be for long. Spinning her around, he attached her hands to the metal hoop with the handcuffs. She wouldn't meet his gaze: her eyes were red and weepy, and she was making a sad snuffling sound. He pulled at her hands to make sure the cuffs were tight enough and then, without another word, he made his way back up the stone staircase to the kitchen.*

As he reached the top of the stairs, he looked back briefly. She really was a beautiful woman, and she had a magnificent body which she clearly looked after. What the hell was she doing with a teacher? She could have done so much better.

When it was her time, he decided, he would make it quick. Probably while she was sleeping. She had suffered enough.

He finally turned the cellar light off and closed the door, tightly locking and bolting it. He listened for a while. At first there was only the sound of her breathing, but then he heard a series of muffled sobs that sounded like her heart was being torn out.

The 'incident' was the shooting of two police officers and the kidnapping of Elizabeth Turner from the local general hospital. By the time Lapslie and Bradbury arrived, the place was teeming with people. Not just the murder squad, SOCOs and uniforms, but more press than Lapslie could ever remember seeing before. At least six TV cameras, countless photographers and more reporters than you could shake a shitty stick at.

After having their names taken and the registration number of their car recorded by the booking officer, Lapslie and Bradbury were waved through and directed to a parking place. After that they were escorted from their car to the corridor where the double murder and the kidnapping had occurred.

Jeff Whitefoot, the police surgeon whom Lapslie had last seen at the decommissioned nuclear bunker, standing over the body of the tramp, was just leaving, grim-faced and as purposeful as ever. Behind him, Jim Thomson, the senior SOCO, appeared, holding two light blue overalls and cover shoes.

'Put these on and keep to the platforms when you're crossing the scene.'

They kept to the platforms, which raised their feet above the floor and stopped them contaminating it. Entering the hospital room, Lapslie was struck by the smell of faecal matter. It was the unacknowledged result of sudden death: the bowels and bladder voided themselves. Nobody ever told the families, of course. It was a secret of the job.

Lapslie stopped by the first body and looked down at it. There were two distinct holes in the head where the bullets had entered, but no obvious exit wounds. There was a look of complete shock on the officer's face. His life had been snuffed out in an instant and he must have had no idea of what had happened to him, yet somewhere deep in his subconscious the fact that he had lost his life so suddenly, so unexpectedly, had sent a shock through the rest of his body. This awful despair manifested itself through his face, twisting it into the ugly mask Lapslie could now see before him. This man was not at rest, nor would ever be: he'd lost too much too early.

Bradbury cut into his thoughts. 'PC Tom Spencer.'

Lapslie nodded. There was nothing he could say. Even now, after all these years and all the death he had dealt with, there was still something appalling at seeing one of your own lying dead, murdered in the service of his community. The truth was, it could have been any of them, at any time.

Bradbury continued: 'He was married, with a young son.'

Lapslie stood slowly, and turned to the second body. The female constable lay flat on her back, her face staring blankly up at the ceiling.

'PC Susan Cradock.'

Despite her efforts to conceal it, Lapslie detected a strong hint of emotion in Bradbury's voice. He looked across at her and caught her wiping something from her eye. 'You okay?'

She nodded. 'Yes.'

'Did you know her?'

Bradbury nodded. 'Yes, I went to her wedding.'

'Good police officer?'

'The very best. Top of everything. She'd have been a chief constable one day, and not because she said the right things, but because she *did* the right things.'

Lapslie looked at her sympathetically. 'I can book you off the inquiry for a few days, if it helps.'

Bradbury's face hardened. 'No. I want this bastard like I've never wanted anyone before. I'll stay until it's over.'

Lapslie looked back at WPC Cradock. Her face seemed so much calmer than Spencer's. It was odd how two people could have died in the same way at the same time and yet look so different. He wondered bleakly whether in death personalities rose to the surface, imprinting themselves one final time.

'Can I have a word, Chief Inspector?'

Chief Superintendent Alan Rouse stood in the doorway, glaring at him. Whatever he wanted to say, Lapslie knew it wasn't going to be good. He followed Rouse out of the ward and into the fire-escape stairwell; the same one Elizabeth Turner had apparently been taken down when she was kidnapped.

'What the *fuck* has happened, Mark?'

'I'd have thought that was self-evident.'

'New question, then: *why* the fuck has it happened? Why only two constables, why wasn't she taken to a safe house? What the hell is going on?'

'She was guarded by two of our top firearms personnel. There were another four police officers outside the hospital. It's more than the book tells us to do.'

'But it wasn't enough, was it, Mark? We have two dead officers and a kidnapped victim, who we *should* have been looking after.'

'Whoever he is,' Lapslie pointed out, staring at the wall, 'he is not your average killer.' He sighed. 'I didn't see it coming. I thought his target would be her husband. It never occurred to me he would go for the wife.'

'No, it didn't, did it?' He made a growling noise, deep in his throat. 'What do you expect me to tell the media? They're all camped outside, waiting for a statement.'

'With respect, sir, that's *your* problem. *My* problem is finding Elizabeth Turner before something bad happens to her.'

'That's not your problem any more. I'm sorry, Mark, but I'm moving you to one side. I want you to be an adviser, not the senior investigating officer.'

Lapslie was stunned. *'What?'*

'It's nothing to do with your judgement, and it won't affect your permanent record.'

Lapslie felt anger growing within him. 'Then why? I'm close to an arrest, sir, I know I am.'

'Even if that was true, I need you to step back. I'm putting Alan Shaw in charge. He's ready for the move up.'

'Why?' Lapslie asked bluntly.

'Because you can't investigate the case if you are part of it.'

Silence, while Lapslie digested the words. 'You've heard about the thirteenth coffin, then?'

'I was told.'

'Who by?'

Rouse hesitated for a moment, obviously wondering whether or not to spill the beans. Eventually, he said: 'Jeff Whitefoot told me.'

'Jeff?' Lapslie sighed. He'd known the police surgeon

for years. It just went to prove that you couldn't trust anyone. 'I can still lead the inquiry. Knowing I might be a target doesn't frighten me.'

'It frightens *me*, Mark. I don't want you front and centre on the inquiry when some madman is taking aim. I can't afford to lose you. I want you somewhere isolated, protected. And need I point out that if you make an arrest, and if it comes out at the trial that you were a potential target, the defence solicitor will call "Foul!" and have the case thrown out?'

Lapslie sighed. He knew Rouse had a point, which was why he hadn't wanted the man to know. 'What about Sergeant Bradbury?' he asked.

'That's up to Inspector Shaw—'

Lapslie cut in. 'Make sure he keeps her on and I'll follow orders like a good little boy,' he said bitterly.

Rouse nodded. 'Agreed.'

Decision made, Rouse put his hand out. 'No hard feelings, Mark. I'm sure it will all be for the best. Shaw will make an arrest. What I want you to do is spend your time going over all your old cases. If this murderer wants you dead then he has a reason, and that reason must have to do with something from your past. Work out what it is.'

Lapslie shook the outstretched hand, turned and walked away without saying anything. He didn't trust himself to be diplomatically correct.

Lapslie knew he needed to get out of everyone's way, and away from the situation. The obvious place wasn't his rather remote cottage, but his boat. Few people knew its mooring place. He had no intention of going to sea, though.

He knew the next part of the inquiry was very much Bradbury's, and she would have to be quick about it. Lapslie didn't trust Rouse, or Shaw. They would want their own favourites in on a high-profile arrest like the one they were hoping for.

Lapslie spent most of the first day with George getting his boat out of the water and onto ramps ready for painting; the only remaining task that George had advised needed seeing to after the recent fix-up. He had picked up enough food to last for a day or so and was happy to sleep inside the boat's cabin overnight. In fact he rather enjoyed the experience. He just needed to keep himself busy until Bradbury turned up with news.

The next day was much like the last. He worked on the boat with George sanding and rubbing, but Bradbury didn't call. In the lull moments his mind drifted to his previous cases, trawling for someone who might want revenge, but it was hopeless. There were too many of them. His thoughts kept on circling back to Elizabeth Turner, kidnapped, and Tony Turner, her husband, who must be frantic with worry. Lapslie was too involved, and it mattered too much. Besides, he thought, what if Shaw did come up with the solution all on his own? What if Lapslie had been barking up the wrong tree all this time? That was the point, he decided, at which he would have to sail away into the sunset.

On the third day, Bradbury finally arrived. DCs Parkin and Pearce were with her. He took Bradbury to one side. 'What the hell are they doing here?'

'They've come to help.'

'Can they be trusted?'

Bradbury nodded. 'They can be trusted. They hate Shaw more than you do. Besides, as far as they are concerned, it's better the Devil you know.'

'Were you seen coming down here? If I were Rouse then I would have a surveillance team assigned to me, just in case the killer switches targets.'

Bradbury indicated Parkin and Pearce. 'Meet your observation team.'

'That must have taken some doing.'

'Just a bit of fiddling with the duty roster.'

Lapslie looked at them for a moment. 'Okay, all aboard and I'll get the kettle on . . .'

'Any chance of a bacon butty, sir?'

Halfway through his second bacon sandwich, Lapslie asked the obvious question.

'So how's Shaw getting on?'

'Reorganizing,' Bradbury replied.

'So . . . breaking up the team?'

Bradbury nodded. 'That's about it.'

Parkin said: 'Oh yes, this somehow managed to find its way into my bag. Must have fallen in as I left the office.' He handed Lapslie two large A4 envelopes. 'It's copies of all the relevant stuff from the inquiry. Names, addresses, phone numbers.'

Putting down her tea and clearing her throat, Bradbury continued: 'We discovered a few more things as well.'

'Go on.'

'Remember the people at Richard Dale's funeral: the ones that had all sat on the same jury?'

Lapslie nodded.

'Well, the trial they were on was in 2004. It was the trial of a man called Edward Dakker.'

'The rapist?'

'The *alleged* rapist. Remember, he was found not guilty.'

Lapslie shook his head. 'Like hell. Especially considering what happened.'

'Anyway, we've managed to track down the names of all the people on the jury.'

'Who were they?'

'Just normal, everyday people called for service, like thousands before and since. Anyway, obviously the evidence wasn't strong enough, so they released him . . .'

Lapslie was disturbed. 'I know, I remember. I was the senior investigating officer. I was gutted when he walked free. Couldn't understand it.'

'Well, whatever the reason, the jury did understand it. They made the decision.'

'But it isn't them being murdered, is it?'

Bradbury shook her head. 'No, it's their children.'

'It's their *what*?'

'Their *children*. Jane Summers, the nurse that was strangled, was, as we know, the daughter of Jack and Amelia Summers, and so it goes on. In every case bar one, our victims are the children of the members of the jury that found Dakker not guilty.'

'You say bar one. Who was that?'

'A model by the name of Clair Brett. She was the niece of a jury member, a man by the name of Colin Brett. Electrocuted and boiled in her own hot tub.'

'Why would Dakker have an interest in revenge? They found him not guilty. Besides, didn't he leave the country?'

'He did. He moved to Australia, where he raped and killed a nineteen-year-old student by the name of Alice Henry. In a church, apparently.'

Lapslie nodded gravely. 'I remember now. If only that bloody jury had done its job properly, she might still be alive.'

'I think that's what her father thought too.'

'You think her father is the killer?'

Bradbury nodded, and gave him an odd half smile. 'I'm sure of it.'

'But we have no suspects by the name of Henry.'

Bradbury continued. 'That's right, but that's only because her mother and father split up when she was small and she used her mother's maiden name of Henry.'

'So what's her real name?'

'Whitefoot.'

'But we have no suspects by the name of Whitefoot either,' Lapslie pointed out.

'But we do,' Emma Bradbury said quietly, 'have a police surgeon by the name of Whitefoot, don't we? Jeff Whitefoot.'

PART TEN

Now that he had decided to readjust his plans and kill the Teacher's Wife, it was only fair that he should make her a doll. He enjoyed making dolls, enjoyed the detailed, careful work that went into them. Of the various arts and crafts courses that had been offered to him by the psychiatrists treating him for depression after the death of his daughter, he had found doll-making to be the most therapeutic. Not that it had brought her back, of course. If it hadn't been for that damned jury, she would be with him now. She might even have given him grandchildren by now.

He had received the latest message from God as he was in the supermarket earlier, stocking up on supplies. This message wasn't indirect, or subtle. This one wasn't capable of being misinterpreted if he wasn't paying attention. It was aimed directly at him. As he had walked past a man pushing a trolley, he had distinctly heard the man say: 'She must give you your daughter back.' He had turned around, shocked, but the man had been looking at the shelves, not at him. He hadn't misheard,

*though, because moments later a loudspeaker had crackled to
life and a voice had said:* 'If a Mr Whitefoot is present,
could he please note that she should give him his daughter back. Thank you.'

*It was clear what God wanted from him. Before killing the
Teacher's Wife, he was to make her pregnant. He was going to
replace the daughter lost to him. Then it wouldn't just be death
that came out of his quest, it would be life as well.* That was
what God wanted. That had been the end of the plan all along,
not something negative, but something positive.

She seemed like a fit, strong girl, so getting her pregnant
shouldn't really be a problem. He was a doctor, after all, and he
had delivered more than a few children in his life, so that wasn't
going to be a problem. He would have to examine her to make
sure she wasn't concealing a contraceptive cap. If she was taking the pill, of course, then its effects would be dispelled very
quickly once she stopped, and there would, of course, be no
morning-after pill.

He had never been one-hundred-per-cent happy about all the
killings. They were necessary, he knew, and God had encour-
aged and protected him all along, but now, at the end of it all,
his journey had led him to life, rather than death. He felt the
same kind of relief that he imagined Abraham had felt when,
ordered by God to kill his son Isaac on Mount Moriah, the

instruction had been countermanded at the last minute. It had been a test of faith, and so was this.

With precise movements he continued making the doll. Because this had been one of the few last-minute decisions he had made in his life, he did not have Elizabeth Turner's clothes, so he was unable to make the doll anything to wear. In the end he decided to use sections of the hospital gown she had been wearing when he took her from the hospital. He had already cut a large chunk of hair from the back of her head and was threading it through the doll's head, so at least he had something of her in its creation.

Keeping her hidden for nine months was going to be the biggest problem. Getting rid of her body at the end should be relatively easy. He would need to buy her some clothes and blankets. Monitor her health, make sure she remained warm and healthy. There was a lot to think about. Once the baby was born he would finish her with a quick injection – probably insulin. Painless and quick. He would do it while she was sleeping.

Then again, he pondered, maybe he should let her live for a while in case something happened to the child and he had to start all over again.

So many possibilities, so many options. For the first time in a long time he felt . . . uncertain. Rather than remaining on the track that had defined his life for so many years, he had options now. Different routes. It would take time to get used to it.

The good thing was that if everything went to plan, then both Tony Turner and Lapslie should be dead before the end of the day. The police would soon get tired of looking for Elizabeth Turner – they always did in cases of disappearance, after the first few weeks had passed by. Then he would be home free. He would, of course, have to make sure they never discovered her body. All that would do was to stir things up again. He would leave the country with the child, set up home in Canada or Australia, where awkward questions would never be asked. Instead of living the rest of his life in misery, he actually had something to look forward to.

He finished the doll and examined it. It wasn't a bad likeness. He was pleased with his work. All he had to do now was make the coffin, and that was it. End of story.

This would be his last doll. He didn't want to make any more; he wanted to finish now. Finish with the killing. With a new grandchild to care for he could at last concentrate on the living. There would be light in his life, not darkness. It was a good feeling.

Standing, he walked across to his writing desk and began to write the last two letters, the ones that would bring an end to everything. Failing to plan was planning to fail.

He smiled to himself as he wrote. If the new child was a girl, and wanted dolls, then he wouldn't make them. He would just buy them.

They were parked just down the dirt road that led to Jeff Whitefoot's isolated house: Pearce and Parkin, armed, in one car; Lapslie and Bradbury in the other. Pearce and Parkin were legally armed, although not legally on duty in the area. Bradbury was illegally armed. Lapslie she wasn't sure about.

As Bradbury came off her mobile, Lapslie asked, 'So is everything still secure with Tony Turner?'

'Yes. They've got his place tied down as tight as a drum. Three men inside guarding, two outside. Whitefoot won't get to him easily.'

Lapslie nodded. As he'd instructed, he'd heard Bradbury inform the team guarding Tony Turner that the likely suspect was Whitefoot, so that they were forewarned who to look out for.

'Let's just hope it's enough.'

Bradbury eased out a slow breath and looked ahead. 'Are you sure this is a good idea, sir? You're supposed to be sidelined. If we notify Rouse, he could have an armed back-up team here within a half-hour.'

'Good ideas aren't always my strongest suit,' he said with a pained smile; then with a graver, less flippant tone, after a moment's deliberation: 'I want Whitefoot. I want him personally. I don't want to read about it on the news, or watch Alan Shaw get the plaudits for bringing him down. I know the man, had more than a few heartfelt heavy drinking sessions with him.' As he said it, he wondered whether that personal connection had blocked him reading the signals quicker: Whitefoot conveniently being at the original bunker scene with the tramp, the inside knowledge, the medical link, Whitefoot being the one to inform Rouse that Lapslie was the thirteenth doll, to get him off the investigation. The signs had all been there if he'd bothered to scratch deeper, and now he was partly blaming himself. He sighed. 'If you want out, go now. I wouldn't blame you. No point dragging yourself down with me.'

Bradbury looked away from him. 'You know I wouldn't do that. Go one, go all. Besides, the job wouldn't be the same without you.'

'What would you do?'

Bradbury shrugged, 'What *do* ex-cops do?'

Lapslie chuckled. 'Run a pub? Become a private investigator? Go into security?'

Bradbury laughed. 'I think I'd go back to college and teach.'

Lapslie was surprised. 'Teach! You'd end up smacking the little shits.'

'I was thinking that infants are much more controllable.'

Lapslie looked across at her. 'You haven't got any kids, have you?'

Bradbury shook her head. 'None that I'll admit to.'

'Thought not. If you had, then you wouldn't think infants would be a pushover.'

'I didn't say—'

Before she had time to finish, her radio crackled into life.

It was Pearce. 'In position. Ready when you are.'

Lapslie pulled the radio from Bradbury's hand. They'd made sure when briefing the team to establish a secure network. 'Make sure your safety catches are off.'

'Thanks for the advice, sir. Wouldn't have thought of that.'

Lapslie smiled. 'Just a well-wisher. Remember, watch the back. Stay in position unless he comes your way.'

'Understood.'

'If you get a shot, don't worry about warning him: just

fire. He's a dangerous bastard. Bradbury and I will swear we heard you shout a warning.'

The reply came back. 'Ten-four. We were going to do that anyway.'

Bradbury pulled the radio back from Lapslie. 'You ask a lot.'

'I ask for justice.'

'With the lives and the trust of your officers.'

'That's part of the bargain,' he said, callously. He indicated the 9mm automatic she held in her hand, low so that it couldn't be seen through the car window, even though nobody was around. 'And where did that come from?'

'It was a birthday present from Dom, okay?'

'I would have had him tagged as a frilly lingerie man.'

'No, that was my present to him.'

Lapslie nodded, smiling. 'Okay, let's get on with it.'

As Bradbury was about to leave he grabbed her arm. 'What I said: the same applies to you. Shoot first . . .'

'Ask questions later?'

Lapslie smiled wolfishly. 'Well, not if you shoot first.'

While Lapslie made his way along the path, Bradbury covered him with her automatic. She was a good shot: had come top in her course. The trouble with courses, she thought, is no one is shooting back at you. She just hoped to God that if the good Doctor Whitefoot did make an appearance, she didn't miss.

A dark thought hit her: what if it wasn't the doctor? What if it was someone else, using the doctor and his links to the murders as a cover? Bradbury had seen that more than once during her career. Although she felt the evidence was good, she had seen better evidence than that taken apart when subjected to closer scrutiny, especially in court. All they had right now was circumstantial evidence, and they were assuming a lot. What if she did shoot and kill him to protect Lapslie? She was holding an unlicensed weapon and they were there in an unofficial capacity. Bloody hell, Lapslie was even suspended. This could all blow up in her face, and she could find herself doing life in Holloway!

During an operation as dangerous as this there should have been a perimeter set-up, Special Ops personnel armed with every weapon known to man, counter-snipers, even the SAS. Yet here they were, the four of them, none of them having fired a gun in a year. Never mind getting sent to Holloway, she thought hollowly, she would probably end up draped in a Union flag, being buried in her local churchyard. How the fuck did she allow Lapslie to get her into these situations? She wasn't covering his life with her 9mm, she was covering his ego. He just couldn't stand to be wrong. He couldn't stand for another detective to take over one of his cases, and worse still, solve it. He was willing to do anything to stop that happening, even break the law, and if it came to it he would put his and more importantly her life in danger. When this was all over she owed herself a serious rethink about her relationship with him.

Pearce and Parkin had already snipped the wire on the fence. Lapslie slipped through and made his way up the path purposefully, watching all the time for any move-ment. There was nothing. The problem was that, given Whitefoot's obvious skill with a sniper rifle, he would be dead and not even realize. The only chance he stood was if he managed to hear the ranging shots and got himself under cover.

Reaching the door quickly, he rapped hard and waited, making sure he stood to one side in case a burst of fire came through the door.

'Jeff? Doctor Whitefoot? It's Mark Lapslie!'

And that, he thought, was the closest to saying 'Police! Open the door!' that he was going to get.

He glanced back at Bradbury, who seemed frozen to the spot, only her arms jerking from time to time as she covered a series of windows with her 9mm. He really didn't know what he would do without her. She seemed to understand and accept him, warts and all. It was like a successful marriage – a professional one, but a marriage all the same. She was even willing to put her life at risk without question. That was loyalty. Who else would do that for him?

When, after a few minutes, no one came to the door, Lapslie knocked again, only this time louder. Still nothing. He stepped back and examined the front of the house for a burglar alarm. There wasn't one, which both surprised and pleased him. Without further ado he smashed the glass in the door, reached in and undid the lock inside. Whitefoot's security was really poor. Lapslie was surprised. Maybe the man just didn't want to draw attention to himself, he pondered. Odd, all the same.

As he began to push the door open he heard Bradbury call out to him, 'Stop, for fuck's sake! Stop!'

The urgency in her voice made him stop at once. Bradbury reached him quickly. 'It was too easy, boss. Are you sure the house isn't booby-trapped?'

It was something that hadn't occurred to Lapslie, but

now Bradbury pointed it out it was bloody obvious. He still needed to get in, he had no choice; there was no back-up for suspended detectives. He looked at Bradbury. 'Get back to where you were.'

'You're not thinking about going in?'

'I have no choice.'

'Yes,' she said urgently, 'you do! What's more important: the fact that he's caught, or that you catch him?'

There wasn't even a moment's debate in Lapslie's mind. 'The fact I catch him.'

'Even if it costs you your life?'

'Yes. Even if it costs me my life.'

It was obvious from her face that she knew there was nothing more she could say.

'Now get back to where you were; you should be safe there.'

Bradbury suddenly leaned forward and kissed him. It was only a quick kiss, but it took Lapslie by surprise.

She looked into his face. 'Don't get the wrong idea: that was just a goodbye kiss.' With that, she turned and ran back to her former position.

Bemused, Lapslie turned and began to feel around the door, searching for tripwires. Bombs were simple; women were complicated. There were no wires. Pushing the door open, he sank slowly onto his hands and knees and crawled inside, searching for any signs of a pressure plate. He took it slowly, feeling his way along the corridor. Finally, and feeling satisfied that there was nothing, he stood. It was time to take a risk. If he was blown apart that was his own lookout. Bradbury and the boys were safe and they all knew enough to nick Whitefoot. Either way, the police surgeon was finished.

He moved slowly from room to room. He wasn't sure what he was looking for: he just knew he would recognize it if he saw it. Nothing grabbed at his attention. No dolls, no pictures, nothing relating to the SAS, just what he would expect an average middle-class doctor's house to be. Finally, satisfied that everything was okay, he waved Bradbury inside.

'So did you find anything incriminating?'

Lapslie shook his head. 'Nothing. Not a damn thing.'

'So there's still a chance it might not be Doctor Whitefoot?'

Lapslie shook his head. 'No, it's him all right.'

'But you haven't got any evidence; how can you be so sure?'

'Gut feeling.'

Bradbury wasn't convinced. 'It's not enough, sir. Just

because he's the obvious one doesn't mean he did it. This could be one big set-up.'

Lapslie looked at her. 'By whom?'

'The real killer. It's been done before. Remember the Bobby Clarke case?'

'That was a one-off.'

'The Jimmy Henshaw job?'

'Another one-off.'

Bradbury wasn't impressed. 'Can't you see what I'm trying to say?'

'Yes, that Whitefoot's innocent.'

'No. I'm trying to say that we don't know for sure he's guilty. It's not the same thing.'

Lapslie knew she meant well, but she was wrong. 'I don't think so.'

'I didn't think you would.'

Suddenly Lapslie's phone went off, making both detectives jump. Bradbury was astonished. 'You left your bloody phone on when there might have been a bomb in the house?'

Lapslie shrugged, and clicked the answer button. 'Hello, Chief Inspector Lapslie. Yes, okay. What? Oh, bollocks.'

Lapslie turned his phone off, pushing it deep into his pocket.

'Trouble at t'mill, sir?'

Lapslie scowled. 'Some bastard has broken into my gaff.'

Lapslie sent Pearce and Parkin back to their section before they were missed, with instructions not to breathe a word of what had happened. He kept Bradbury with him. Guessing that there might be some uniforms at the house, he left Bradbury at the bottom of the drive and told her to make her way up to the cottage through the woods. He was right; there were two section cars, a traffic car and a dog van waiting for him when he arrived.

Lapslie stepped from the car and was greeted by a middle-aged traffic constable.

'Afternoon, sir. Sorry about this. We haven't been in yet. We're waiting for Scene of Crime to arrive.'

'Well, I'm not waiting. If some bastard's been in my house I want to know why, and what's gone.'

As Lapslie walked past him the traffic officer tried to dissuade him. 'Not sure that's advisable, sir. You might be walking across evidence.'

'Okay, you can all go. Thanks for turning up. I'll take full responsibility for the scene. I'll wait for Scene of Crime here.'

Without another word, they all jumped back into their vehicles and drove away. As Lapslie watched them disappear along the drive he noticed Bradbury emerge from the woodland that surrounded his cottage. He waved her towards him before going into his house to see what had happened and what, if anything, had been stolen.

A rapid search established that this, as Lapslie expected, was no ordinary burglary. It had been done for a reason. If Whitefoot had wanted to burgle his home he would have been in and out without disturbing his alarm system. There had to be a reason for this.

As Lapslie walked into his bedroom, he saw the reason. Lying on his bed was a doll – a woman in hospital clothing. Next to it was a letter. The woman, he assumed, was meant to be Elizabeth Turner.

He picked up the letter. It had been typed and there was no envelope. There would be no DNA, no fingerprints, nothing that might help prove who had sent it. Whitefoot knew all the tricks.

Lapslie unfolded the letter and read it.

As you may know, I have Elizabeth Turner. She is unharmed at the moment, and she will remain that way if you do as I tell you. Go to the church where I murdered the young bride at 3 p.m. and wait. I will contact you. There is no point in me telling you not to tell anyone, as I know your arrogance will not allow you to do that anyway. We are of a type, you and I.

Lapslie read through it again. As he did, Bradbury entered the bedroom.

'Anything interesting?' He handed her the letter. She read it in seconds.

'You're not going, are you?'

Lapslie nodded. 'I don't see any alternative. Not if I want to keep her alive.'

'That's irrational thinking. He'll kill her, and kill you too. Why wouldn't he?'

He knew Bradbury was probably right. 'What choice do I have?' he asked heavily. 'If I don't, he will kill her. If I do, he might kill her. It's a case of maximizing reward against risk.'

'He can kill you from a mile away. You won't see it coming; you won't know—'

Before Bradbury had time to finish the bedroom window suddenly shattered. Bradbury fell backwards, behind the bed. Lapslie threw himself onto the bedroom floor.

'Emma! Emma, are you okay?'

'Shaken,' she called back, 'but uninjured. I think. Dropped my gun, though.'

Another window smashed, and a large section of plaster was blasted out of the opposite wall, crashing to the floor and shattering. This was followed by a third and fourth shot which smashed into various parts of the room.

Lapslie crawled back to his bed and picked up Bradbury's 9mm automatic. He made sure there was a cartridge in the chamber before looking around the room for possible entry points. There were several. He would just have to hope to luck.

A voice from somewhere on the ground floor called up to him. 'Hello! Hello! Scene of Crime here! Anyone there?'

'Get down!' he yelled, 'for fuck's sake, get down!'

Lapslie heard the sound of footsteps moving up the stairs. SOCO, or killer? He levelled his gun at the point where he thought the person's heart would be. He would fire twice and then hold.

Before the person reached the door, Lapslie called out again: 'I'm Chief Inspector Lapslie. Do not come into the room or you will be shot.' His voice was shriller than he would have liked.

A voice came straight back. 'Okay, sir. Understood. What do you want me to do?'

'Walk towards the door with your hands high above your head.'

A man appeared in the doorway with his hands up. He was wearing white coveralls.

'Okay,' Lapslie went on, 'throw your ID over to me.'

The man reached into his pocket with one hand.

'Carefully.'

He threw his ID over to Lapslie.

'Okay, hands back in the air.'

He did as he was told. Lapslie picked up and examined his ID. It seemed fine. Besides, he was now sure of two things. One: the killer wouldn't put himself at this much risk. Two: if he were still outside, the SOCO would be dead. Whitefoot was just sending a message.

The police surgeon had made it very personal, and he was going to pay for that.

As Jeff Whitefoot drove away from Lapslie's house, he felt a strong sense of satisfaction. He could have killed Lapslie there and then, but that would have been too easy. Besides, there were some vital issues he wanted to vent to Lapslie directly beforehand. He was sure Lapslie would turn up at the church in the hope of saving Elizabeth Turner. He had that kind of personality. He was also sure it would be there that he would kill him.

It had to be at the church, of course. That was where he'd tried to implicate Stowell, and when Lapslie had first become alerted to the murders, and that was where it had to end.

Before that, however, he had Tony Turner to consider. If all went well he would kill the Teacher first, then move on to Lapslie. Elizabeth Turner was already packed up and ready to go. He would really have to care for her for a while. Picasso had children at seventy, so he should have no problem at all. And, of course, God wanted it to happen, so it would happen. He could have a new family soon, making up for all the years he had gone without. Maybe the pain would then diminish. Maybe it would disappear altogether.

Failing to plan was planning to fail. How well he had planned everything, and now he was almost there. My God, he pondered, he was a genius. In less than twenty-four hours he would start his life all over again. No more killing. Just life, and more life.

Outside his cottage, Lapslie breathed in deeply, letting the cool early evening air fill his lungs.

His phone began to ring. He looked to see who it was. *Unknown.* He considered for a moment whether to take the call or not. What the hell? If he didn't want to talk to them he could always hang up.

'DCI Lapslie? It's DC Pearce, sir. Can I ask, with respect, sir, what the fuck is going on?'

'Someone shot at us. Look, you and Parkin need to get out of it. Plausible deniability. I don't want you involved. No point dragging you down with me.'

'We've already gone, sir. We're about a mile away, just outside Great Chesterford. What do you want us to do with the guns?'

Lapslie thought for a moment. 'Take them apart and throw the bits in various lakes and rivers.'

'Understood.'

There was an awkward pause, which Lapslie picked up on. 'Was there something else?'

'I know this isn't a good time to tell you, but we've just heard that the teacher, Tony Turner, has gone missing. It's been reported on the radio.'

Lapslie was taken aback. 'I thought he was surrounded by security. How the fuck has that happened?'

'He ran.'

'He *what*?'

'Apparently he ran away from them, and the SOCO team lost him.'

'Why the fuck did he run?'

'No idea, boss. Sorry.'

Lapslie thought for a moment. Ideas and concepts shooting though his brain like shooting stars. Finally he came to a conclusion.

'Okay, meet me at his place in thirty minutes. If I'm right, I think I know why he ran.'

'Ten four, sir.'

Lapslie hadn't quite finished. 'One more thing.'

'Yes, sir.'

'Ignore my previous order. Hang on to the guns.'

It took Lapslie forty-five minutes to get to Tony Turner's house. Carl Pearce and Dave Parkin were already there. He waved them across and they climbed into the back of his car. 'So, how's it looking?'

'They've pulled off most of the security: just left a woodentop on the door.'

'Can we get rid of him for fifteen minutes? I need time to get inside and have a quick look around.'

Pearce nodded. 'Not a problem.' Jumping from the car, he quickly disappeared around the front of the house.

'Dave.'

'Sir.'

'I want you and Carl to search upstairs: there are only two bedrooms and a bathroom. I've been here before. Social occasion.'

'Anything and everything, boss?'

Lapslie nodded. 'Sort of. I'm looking for a note or a letter. It might not be there – he might have taken it with him – but I need to be sure.'

Parkin was a bit confused. 'What kind of note?'

'You'll know it when you see it. Can you tell Carl?'

'No worries.'

Carl Pearce suddenly appeared again by the side of the car. Lapslie looked up at him. 'Got rid of him?'

He nodded. 'Her, actually. Sent her to get me some fags. She was a Special. You know what they're like: keen to please. Good news is, she gave me the key to the front door.' He held the key up triumphantly.

'How long do you think we have?'

Parkin looked at his watch. 'Well, the shop is about half a mile away. I told her not to rush, but she probably will. She's that eager. So I'd say twenty, maybe thirty minutes, tops.'

Lapslie nodded. 'Well, let's get on with it then. Carl will brief you.'

The three detectives made their way to the front door

and let themselves in. Pearce and Parkin made their way up to the bedrooms while Lapslie began his search downstairs.

He started with the waste-paper bins, and struck lucky. What he was looking for was sitting right on top of a pile of other disregarded papers. It was, he thought, some kind of sign.

Opening it out flat, he began to read:

If you want to see your beautiful wife alive again, go to St Mary's Church in Finchingfield. I will be waiting there with her at 3 p.m. If you do not follow my instructions to the letter, I will first torture her and then kill her in the most painful way I can imagine. After all the work that I have done, I have a very strong imagination.

It wasn't signed, but Lapslie knew who had sent it.

Lapslie looked at his watch. Ten minutes to three. He knew he would have to do the last part himself. He couldn't involve Parkin and Pearce any further. He had a feeling this was going to be the final act, one way or the other. If anyone was going to end this it had to be him, and he didn't want anyone else to die with him.

Pushing the letter into his pocket, he slipped out of the house and back to the car, leaving his two colleagues still searching the upstairs rooms. Once in the car he checked Bradbury's automatic before driving off in the direction of St Mary's.

The church car park was empty when he arrived. Nobody about, not a single car there. Making sure his 9mm was not on safety, he made his way towards the church. The automatic made him feel more secure, but that was an illusion. If he was going to be killed then it would be from a mile away, and he wouldn't even hear it coming. Still, he thought, there was something reassuring in being dead before you knew it.

Lapslie walked around to the far side of the church, away from the main door. There he found the small door that must lead into the vestry. He tried it, but it was locked. Walking back to the front of the church would make him an easy target, so the only safe way now was through that door, and damn the blasphemy. Stepping back, he kicked hard at the lock. After three or four heavy kicks, the door finally gave way, and he could step inside.

Walking through the vestry to the main door into the church, which was also locked, he slid the large bolts across and managed to push it open. He didn't want to open it fully: just enough for him to squeeze through and still remain low enough not to make an easy target. The door creaked slowly open.

Lapslie looked outside. At first it seemed clear, but then he noticed, slightly to the right of the door, a shoe, or rather a Doc Martin boot. He crawled out slowly and pulled at the boot. It was heavy, and Lapslie quickly realized it was attached to a body. He had a good idea whose body it was.

Keeping low to the ground, he crawled out through the nave of the church until he was fully over the body. When he got level with the head, he twisted to face it. Any hope he had of identifying the body was quickly dispelled. What was left of the face was just a bloody mess, with few, if any, discernible features to go by. Near the top of the head was one of the small coffins. Lapslie reached out and grabbed it, pulling it to him and opening it. Inside was the doll of the teacher. It was either the same as, or identical to, the one he had seen in the bunker. If there had been any doubts in his mind before that this body, or what was left of it, was Tony Turner, then this doll quickly dispelled those.

It struck Lapslie with crushing force that with the death of Turner he was the only one left. He was to fill the thirteenth coffin.

Keeping hold of both the doll and the coffin, Lapslie began to crawl back towards the vestry and the protection it allowed. As with the concept of medieval sanctuary, part of him felt that once inside the vestry he would be safe.

As he was still crawling across the nave of the church, only yards from the vestry door, he suddenly felt an object being pushed into his back.

'That's far enough, Mark. No sanctuary for you, I'm afraid.'

Lapslie rolled over, and came face to face with Doctor Jeffrey Whitefoot. The police surgeon was holding a sniper's rifle, the barrel pointed at Lapslie's face. For some reason, Lapslie didn't feel afraid. If anything, he felt a strong sense of calm. Like a man coming to the end of a long journey of discovery to find the truth. Despite the calm, he carefully felt the outside of his pocket to make sure he could feel the shape of the automatic pistol. As the Arabs say: trust in Allah, but always tie up your camel.

'So, it *was* you. I was hoping it wasn't.'

Whitefoot nodded. 'It was me. It always was. You came very close, Mark, very close, but God just wasn't on your side.'

Lapslie knew he was finished. He just hoped that, given the information they already had, even fools like Rouse and Shaw would be able to track Whitefoot down.

'So why the children, Jeff? Why not the jury members themselves?'

'Two reasons. First, if I had gone after the jury members themselves then someone would have realized pretty quickly what the connection was between the victims. Going after their children muddied the waters a bit, especially since some of them had married or otherwise changed their names. And second, of course, I wanted them to suffer as I had. I wanted them to know what it was like to lose a child.' Whitefoot smiled, but there was no humour in his expression. ' "Suffer the little children",' he said quietly.

'You're misapplying the quotation,' Lapslie pointed out.

'It's not a quotation,' Whitefoot said, 'it's the actual Word of God. And believe me, I know what God wants me to do, much as it might pain me from a personal point of view.'

'Those people were pure innocents; nothing to do with the death of your daughter ...'

'Nothing to do with it!' Whitefoot screamed. 'Their parents released a man who murdered my daughter! He raped her, he tortured her, then he killed her! He made her suffer for as long as he could, then he killed her as if she was *nothing*!'

'And you did the same to their children.'

His voice had regained its eerie calmness. 'I didn't torture them or rape them. They died quickly, and mostly painlessly. I made sure of that.'

'You're as bad as the man who killed your daughter. Do you think she would have wanted that?'

'She was dead, Mark. I don't think she wanted anything any more.'

'So you killed twelve innocent children out of your own warped sense of justice.'

'Yes, justice. That's a very good word, Mark. Justice. The parents felt what I did. They were as responsible for the death of my daughter as the evil bastard that killed her.'

'And what about all the other people you murdered along the way? The police officers, Major Thomas's girlfriend ... Elizabeth Turner?'

'That's the fault of the jury members. If they had made the right decision then none of this would have happened. I would have been happy with life. I would have accepted what had happened. But no: they let him go to kill again. People should realize that they can't make those kinds of decisions without being responsible for the outcomes.' He looked around. 'It happened in a church, Mark, did you know that? She'd run there for sanctuary, for protection, but there wasn't any. He raped and tortured and killed her on the altar. On the *altar!*'

Lapslie moved his hand down towards his automatic. He knew there was no chance of pulling it out of his pocket; he would just have to try and fire it while it was still there and trust to luck, and whatever divine influence happened to be pointing his way.

'What about me? Why do I get a coffin?'

'The evidence you gave in the case was pathetic.'

'I told the truth. We didn't have a lot, Jeff. It was a risky prosecution at best.'

'You could have stitched him up if you had wanted to. I know you've done it before. You've gone as soft as those bastards in Parliament. If you'd said he had admitted it then he'd have gone down . . .'

'But he didn't.'

'Maybe not, Mark, but you could have *said* he did. The police used to do that. They kept the scum off the street any way they could.'

'And put a lot of innocent people in the nick, who then got off on appeal and undermined the honesty of the police. Not a good policy in the long term, Jeff. It only leads to more killers being released.'

'I couldn't give a damn about other killers, I only care about this one, and you helped to let him go.'

Lapslie finally managed to get his hand around the butt of his gun in his pocket. All he had to do now was get his finger even partially around the trigger and he would be in with a chance. Or maybe just blow his balls off, depending on the orientation of the gun. It was difficult to tell.

'Take your hand away from the pistol in your pocket.'

Whitefoot pulled his rifle up to his shoulder and pointed it directly at Lapslie's head. Lapslie's last chance had gone.

'Why the dolls?' he asked quickly. 'What was the point of that?'

Whitefoot stared at Lapslie for a long moment. 'That's

what she looked like, when I saw her in the mortuary in Sydney. Like a doll. Not like my daughter at all. Like a broken doll.'

As Lapslie watched, Whitefoot's finger begin to tighten around the trigger. Lapslie closed his eyes convulsively. His final thoughts were of his children.

He heard the shot: a deafening report. A salty, syrupy wash of flavour flooded his mouth. He was drowning in it. Everything they had said about being shot at close range was wrong. You *do* hear the shot that kills you.

It took a moment, but Lapslie suddenly realized he was still alive. He opened his eyes. Standing before him now was not Jeff Whitefoot, but Colonel Andrew Parr. He was standing over Whitefoot's body, and he had a gun in his hand.

'He wasn't as good as he thought he was,' Parr said calmly. 'But then, none of us are, I suppose.'

Lapslie was speechless.

'Cat got your tongue, Chief Inspector?'

Lapslie began to pull himself to his feet, unsure what to say, and still in shock. 'Thanks?'

Parr smiled. 'My pleasure. Won't be able to take the credit though, old boy. I shot him at close range, so we can mark it off as a suicide. Man kills his last victim and then, his task completed, kills himself. Police arrive late at the scene . . . I think you can fill in the gaps.'

As he was speaking two men arrived, dressed in white overalls. Lapslie was confused. What the hell were they doing there?

Parr read his thoughts. 'It's okay, old boy; they're not SOCOs. They're with me. They should have the scene sorted in a few minutes. In the meantime, I think you had better come with me.'

As they walked away, Parr took Lapslie's arm. 'Are you okay?'

Lapslie nodded. 'A bit shaken up, but fundamentally okay. How did you know?'

'We had our concerns about Whitefoot for a while. He trained with the regiment, you know? Spent fifteen years with us before leaving and retraining as a doctor. It was your Sergeant Bradbury that finally put us onto him. She called me. Anyway, he took some tracking down, but we finally got on to him.'

Lapslie nodded, still trying desperately to put the pieces in place. He wasn't the only one to have missed the early signals with Whitefoot, but then policemen with past Army backgrounds were a fairly common occurrence; no doubt it was also what had led White-foot to try and put Mike Stowell in the frame.

'But not soon enough to save Turner?' Lapslie asked, shaking the woolliness from his head. He was still phys-ically and emotionally numb.

Parr grimaced awkwardly, 'Unfortunately not. The final meeting place here caught us on the hop as much as Turner giving the slip to the police cover. Thing is, we have to keep this quiet. Can you do that effectively?'

Lapslie nodded slowly: Special Forces were covering up after one of their own who had gone rogue; getting in their way could end up messy.

'Do I have much choice?'

'Well, if you're unhappy with the suicide closure, you could, I suppose, say it was SCO19 or some other armed back-up officer. But that would mean someone else your end stepping up to the plate for that, because you under-stand I can't be involved.'

'Yes, I understand.' And even if there was agreement from Shaw and Rouse, finding that person to step for-ward would be equally problematic, with the possibility of a Menendez-style inquiry hanging over them. Lapslie nodded soberly. 'Given everything, perhaps suicide is the best option.'

They finally arrived at Lapslie's car.

'Well, this is it, old boy. Drive safely.' He put his hand out. 'Thanks for all the help. You really are a first-rate detective, but you're probably somewhat rattled by this close call now. If I were you, I'd leave it to Superintendent Rouse and Inspector Shaw to tie up the final loose ends.'

'What? And give them the chance of grabbing any of the glory?' Lapslie grinned crookedly. 'No, I'll see it through to the bitter end. On which front – how do you see the paper trail running?'

'From our end, we'll sanitize any involvement with Special Forces, but Whitefoot will still be down as Army. Quite common for many a policeman or police medic.' Parr looked briefly behind them with a pained expression. 'My men here will make it look like suicide for forensics. And the rest of it, I daresay, can run as is.'

Lapslie nodded thoughtfully. 'My men have been searching for Turner's wife, but no joy as yet. Any thoughts your side on what might have happened to her?'

'Unless she surfaces soon, I fear the worst, I'm afraid,' Parr said, grimacing.

Still trying to get full clarity on this sudden sea-change in events, Lapslie put his hand out to shake Parr's, then climbed back into his car and drove away. And as everything finally gelled halfway back to station HQ, he started to draft his report in his mind.

Charlotte boarded Lapslie's boat without difficulty before helping him stow the picnic, two bottles of wine and a selection of waterproof clothes. Lapslie used the small inboard motor to get them away from their mooring and along the river, out to the North Sea. Charlotte seemed to know everything that was needed before he even had a chance to ask. With the wind behind them and the boat in full sail, the Mazury seemed to zip along effortlessly.

Lapslie had spent two days tying up the loose ends of the investigation and making his reports, then had arranged the day's sailing with Charlotte. One urgent concern was that Elizabeth Turner was still missing, but with a third of his squad assigned to search for her and every police station in Essex duly notified, there was little he could do to further that. Despite Rouse's complaints about the manpower and resources that the investigation had so far eaten up, he was duty bound to extend them a while longer – the only thing to put a faint smile on Lapslie's face, counter that nagging loose end and sour taste that they hadn't been able to save Tony Turner, and now might fail to save his wife as well. Bittersweet; hopefully the only taste to assault his senses during the day's sailing.

At first Charlotte had seemed content to sit on one of the small seats at the side of the boat, but after half an hour she moved her position and sat between Lapslie's legs, her head resting against his body. Lapslie was surprised, but didn't mind. He put an arm around her and she pulled it into herself, slipping her slim fingers through his.

They sailed for several hours, but the time went so quickly that he hardly noticed. Thankfully there was no storm this time, or storm clouds on the horizon. They moored up a few miles along the coast to have their lunch. After eating and chatting for a while about his cases and her hospital career, Lapslie decided to go for it.

'Can I ask you something, Charlotte?'

She looked at him and smiled. 'Why is an attractive doctor like me going out with an older man with neurological problems?'

'Well, to be honest, yes. How did you guess?'

'Elementary, my dear Lapslie. A few moments ago we were speaking about boats and laughing about stupid experiences, and then your face suddenly became very earnest. I guessed it might be bothering you.'

'It does, a bit.'

'Age is just a number.'

'But in our case it's a big one.'

'Twenty years is nothing.' Her expression turned serious. 'Don't worry: I'm not looking for someone to replace my dad. I've had young men hit on me most of my adult life and a bit before, but they bored me. I tried being with one that bored me a little less, but it didn't work out. It wasn't what I wanted . . .'

'And I am?'

She looked at him for a moment. 'Right now, yes. Who can say what will happen in the future? Right now, you are right for me. You make me feel secure, and I'm happy when I'm with you. Is that okay?'

With that she took Lapslie's head and pulled it to her, kissing him warmly and long.

'How would you feel,' he asked, breaking away, 'if I named this boat after you?'

'It has a big stern and it wallows around in the water like a pig,' she said. 'I would be offended.'

'Well, put like that, I'd have to break with centuries of seagoing tradition and call it the *Alan Rouse*.' He smiled broadly and she chuckled. 'But if I put it to you another way: that on a fine day with a fair wind, it's sleek and glides through the waves like a mermaid . . .?'

She smiled, glancing slyly towards the cabin below. 'Keep up the sweet talk and I might just consider it.'

Elizabeth Turner managed to roll onto her side. She was tied so tightly she couldn't move. He had tied her hands behind her back, attaching them to her legs and forcing them upwards. He had then looped a cord around her neck, so that the more she struggled the tighter it got. Finally he'd taped up her mouth so that she couldn't make a noise.

He had told her that he would only be a few hours, and then they were moving on. Where, she had no idea. All she was concentrating on at this point was surviving from moment to moment, and she would do whatever she had to do to achieve that.

She didn't have a watch, and there was no clock in the cellar. The only light came from a small oblong window high up, through which she could see only a few yards of overgrown grass. Time passed slowly, but she thought it had been more than two days now since he had left. And towards the end of that second day, with the moisture from her mouth, the tape began to loosen and she managed to wriggle her lips and gnaw and spit part of it away.

She spent the next few hours crying out until her voice was hoarse, but no answer returned. She was dehydrated and ravenously hungry. Where the hell was he? He was normally such a methodical man, but now he had vanished.

She had tried to struggle free, but had only managed to make the cords tighter and make them cut deeper into her wrists, ankles and neck. How much longer would he be? How much longer could she survive? She knew the house was isolated, with few people having any idea who lived there. He'd told her so. She would just have to wait and endure the situation until he returned, or . . .

She blacked out at last, a welcome release in many ways. And when she awoke again, it was to the sound of a dog barking in the distance. At first she thought it was part of her dream, but then, as she peered up towards the light, she realized the sound was coming through the small oblong window. She couldn't stand up to see through the window, but she could at least try calling out again. She cried out with all her might, praying that there was enough strength left in her voice for the dog's owner to hear her.

Nothing, only the sound of the dog's continued barking.

She tried again, and again, becoming more frantic each time; and just as she feared the last of her voice was going, she finally heard a faint, distant voice in response.

Hope.

ACKNOWLEDGEMENTS

Thanks to my friend and fellow pen smith, Andrew Lane, who always entertains. My agent (United Agents) and friend, Robert Kirby, without whose patience and belief there would be no book. To John Mathews for his remarkable writing talents; Stef Bierwerth, my editor, for all the time and trouble she took to make the book as good as it could be; David North (Quercus) for all the time and trouble he took to keep the series running – much appreciated; Mark Smith, whose foresight started it all, many thanks; and to Quercus for publishing the book.